BROKEN

THE WATCHER CHRONICLES
BOOK 1

BY
INTERNATIONAL
BESTSELLING AUTHOR

S.J. WEST

CONTENTS

COPYRIGHTS

Cover Design: coversbyjuan.com, all rights reserved.
Interior Design & Formatting: Stephany Wallace, all rights reserved.
Proof Reader: Kimberly Huther.

ublished by Watchers Publishing January, 2013.
www.Sjwest.com

BOOKS IN THE WATCHER SERIES

The Watchers Trilogy

Cursed

Blessed

Forgiven

The Watcher Chronicles

Broken

Kindred

Oblivion

Ascension

Caylin's Story

Timeless

Devoted

Aiden's Story

The Alternate Earth Series

Cataclysm

Uprising

Judgment

The Redemption Series
Malcolm
Anna
Lucifer
Redemption

The Dominion Series
Awakening
Reckoning
Enduring

The Everlasting Fire Series
War Angel
Between Worlds
Shattered Souls

OTHER BOOKS BY S.J. WEST

The Harvester of Light Trilogy
Harvester
Hope
Dawn

The Vankara Saga
Vankara
Dragon Alliance

War of Atonement

<u>Vampire Conclave Series</u>
Moonshade
Sentinel
Conclave
Requiem

<u>Circle of the Rose Chronicles</u>
Cin D'Rella and the Water of Life
Cin D'Rella and the Golden Apple
Cin D'Rella and the Lonely Tower.
(Coming Spring 2019.)

ACKNOWLEDGMENTS

I would like to express my gratitude to the many people who were with me throughout this creative process; to all those who provided support, talked things over, read, wrote, offered comments, allowed me to quote their remarks and assisted in the editing, proofreading and design.

Thanks to Kimberly Huther, my proofreader for helping me find typos, correct commas and tweak the little details that have help this book become my perfect vision. Thank you to Stephany Wallace for creating the Interior Design of the books and formatting them.

Last and not least: I want to thank my family, who supported and encouraged me in this journey.
I apologize to those who have been with me over the course of the years and whose names I have failed to mention.

CHAPTER 1

The world my parents knew doesn't exist anymore. On the night they were taken from me, the people of Earth learned definitively that we are not alone in the universe. A permanent ripple of white light now laces the sky, like a silky ribbon of fate, reminding any remaining disbelievers that their lives could be irrevocably changed in an instant. Day or night, you can see the Tear, which has literally transported people off our world, like my parents, and substituted people and creatures from alternate realities and distant planets in their place.

All our scientists have been able to tell us is that what we perceive as a Tear in the sky is actually one end of a wormhole, but none of them can explain where the Tear came from or how it chooses its victims. Even with our advanced, modern science, no one can find a way to stop the wormhole from opening and ripping our loved ones from our lives, casting them out into the unknown.

"Don't get your hopes up, Jess. You know the chances of them ever coming back are slim."

I look at my best friend, Faison, in the dim light cast by the moon and the Tear in the sky. Her perfectly-braided auburn hair hangs over her right shoulder against the emerald green of the scrubs she is wearing. Faison is the classic version of a true southern belle, a status in our circle of friends I could never quite seem to achieve no matter how hard Mama Lynn, the woman who raised us, tried to make me into one.

We are sitting on a red and black plaid wool blanket in the middle of my parents' land. On the night of their disappearance, my parents and I had been looking up at the sky because we were actually going to be able to see the Aurora Borealis in the Deep South. It was supposed to be an event caused by the after-effects of a large solar storm, which no one would ever see again for a thousand years.

December 20, 2012, just before Santa had a chance to visit seven-year-old me, is the date I lost my parents.

At exactly seven o'clock in the evening, the ripple appeared in the sky and opened to reveal two planets, one blue and one orange. When I reached out to my parents for comfort, thinking the world was about to end, I found only empty warm spots on the blanket where they had been lying only moments before.

Every year since then, the ripple has opened at the exact same time and date that it first happened. Sometimes those who were chosen from our planet return to the spot they were taken from. So, every year, I come back to my parents' home, hoping to win the lottery of their safe return.

I glance down at my phone and see it's a minute until seven. I reach for Faison's hand. She clasps mine tightly, neither of us knowing if one, both, or neither of us will be chosen to travel through the Tear this year.

The Tear opens, showing only blackness on the other side. For 15 years, we have seen various worlds and distant constellations through the ripple, but never absolute darkness. The other side of the Tear looks void of anything, a great expanse of nothingness. I suddenly consider the absurd possibility that we won't have to deal with any new Tearers this year. The idea almost makes me laugh. The odds it would take for us to get that lucky don't exist in the real world.

"What do you think is comin' through?" Faison asks, her hand squeezing mine tighter with justifiable worry.

"Your guess is as good as mine," I say, reaching for the plasma pistol in front of me with my free hand, "but you're safe with me."

"I know I am, Jess." I hear the tease in Faison's voice just before she says, "Even if you are 120 pounds of nothin' and can't scare a fly."

I shake my head in feigned disappointment, keeping my eyes on the Tear as it closes. "Geez, no respect for Watcher agents these days, not even from the best friend of one."

"Well, if you actually ate something every once in a while, maybe you wouldn't look like a bag of bones. I don't know how Tearers are supposed to be frightened of someone who looks like a brown-haired Barbie doll."

I just sigh and stand up, pulling Faison swiftly to her feet with a jerk of my arm.

"Listen, I know you don't like me being an agent, but it's what I've chosen to do with my life. Mama Lynn understands why I have to do it. I don't know why you refuse to."

Faison crosses her arms over her ample bosom. If I look like Barbie, Faison's curves make her look like a Playmate of the Year.

"Mama Lynn thinks the world rises and sets just for you; of course, she wouldn't second-guess what you decided to go and do with your life. I just want you to know that you're not foolin' me, Jess. I know you think working for the Watchers will help you find a way to get your parents back."

"You don't know it won't," I say defensively.

It's an old argument between Faison and me. I know she doesn't think working for the Watchers will help me find my parents, and I can't deny she might be right. But the odds are 50-50 as far as I'm concerned. As long as there is a chance I can get them back, I'm going to take it, no matter the cost.

"I need to get back to the station," I tell her. "I'm lucky they let me come here this year as it is. Rookies don't usually get to take time off on this night."

Faison bends down and picks up the blanket from the grass, folding it into a neat square.

"Call Mama Lynn and make sure she's ok first," Faison instructs. "Then you can drop me off at the hospital. They asked all the nurses to come in for the first few hours after the Tear opened."

I scroll down my contact list to Mama Lynn's number, and tap her name twice to place the call. She picks up on the second ring.

"Jess?"

"We're both fine," I immediately reassure her. "Are you ok? Did anything happen at home?"

"No, I'm fine. George came over to keep me company while it opened. You two be careful out there," Mama Lynn says, "and tell Faison to call me when she gets to the hospital."

"Yes, ma'am, I will."

"Love you kids. You watch your back tonight, Jess. Who knows what came through this time."

"I know. I'll be careful. Just make sure you stay inside and keep the doors and windows locked. Don't let anyone try to come into your house until the Agency is able to do a threat assessment. In fact, why don't you get George to stay with you tonight? That way I won't worry about you."

"You tell me that every year," Mama Lynn says, with a smile in her voice. "I'll ask George to stay with me just so you don't worry. I love you girls."

"We love you, too."

"Oh, Jess?"

"Yes?"

"Don't forget we're all supposed to go see Uncle Dan tomorrow evening. They don't think he'll be with us much longer," I hear the strain in Mama Lynn's voice, as if she's trying not to cry. "I sure would appreciate it if you and Faison would go up there with me this time and say your goodbyes."

"All right, we'll go with you," I tell her, even though I feel like the loss of Uncle Dan is simply granting us one less asshole in the world.

"I know the two of you had a falling out before his accident," she says, "and I still don't need you to tell me what happened, but maybe you could find a way to forgive him for whatever it is he did to you before he passes away."

That's never happening, I say to myself but not to Mama Lynn.

"See you tomorrow, Mama Lynn."

"Ok," Mama Lynn sounds disappointed, but I know it's better than her knowing the real reason I can't mourn the loss of Uncle Dan.

When I end the call with Mama Lynn, I tell Faison, "She wants us to go pay our respects to Uncle Dan tomorrow."

"Pfft, the sooner he dies, the better off we all are," Faison says. "Especially you."

"Sometimes," I say, pausing to pull my thoughts together, "I want to tell her what her brother did, but then I realize it wouldn't do any good. It would only cause her pain."

"But maybe you need to tell her," Faison urges. "Maybe it's time you told someone else besides me."

"You know the only reason I told you was to make sure you never went over to his house alone."

"I know, Jess," Faison puts her free hand on my arm, "and I know what you did to protect me from him."

"I love you," I tell her, "and if he had laid a hand on you, I couldn't have lived with myself."

"I wish we had told someone back then what he was."

"We were kids," I say by way of an explanation. "You don't expect someone you trust to hurt you on purpose."

"I know, but..."

"Let's just forget about it," I say, putting one of my arms around Faison's shoulders. "Come on; we both need to get back to work."

By the time I drop Faison off at the hospital where she works, I've already received a call from the head office in Memphis about disturbances caused by the new Tearers in the northern part of Mississippi, where I'm stationed. I'm given directions to a home in Tunica where a man reported a Tearer holding his daughter hostage, demanding to be sent back home.

It isn't uncommon for Tearers to become a tad psychotic when they reach their final destination. Being taken completely away from your own reality against your will can do that to a person. Most Tearers end up accepting the government's assistance with setting them up in a home of their own and finding jobs for them. It isn't much different from the witness protection program. Some Tearers never acclimate to their new homes, though, and have to be dealt with by Watcher agents like me.

Being an agent is a fairly thankless job. The general public fears us because we are a law unto ourselves. All Watcher agents are placed under the jurisdiction of one Watcher. There are five Watchers in the U.S. alone and 174 more stationed around the world. No one knows where the Watchers came from or who or what they are exactly. All we know is that the governments of the world trust them completely. They look human, but we all know they aren't. Some speculate they're demons bent on destroying us, while others think they're our saviors sent in a time when the world needs heroes. All I know is that they're different, just like the Tearers are different, and that they were living on our planet long before the ripple ever appeared.

Since I was a small child, I have unknowingly been aware that there are people living on our planet who don't belong.

My father is one of those people.

I didn't realize what I was seeing at the time. I just thought the faint golden halo which perpetually surrounded my dad meant he was special. When I was old enough to ask him why he glowed and no one else I knew did, he simply told me it was because I could see the truth of things. He asked me not to let anyone else know what I could see and I never did, not even Mama Lynn or Faison. It was our secret, and I was thankful he advised me to keep my peculiar ability to myself.

It wasn't until I saw my first Tearer and Watcher that I realized my father was right; for some strange reason, I *could* see the truth of things. Tearers don't glow blue like Watchers; those who are brought to Earth through the Tear glow red, making them stand out in a crowd for my eyes. As a

Watcher agent, my unusual talent comes in handy. It helped me rise through the ranks of the organization faster than any other agent my age. No one else in my class has a class-one rating in identifying Tearers; only me. Some of my colleagues think I am a Tearer, but the Watcher I work for knows better.

When I reach the house on Bankston Street, I park in the driveway and make a quick survey of the surrounding area. The house is a regular ranch-style brick home. There's a cedar playset in the lot beside the house, a red F150 double-cab parked in the garage, and a white steeple church across the street. I can hear frantic yelling coming from inside the home, but the voices are too muffled to make out the exact words.

I step out of my Watcher-issued black Dodge Phoenix when I hear the distinct pop of a Watcher phasing in behind me. All Watchers have the ability to teleport wherever they want, whenever they want. It comes in handy.

"So what's the situation exactly?" I ask, turning to face the Watcher of my jurisdiction while I put my Kevlar vest on over the black leather jacket of my Watcher uniform.

Isaiah Greenleaf stares in the direction of the house before answering me.

The first time Faison saw Isaiah, I thought she was going to faint. She called him the prettiest black man she'd ever seen. Mama Lynn said he was pretty enough to be a movie star. But the strange thing is, if you were to round up all the Watchers in one room, you would have a hard time deciding which one of them was the most gorgeous. They all have an unearthly beauty that would have separated them from us regular humans anyway.

"Jonas Hunt, his wife, and daughter, were gathered around their dining room table, holding hands and praying when the Tear opened," Isaiah tells me as his gaze finally turns in my direction. "When it closed, the wife was gone, and a Tearer sat in her place. The Tearer freaked out, like most of them do, and put a knife to the little girl's throat, demanding to be returned to his home. That's all I know."

I grab my plasma pistol from the passenger seat and slide it into the holster on my right thigh.

"Ready when you are, boss."

Without another word, Isaiah and I make our way to the front of the house and ring the doorbell. It's standard protocol to announce our presence before actually entering a situation involving a Tearer. Taking a newly-deposited Tearer by surprise isn't wise, because you never know what you're dealing with until you meet them.

We don't wait for someone to answer the door. That would be ridiculous, considering the situation. Isaiah opens the door a crack and yells, "Watcher Greenleaf and Agent Riley coming in!"

Isaiah pushes the door completely inward, revealing the entire situation in one glance. Directly across from the front door through the living room, the dining area of the house is in plain view. The Tearer is a man of average height and build, with brown hair, wearing jeans and a plain white T-shirt under a thin blue jacket. An ominous red glow only I can see pulsates around him, yet something seems odd to my eyes; the red is a darker hue than usual for some reason.

The Tearer is holding a girl of about five in one arm, while pointing the edge of a long kitchen knife against her throat. The father of the girl stands anxiously on the opposite side of the table, helplessly watching his daughter sob uncontrollably.

"Please, help her," the father begs us, chancing a frantic glance in our direction.

With the cool assuredness only Watchers seem to possess, Isaiah walks through the living room to stand beside the distraught father.

"Everything will be all right," Isaiah says. His silky voice is like a healing balm meant to bring calm to the tense situation.

"Send me back home," the Tearer demands, the hand with the knife visibly shaking. "I want to go home now!"

Isaiah looks at the man. "You know we can't do that. You've more than likely had this type of thing happen on your world, too. The same rules apply here. No one controls the Tear."

"My wife," the man's voice trembles with grief, "my kids. They need me!"

"What's your name?" Isaiah asks.

"Owen."

"Owen, if there was any way we could return you home, we would, but holding this man's daughter hostage isn't earning you any points on this planet. I'm not sure where you come from, but I feel sure if someone was doing this to your family, you wouldn't stand for it."

Owen's eyes fall to the knife in his hands, just before he lets it drop to the floor and releases his hold on his hostage. The girl immediately runs to her father.

Owen sits on the kitchen floor, completely dejected. "What am I supposed to do now?"

I step up to his side to do what I've been trained for.

"Come with me; we can help you start a new life here. You're not alone."

Owen looks up at me, his eyes devoid of hope. "Without my family, what's the point?"

"Maybe someone from where you came from is here, too. You'll never know until we get everyone's information into our database." I hold out my hand to him. "Come on; let's see if we can find your family."

A spark of hope lights Owen's eyes. He takes my offered hand and stands to follow me out of the house.

Isaiah stays behind to make sure the Hunt family is all right, and gives them our number if they want free counseling. I know from experience that the counseling will be useless; no one can help you get over the fact that your family member was sucked through a wormhole to points unknown. At least if they had died naturally, you would have something physical to prove they once existed, a body or ashes, something to mourn over. Having someone ripped from your life without explanation, and not knowing where they are or if they are even still alive, is a hundred times worse.

I help Owen into the backseat of my car and head towards the Tunica Watcher Station. When I glance in my rearview mirror, I see him staring out the window at the flat farmland on either side of Hwy 61. During the winter, most of the Delta looks like a barren landscape in some post-apocalyptic movie. With the trees bare of leaves giving the illusion of skeletal figures, I can only imagine what our unearthly guest thinks of his new home.

"Do you mind me asking the name of your planet?" I ask. It's the first question all Tearers are asked. That way, we know whether or not they are alien or simply from a parallel universe.

"Earth," he replies, never taking his eyes off the world outside.

"This is Earth, too. What was your Earth like?"

"Nothing like this one."

"What's different?"

The man meets my eyes in the rearview mirror. A passing car's headlights illuminate his face for a fraction of a second, but that's all I need to see that his eyes have turned completely black and glossy, like pieces of marble.

"They weren't as gullible as you."

Before I know what's happening, he thrusts his arms through the Plexiglas which separates the front seats from the back, passing his hands and arms through the inch-thick plastic like it isn't even there. I slam both feet on the brakes just as his fingers are about to wrap around my neck. The force of my rash move causes the car to skid off the road, slamming us into a power pole along the highway. The airbag deploys and slaps my face like someone just kicked a soccer ball into it. As quickly as it inflated, the airbag deflates, giving me time to unlatch my seat belt and stumble out of the car.

I feel disoriented from the impact, but have enough sense left to draw the plasma pistol from my thigh holster and point it at the car.

The back passenger door blows off its hinges, soon followed by Owen.

"Hands over your head!" I yell, trying to keep the gun steady while I try not to pass out.

"Now, why would I do that?" Owen walks steadily towards me, no hesitation in his steps.

"Stop where you are or I'll shoot! This is your last warning!"

Owen doesn't stop; I know if he reaches me, I'm dead. I shoot.

The ball of plasma bounces off his face and dances off into the night sky, exploding into a shower of light like a sparkler on the Fourth of July.

Before I even have a chance to get off another shot, Owen has one hand around my throat and uses his other hand to yank the pistol out of my grasp. I desperately try to pry his hand away from my throat, but it's like his fingers are welded to my skin.

"Now just be still," he whispers in my ear. "This won't hurt much as long as you don't try to fight me."

The words are anything but comforting. Owen brings my

body closer to his, like he's about to hug me. I feel more than see the right side of my body begin to meld with Owen's left side, like two candles melting into one another. I grab him by the shoulders and desperately try to push him away, but the added pressure only causes me more pain.

"Stop resisting," he murmurs, as though he's receiving pleasure from the process.

My mind rejects what I'm going through. I feel like someone who's stepped into quicksand, without anything around to use as a handhold. I don't know what's happening, and I'm not completely sure I want to.

His shoulders begin to tremble beneath my hands, causing my whole body to vibrate like a tuning fork. He finally starts to scream as loud as I am, and thrusts me away from him, causing me to fall ungracefully onto the ground. When I look back up at him, I see that half of his body is missing…the half mine occupied only moments before.

"What did you do?" he shrieks, like I should have all the answers.

My eyes feel like they're about to bulge out of their sockets as I continue to stare at him, unable to move or even take a breath to fill my burning lungs.

Owen falls down on the one knee he has left, screaming in agony before exploding into a pile of black ash.

I hear the distinct pop of a Watcher phase in behind me. I assume it's Isaiah, so I relax, comforted by the fact that he will know what to do next, because my mind is a maelstrom of confusion.

I finally find it possible to take a deep breath, but impossible to say anything to Isaiah, who is strangely silent and still behind me. I turn my head to look up at him.

It's not Isaiah.

I scramble to my feet to face a Watcher I've never seen before. Everyone in America knows what the five Watchers who help protect us look like, and this one isn't one of the five. I know what many of the Watchers from overseas look like, and can't seem to place him as one of those either.

In the dim light of night, his pale face glows softly. His grey wool button-down coat flutters in the wind around his legs. Like all Watchers, he is handsome, but, unlike other Watchers, his face isn't perfect. A deep scar mars his face, running from right above his left eye to below his cheekbone… an imperfection no Watcher I've ever seen has.

His eyes stare into mine for a moment before moving to the pile of ash still on the ground behind me.

"Who are you?" I demand.

"Mason Collier," he replies. His eyes slowly travel back to me. "More importantly," he pauses, tilting his head and narrowing his eyes in on me, "what are you?"

CHAPTER 2

"What *am* I?" I repeat, feeling slightly offended by the question, considering who is asking it. "Shouldn't that be my question to you?"

The corners of Mason's mouth twitch like he wants to smile. "Touché, Agent...?"

"Riley. Jess Riley."

He's silent for a moment, looking me up and down with one glance, like he's trying to detect something special about me.

"Has anything like this ever happened to you before, Agent Riley?"

I take a deep breath and say, "No," while sliding my pistol into the holster on my thigh. The steely weight of it against my leg brings a strange sort of comfort to me. "I can't really say I understand what just happened, to be honest. I was just doing a routine transport of the Tearer to my station when he attacked me."

Mason crosses his arms in front of him. "He wasn't a Tearer. He was changeling."

"Which is what, exactly? An alien?"

"No, it's a type of demon that is almost impossible for even someone like me to detect."

"A demon?" I ask, thinking he's making some sort of joke. "There's no such thing."

"You say that like you know it for a fact," he comments, tilting his head at me. "Why?"

"Demons are mythological creatures. If demons are real, then there would have to be a God, too."

This time it's Mason who looks completely confused.

"You don't believe in God?"

"If a benevolent God actually existed, He would do something about that," I point directly above us to the Tear.

"What if He's leaving it there for a reason?"

"It would have to be a pretty damn good reason."

I don't feel like having this discussion with a complete stranger. Mama Lynn's already tried to persuade me God had a purpose for putting the Tear in the sky, but none of her Bible-thumping religious mumbo jumbo ever convinced me the God she loves and believes in so blindly could have a good enough reason to take my parents away. I can't place my faith in a higher power that could be so heartless and cruel for its own nefarious purposes.

"Greenleaf is the Watcher for this part of America, isn't he?"

"Yes; I actually thought you were him when you phased in behind me."

Mason holds one of his hands out to me, and I automatically shake it, thinking he intends to leave me and search for Isaiah to inform him of my situation. Instead, I instantly find myself standing in the middle of Isaiah's office, at Watcher Headquarters in Memphis.

I stare at Mason with eyes wide, and yank my hand out of his before he has a chance to whisk me off somewhere else.

"I didn't know you guys could take someone else along with you," I say, feeling like I need to explain why I might look like a startled rabbit.

"We don't share the knowledge with many people," Mason tells me.

"Why not?" I ask, walking over to the glass wall of Isaiah's office, which looks out over the Mississippi River. I feel a need to put as much distance as I can between Mason and myself. "Afraid people will start bugging you for rides?"

Mason smiles sardonically. "Something like that."

I hear the distinct pop of a Watcher phase in, and silently let out a sigh of relief when I see Isaiah's reflection in the glass.

Isaiah's gaze is immediately drawn to Mason like a magnet to metal. My mentor for the last year does something I have never seen him do before. He instantly drops to one knee in

Mason's direction and bows his head. It's the first time I have ever seen a Watcher show complete humility towards anyone.

Mason walks over to Isaiah. His gait reminds me of a white tiger I saw once in a zoo. Confident isn't exactly the right word to describe it. It's more like he knows he is the most powerful being in the room, but lacks the arrogance usually associated with such a fact.

Mason steps up to Isaiah and places his hand on my mentor's head.

"Rise, Isaiah," Mason's words are gentle, like he's talking to a trusted friend.

Isaiah stands and meets Mason's eyes.

"May I ask what has brought you here?" Isaiah's voice holds a note of uneasy reverence, a warning to me that Mason's presence bodes danger.

"I came to tell you I'm recruiting one of your agents," Mason briefly looks over at me before returning his attention back to Isaiah.

Finally noticing I'm in the room, Isaiah stares at me with a confused frown on his face.

"Why do you want Jess?" Isaiah asks.

"She just killed a changeling demon without even trying or knowing what it was. I think she might be useful in helping us solve the puzzle we were asked to deal with."

"She killed a demon?" Isaiah asks in surprise, obviously thinking he heard Mason wrong.

Mason nods once.

Isaiah looks back over at me. "What are you, Jess?"

My temper flares at the question.

"I'm getting really tired of being asked that like I'm some sort of freak. Isaiah," I take a step forward, "what's going on? You don't really believe that man from the Hunts' home was a demon, do you?"

"What happened exactly, Jess? Tell me everything."

I tell Isaiah what there is to tell of my story. He listens to my words closely, like he doesn't want to miss a single syllable.

"Then Mason showed up and brought me here," I say, finishing a story that sounds completely absurd to my own ears, even though I was the one who lived through it.

Isaiah is silent after my tale, which causes me more worry than anything else.

"From your file," Isaiah finally says, "I remember reading that your parents were taken through the Tear when you were very young."

"Yes, when I was seven."

"So, they were among the first to be taken?"

I nod.

"Did you go live with relatives afterwards?"

"No. The government wasn't able to find any family on either my father or mother's side. I was put into the foster care system like a lot of other kids who lost their parents that night. I got lucky, though, and was adopted by the foster parent I was placed with."

"Then you don't have any living relatives?" Mason asks.

I shake my head. "Not that I know of."

Isaiah and Mason glance at one another like what I've said confirms something they are both thinking.

"What is it?" I ask, not appreciating being left out of the loop, especially when I'm at the center of it. "What do the two of you think I am?"

"We've only encountered a human who can kill the way you did once before," Isaiah says. "Jess, did your parents have any friends who used to come over to the house? Any work colleagues? Anything at all that you can tell us about the people they associated with?"

I shake my head, realizing for the first time how sheltered life with my parents had been.

"How did they make their money?" Mason asks.

"I was just a kid," I reply. "I didn't worry about things like that."

"Did they work from home or go somewhere to work?"

I thought back through my childhood, trying to piece together what memories I had of my parents.

"I don't remember them ever working. I was home-schooled by my mother, and my father was always in the house. I never saw him leave home to go to work. I guess he could have worked from home or something, but I honestly don't know. What I do know is that whatever they did to earn money must have been lucrative."

"What makes you say that?" Isaiah asks.

"Because, when I turned 18, a lawyer came to see me and told me I was a millionaire."

"Why weren't you given the money when your parents

disappeared?" Mason asks. "With that sort of trust fund, you should have stayed out of the foster care system."

"He said my parents set up the account and conditions of disbursement when I was born. I guess in all their planning they never thought they would be sucked up by a wormhole and leave me an orphan," I say defensively on their behalf.

"Even so," Isaiah says, "all those taken through the Tear are declared legally dead. All of their financial wealth should have been given to you."

"They're not dead," I remind him.

"To this world they are," he, in turn, reminds me. "All of their financial property should have reverted to you."

I shrug. "All I can tell you is that after the government liquidated their assets, I was told I had a little over a hundred grand. I don't know why my parents didn't have more than that in the bank. All I know is that the government deposited the money they could find in a savings account for me, and the bank was directed to make good on the taxes on my parents' house and land, since I refused to sell them."

"So, you really don't know anything about your parents' past," Mason states.

"No, I guess I don't," I answer, keeping the secret about my father to myself. I know that's what they're fishing for: the real reason I'm different, more than likely the reason I was able to kill this so-called demon.

"Could either of you have killed that thing?" I ask, doing my own sort of fact finding.

"We can't kill demons," Isaiah answers. "That's why we're

trying to figure out how a regular human could have. Has anything out of the ordinary ever happened to you before now? Can you think of anything else that's different about you, Jess?"

I shrug my shoulders, not willing to trust them completely. My father told me to keep my secret to myself, and that's exactly what I've done all these years. I've always assumed my father would have explained why I could see 'the truth of things', as he put it, when I was old enough to understand. He simply wasn't given the chance. I wasn't going to divulge the information to them so readily, not until I understood what I was first.

"Not much else I can tell you, other than what you already know from my file," I say, and leave it at that. Lies get more complicated when you try to elaborate on them. I figure the less I say, the safer I am.

Both Mason and Isaiah look at me as if they know I'm holding something back from them, but neither seems ready to call me out on my small lie.

"Well, I'll figure out how you killed the demon," Mason says, completely confident in his statement. "In the meantime, I still want you to join my group."

"Which does what, exactly?"

"We're trying to find a way to seal the Tear."

"Seal it?" I look to Isaiah for confirmation. He nods his head, though something in his eyes tells me he's not confident Mason will ever be successful in his task.

"How do you intend to seal the Tear," I ask Mason, "and what makes you think I can help?"

"I'm not sure you *can* help," he admits. "But there is definitely something unique about you, and, considering the types of creatures I usually end up dealing with, you might prove to be useful to me."

I feel slightly offended at the way he makes his statement. I cross my arms over my chest and automatically take a defensive stance. "What makes you think I want the Tear closed?"

Mason frowns. "Weren't you the one who blamed God for not closing it just a few minutes ago? I assumed you would be more than willing to help."

I shake my head slowly. "No, I never said I wanted it closed. I said I blamed Him for not doing something about it."

"Your logic is confusing," Mason admits. "Can you explain exactly what the difference is?"

"I want my parents back. I can't have that if the Tear is closed. If there is a God, then I blame Him for letting it be put there in the first place. The world's got enough problems without having something like that hanging in the sky and randomly destroying people's lives."

Mason takes three slow steps towards me. "What if I promise I'll do everything I can to help you find your parents?"

"Mason…" I hear the note of caution in Isaiah's voice, and instantly know he doesn't think Mason can fulfill such a promise.

"You don't know it can't be done," Mason tells Isaiah almost harshly.

"Have you ever been able to do it?" I ask, my arms dropping to my sides, daring to hope after all these years that I might actually have a way to get my parents back.

"Not yet, but that doesn't mean it's impossible."

I look to Isaiah and see the creases of his troubled brow. My mentor looks me in the eye, unwilling to voice the warning I see on his face. When I look back at Mason, his earnest expression makes me want to believe in his promise. He is giving me hope. It might be a fool's hope, but it's the only time anyone has ever offered me a real opportunity to find my parents. I don't have to just sit around and wait once a year, hoping they make it back home to me by chance.

"I'll help you," I hear myself tell Mason. "I'll join your team."

Mason holds out his hand, as if he wants a handshake to seal the deal. Without hesitation, I place my hand in his and instantly find myself standing somewhere that isn't Isaiah's office.

I'm really gonna have to stop shaking his hand.

CHAPTER 3

"I wish you would stop doing that," I say, yanking my hand from Mason's grasp, "or at least give me a warning before you phase me somewhere."

"Sorry," Mason looks almost amused by my rebuke. "I really don't mean to keep startling you. Traveling this way is just part of who I am. It's not something I think about."

"Well, start thinking about *me* if you want me to work for you."

Mason gives me a lopsided grin.

"Do you find scaring me to half to death funny?" I ask, feeling my temper begin to flare.

"No," Mason shakes his head sincerely, "of course not. I'm just not used to people talking to me like an equal. Most people feel humbled in my presence, especially humans, yet you don't seem affected by me in the slightest."

This fact seems to befuddle Mason.

"Is that why Isaiah dropped to his knee so quickly when he saw you? Do regular Watchers feel humbled by you?"

"I'm Isaiah's superior," Mason says with no arrogance attached to the words, just fact. Mason shrugs off his coat, revealing a slim-fitting black pullover sweater and jeans underneath.

"I didn't know the Watchers had a superior, until now," I say, finding myself slightly distracted by the way Mason's sweater clings to his muscular torso as he moves.

"Not many people do," Mason says, tossing his coat onto the leather couch we're standing by.

"Why keep it a secret?"

"Sometimes it's better when people don't know everything."

"Too many questions?"

"Exactly."

"So, where are we?" I ask, looking at my new surroundings.

"My home."

Mason's home looks like something you would see in a magazine titled *Log Cabins of the Rich and Famous*. We're in a living room area with walls made from large pine logs. The outer wall to my right is made entirely of glass, acting as a picture window, but the view is obscured by the darkness of night. A stone fireplace hugs one corner, and it's lit with a blazing fire, providing enough heat to keep the room we're in toasty warm. The couch and chairs in the room are made of brown leather, and there's an actual white bearskin rug on the floor in front of the fireplace.

"Which is where, exactly?" I ask.

"Near Denver, Colorado. We can find you appropriate accommodations in the city tomorrow."

"No."

Mason looks confused again. I seem to have that effect on him, and I get the sense he's not used to being confused by many people.

"No?" he asks, trying to confirm he heard me correctly.

"I have a home, and I'm not going to leave it."

"That would make it rather difficult for you to come into work," he tries to reason.

"Then I guess you'll just have to come and get me every day, because I'm not leaving my family."

"Do you mean your adoptive family?"

"They're my family, adopted or not. Plus, I like where I live. I like my community. I'm not going to give up my life just to work for you. If you're expecting me to, then I'll have to back out of our agreement."

"I guess I have no choice but to do as you ask," Mason says, resigned to his fate.

"You were right."

Mason cocks his head to the side. "Right about what, exactly?"

"Letting people know you can phase with them does lead to them asking for free rides."

Mason chuckles. It's a nice sound, which sets me more at ease. It's the first time he's looked halfway human.

"Why are we here?" I ask.

"It's also my group's base of operations. This is our busiest night of the year, as you might imagine."

"So what exactly are you guys doing to find a way to seal the Tear?"

"We've been following the person responsible for its existence," Mason says, pushing up the sleeves of his sweater to mid-forearm. "Would you mind if we talked while we walked?"

He doesn't wait for me to say ok before he starts walking out of the room. I decide not to move an inch. Rudeness has never gone a long way with me, and I find Mason's action rude. If he had been Isaiah, I would have done whatever he said. I mentally try to shift gears making Mason my new boss, but find the task harder than I expected.

Isaiah was always thoughtful of others, never having to force people to do what he wanted. Almost every agent I know under his command just wants to gain his approval. But, with Mason, I feel no need to please him. On the contrary; I feel like I'm on equal footing with him, which seems odd since he's Isaiah's superior. It's obvious he doesn't feel the same way, something which will have to be corrected if I'm going to work with him.

Mason notices I'm not following and stops in the doorway of the room to look back at me.

"Is something wrong?" he asks.

"How truthful will you be with me while I'm working for you?" I ask.

"I will tell you everything you need to know when you need to know it," Mason says, turning around to face me while crossing his arms over his chest.

"Then tell me what you are. Who or what are the Watchers?"

"That isn't something you need to know right now. There are only a handful of humans who know the answer to that question, including the leaders of the world. We had to tell them the truth to gain their trust."

"But you don't have to tell me?"

"No. It's not something you need to know to do your job, especially not on your first night working for me. In time, after I know I can trust you, I will tell you."

I feel like that's the best I can get for the moment and decide to follow Mason blindly down the rabbit hole.

We end up going to the end of a hallway where the doors of an elevator stand. Once inside the elevator, we descend to the basement floor. When the doors open, they reveal something I've only seen in TV shows and movies.

The far wall is home to a multitude of holographic displays, showing what looks to be a variety of Watcher agents like me helping Tearers all over the world. A young man with dark brown hair who is dressed in a red T-shirt, jeans and white sneakers sits in front of a touch-screen control panel, moving his fingers across it with incredible speed. A black haired man in a well-tailored black suit hovers over the younger man, studying the holographic images like he's looking for something in particular.

To the left of the elevator is an area that looks straight out of some mad scientist movie. It's a glass room with scientific equipment neatly arranged on black marble countertops. A man and a woman, who both look like they are around the age of 30, instantly stop talking to one another when they notice us walk into the room. The surprised looks on their faces almost makes me want to laugh. I instantly get the feeling that new people aren't an everyday occurrence in Mason's little group.

"It's about time you got back," the man in the tailored black suit says without turning around. "What did you find?" The man pivots on his heels and faces us.

His pale green eyes instantly land on me. He's handsome with naturally wavy, jet black hair expertly parted to the side. His face is clean-shaven and his suit is expensive, indicating he might be someone with money. When he looks at me, he's careful not to give anything away, but I can tell he's surprised by my presence.

"Nick Summers," Mason says to the man, "I would like to introduce you to Jess Riley. She'll be joining the team."

"Watcher agent?" Nick asks Mason, taking in my uniform.

"Yes," I reply, not seeing why I should be talked about like I'm not in the room. "Do you have a problem with that?"

Nick's expression is guarded as he studies me. "No, but I would have preferred to vet you myself before allowing you to come here."

"I was vetted by the Watcher Agency when I joined," I tell Nick.

"I like to do my own investigations, Agent Riley. I feel safer if I know who I'm working with." Nick looks to Mason. "Why her?"

"She killed a demon."

A look of shock passes over Nick's face for a second before he's able to hide it.

"You actually killed a demon?" the young man at the control panel spins around in his chair to get a better look at me.

The boy doesn't look much older than 17. His chocolate brown eyes stare at me like I'm the eighth wonder of the world.

"Stop ogling her, Joshua," a female voice with a British accent says behind me. "We don't want to give her the wrong impression about us right off the bat, you git."

I turn to see the girl from the glass room standing a few feet away. Her light brown hair hangs halfway down her back in soft curls. She's wearing a pair of black rectangular glasses and a white lab coat, with a pink ruffled shirt and regular jeans underneath.

"Jess, I would like you to meet Angela Westwood. The man conspicuously peering at you from the lab is a brother Watcher and Angela's father, Allan."

"Sorry," Angela says, extending her hand to me, which I automatically shake. "I should have introduced myself. We don't get many new faces down here. Well, none really. So, how were you able to kill the demon?"

"I don't know," I tell her, feeling myself relax for the first time in Mason's secret lair. "It wasn't something I was trying to do."

"Pull up Jess' recording," Mason tells Joshua as he goes to stand next to him and Nick. "Start it at around 7:45pm, central time."

Joshua spins back around in his chair and does something that instantly projects my car on the screen, driving down Hwy 61. I watch as the altercation with Owen unfolds before me like a movie. I hear Angela gasp beside me when the demon turns to ash.

When Mason appears in the scene, he tells Joshua, "You can stop it there."

I wait to see if any of them can offer an explanation as to how I was able to kill Owen, but silence reigns eternal in the room, until I hear a new voice speak through an intercom system.

"I would like a sample of her blood, please."

Everyone looks in Allan's direction, and I realize it was he who must have spoken.

"Do you think she's a hybrid?" Mason asks.

"Hard to tell from just looking at someone," Allan says. "But an analysis of her DNA will tell us definitively."

"Do you mind?" Mason asks me, more as a perfunctory question than a real concern.

"Yes, I do mind, actually," I say. "I don't know any of you. I'm not some lab rat to be prodded and poked at."

"Do you have something to hide?" Nick asks me, instant suspicion written clearly on his face.

In truth, I fear what they might find out. I've always known my father was different in some way, and feel sure that, if they try to do a genetic profile on me, his secret will be discovered. I can't willingly let that happen, not after the promise I made to him.

"Do you?" I counter, not seeing why I should let them know everything about me when I know nothing about them.

Nick looks at Mason. "You're not going to just tell her everything, are you? I would feel a lot more comfortable if I could vet her before giving her any classified information. Plus, you know I have to ok it with Washington first."

"What is your job here, exactly?" I ask Nick, wondering why he's so concerned about my trustworthiness when none of them have proven theirs to me.

"Nick is my liaison with the President," Mason tells me. "He makes sure your government stays out of my way and smooths over any ruffled feathers when needed."

It's not hard for me to imagine Mason ruffling the feathers of the government's bureaucracy. He doesn't strike me as someone who lets red tape prevent him from doing what needs to be done.

"I'll tell Jess what she needs to know when the time is right," Mason says to Nick, looking the other man in the eye to make sure he understands his position.

"I would like to know one thing," I say. "Can you tell me how you just happened to find me in the middle of nowhere tonight?" I ask, looking at the holographic displays of the other Watcher agents all over the world. "It had to have been like looking for a needle in a haystack, considering what tonight is."

Mason looks at me, and I'm not sure he's going to answer my question. Finally, he says, "I felt you."

"What do you mean, you felt me?" I ask, feeling a little odd about his choice of words.

"I was able to detect you when you began to use whatever power you possess to fight off the changeling. It was like a great disturbance in nature pointing me to exactly where you were."

A vision of Obi-Wan Kenobi pops in my head and I hear him say, "I felt a great disturbance in the Force." I almost smile, but don't want to explain to Nick why Mason's statement would cause such a reaction. He's suspicious of me enough as it is. I don't feel like divulging the very personal fact that I am a sci-fi geek. That is privileged information which is only on a need to know basis, and Nick definitely doesn't need to know.

"Have you ever felt a disturbance like that before?" I ask.

Mason is silent for a moment before saying, "No."

"You do realize," Nick says, "that when you became a Watcher agent, they took a sample of your blood. Whether you give it to us now willingly or not, we'll still be able to run your DNA through our system."

I curse to myself. I'd completely forgotten about that.

"They've already tested me then," I say. "What do you think you can find out that they didn't?"

"There are certain markers," Allan says from his glass-enclosed room, "which a regular DNA profile wouldn't check for. I, on the other hand, know what differences to look for."

"What do you think you're going to find?" I ask.

"It's possible, though unlikely, you fit a profile we've encountered once before," Mason tells me.

"What makes you think I'll be like this other person?"

"Because she's the only other human we know of who can kill the way you did tonight," Mason says. "We would like to either confirm or rule out that possibility. If we can rule it out, it will allow us to focus on what really makes you different."

"You can either cooperate," Nick says, "or we can get your stored blood sample from the Agency. It's up to you."

My heart sinks because I know he's right.

"Take it," I say, stripping off my Kevlar vest and jacket to roll up my right sleeve.

Angela walks back into the glass room where her father is and returns with everything she needs to take a sample of my blood. She points to a seat by Joshua for me to sit in, and I rest my arm on the control screen the boy genius uses to spy on Watcher agents like me.

While she's filling five empty test tubes with my blood, I ask, "So, is this what you guys do all day? Sit here and watch agents with your super spy satellites?"

"I wouldn't exactly call it spying," Mason says, sounding

slightly offended. "We look for anything out of the ordinary which might help us discover how to close the Tear."

"How long have you been trying?"

"Since it opened."

"So, in 15 years, have you found out anything?"

Mason's eyes shift away from mine, and I instantly know my question has hit a sore spot.

"No," he finally answers.

"Nothing?" I ask a bit flabbergasted. "Nothing at all?"

"We've found things but nothing to help us seal the Tear. We know the answer is here on this planet, but, to be honest," he says, looking back at me, "you're the first real lead we've had so far. At least, I hope you are."

My grand vision of this group being able to help me find my parents suddenly evaporates. If I'm the only real clue they've been able to find in 15 years, maybe they don't know what the hell they're doing.

"You people don't strike me as being incompetent," I say. "You must know something."

"What we *do* know for certain," Mason says, "is that the person who made the Tear visits almost every Tearer who comes through each year."

"Is he looking for someone in particular?" I ask.

Mason smiles like he's proud I thought to ask such a question. "That's what we have been assuming."

"Do you know if he's found who he's looking for?"

"He hasn't tipped his hat one way or the other. He only visits them once. There is never a second visit. Either he hasn't found who he's looking for yet, or he has and knows we're watching him."

"Who is *he* anyway?" I ask. "Some genius mad scientist you guys couldn't find a way to control?"

"Genius, yes," Mason says, "mad, certainly, but not a scientist. He's something similar to a Watcher, but not quite that either."

Angela tells me I can roll down my sleeve as she takes my blood to the glass room where her father is located. I watch as she walks in and hands him the tray of vials. Allan immediately sets to work to figure out what makes me so special.

I stand up and button my sleeve. "You know, it's going to be hard for me to work for you if you can't tell me everything. I'm pretty smart," I say. "I might be able to help you figure things out if you give me all the information."

"In time, Agent Riley," Mason says. "Let's see how things work out first. Trust is earned, not given."

"Yes, it is," I agree, staring at Mason.

He grins, hint taken.

"I will need for you to take me to your home," Mason informs me.

I feel my forehead crinkle. "Why?"

"If I'm going to have to be your private phasing chauffeur, I need to know where you live. I can only phase to places I've been to."

"I didn't know that."

"It's possible I've been where you live, just like I was able to phase to your location tonight. What city do you live in?"

"Cypress Hollow."

"Never heard of it. I presume it's near Tunica in Mississippi?"

"You presume correctly."

"Be right back," Mason says, phasing somewhere.

"I wish I could say it was nice to meet you," I say to Nick, "but I try not to lie if I can help it."

Nick raises a dubious eyebrow at me.

I hold out my hand to Joshua. He smiles up at me and shakes my hand. From the adoring way Joshua looks at me, I get the feeling most people don't talk to Nick like I just did. I almost feel bad about it, but can't quite make myself feel ashamed enough to take it back.

"Don't let them keep you up too late," I tell Joshua with a wink.

"Yeah, well, I have my stock of Red Bull handy in the fridge," he says, giving me a shy smile before turning back to his work.

Mason reappears, buttoning the top button of his coat, which reminds me to put my own jacket back on. He holds his hand out to me.

"Shall we?"

I put my hand into his and find us standing in the Watcher station in Tunica.

It's a madhouse as usual on a night like this. Most of the Tearers are upset, some to the point of being inconsolable. As I look into the glassed-in waiting room, which looks a lot like a police precinct with its array of desks and computers, I see some of my fellow Watcher agents trying to console the Tearers placed in their care.

At the front desk, Albert, our dispatcher, looks up from his computer screen. Not being an agent, Albert isn't forced to meet the physical requirements Watcher agents have to adhere to. We are all required to maintain a healthy weight and be able to physically deal with the demands of our job. At almost 270 pounds, Albert is sometimes called 'Fat Albert' by some of my colleagues, a nickname I have never used myself.

"Hey, Jess," Albert's eyes look from me to Mason, and I see him visibly flinch slightly when he sees the scar over Mason's left eye. "Who's your friend?"

"No one of importance," Mason tells him, apparently wanting to keep his identity concealed.

"I guess you heard about my accident?" I ask Albert.

"Yeah, Isaiah told us about it; said you were all right, though." Albert walks to a lock box on the wall and picks out a set of car keys. He walks back to the counter and hands them over to me. "He said you would need a new car too. We already sent out a road crew to clean up the mess. Can you tell me what happened? Isaiah wouldn't go into too much detail."

"Sorry," I reply, truly apologetic. "If he didn't say much, I probably shouldn't either."

"Ok, Jess," Albert says, clearly disappointed, but understanding you should never overstep your boundaries where a Watcher is concerned.

"I won't be around much anymore. I've been reassigned to another project for a while," I say, realizing for the first time I won't actually miss working with many of the people at my station. Albert is the only one I've ever considered a friend.

"Yeah, Isaiah told me that too. Sure gonna miss seeing you around here," Albert says, and I know he's sincere in his sentiment.

"I'll come by to see you when I can," I tell him. "I haven't forgotten about my promise to bring you some of Mama Lynn's sugar cookies when she gets around to baking them."

Albert smiles and rubs his rotund belly. "I really shouldn't, but you know how I love her cookin'. I won't complain at all if you bring me a tin full."

I smile at Albert. "You can count on it."

I wave goodbye and Mason follows me out the front of the building to the parking lot.

When we get into the new Dodge Phoenix, the automated system asks, "What is your destination, Agent?"

"Manual control," I tell the computer.

"Switching off automated driving system. Manual control enabled. Drive safely."

I crank the car and leave the parking lot to head south down Hwy 61 again.

"You don't let the computer drive for you?" Mason asks.

"I don't trust computers that much. They're not infallible. Plus, I like to feel in control of where I'm going."

"Can't say I'm too surprised to hear that."

I glance over at Mason, and see he's actually grinning at his own conclusion about me. The expression makes him look more relaxed, and I find myself wondering how often he lets himself smile.

He must feel me staring at him, because he turns his head to look at me. I quickly look away, feeling slightly flush for being caught.

"Does it bother you?" he asks in a low voice.

I glance in his direction briefly before returning my eyes to the road.

"Does what bother me?" I ask, not having a clue what he's referring to.

"My scar."

Out of the corner of my eye, I see him absently touch his only visible imperfection.

"No," I answer truthfully, "it doesn't bother me. Does it hurt?"

"It did when it was first made," he confesses, letting his hand fall back onto his lap as he continues to look at me.

"If it bothers you, why not go to a plastic surgeon to have it fixed?"

Mason lets out a harsh laugh and turns his head to look out the window.

"It's not that kind of wound," he says. "I'm the only one who can heal it."

I have no idea what he's talking about but decide to let the matter drop. I feel like I might be delving into a deeply personal matter that is none of my business, considering we've just met one another.

I turn off Hwy 61 onto Cypress Lane. The town I live in

is small, and only has one traffic light and one convenience store. Being so close to Tunica, the children are allowed to go there for school since Cypress Hollow is unable to sustain one. As we come to the red light in the middle of town, I slow down and come to a stop to wait for it to turn green.

"What is that?" Mason asks, confusion in his voice as he continues to look out his window.

I glance over. "It's our convenience store."

"Why does it have those large pink dog paw cut-outs mounted on top of it?"

"Beau just never took them off when they shut down the dog-grooming business after his dad died. That's why the store's called Paw Paw's."

I hear Mason let out something close to a real laugh, but it's so short I'm not sure if I imagined it or if it really happened.

The light turns green, and I drive through until I approach the street I live on, Willow Bend.

There are no people out tonight, because anyone with a lick of sense knows you shouldn't be out on the night the Tear opens. The streetlights illuminate the quaint neighborhood I reside in, with its white-picket-fenced-in homes and Christmas-decorated lawns. I see Mama Lynn's house at the end of the street and almost reach for my sunglasses.

For years, Mama Lynn and Margaret Lawson have had a silent duel over who could place the most Christmas lights on their homes and in their front yards. Since they live right across the street from one another, the end of our neighbor-hood never goes dark during the Christmas season.

"Isn't that against your laws?" Mason asks me, looking straight ahead at Mama Lynn and Ms. Margaret's homes.

"Not really," I say. "I suppose if they lived in the middle of the neighborhood instead of at the end of a dead end street there might be some complaints. But Mama Lynn and Ms. Margaret have been decorating like that for years now. Everyone expects it."

I pull into my red brick driveway.

"You have a nice home," Mason says, looking at my house.

"Thanks; I just had it built last year."

I had to buy two lots to build my dream home but money wasn't a problem, thanks to my parents. The large, country-style, light olive-painted clapboard house with white trim was exactly what you would expect to find in a quiet southern neighborhood like mine. With its three bedrooms, vaulted ceiling great room, and large kitchen, it was a home I felt comfortable living in, and one I could see raising a family of my own in one day.

Mason gets out of the car and follows me as I walk up the brick sidewalk and steps. I turn around to face him when I reach the porch.

"What time should I be ready for you to pick me up in the morning?" I ask, wanting to make our goodbyes on the porch instead of inside the house.

Since he said he could only phase to places he'd been to

before, I quickly came to the decision I would not let him inside my home. All I needed was for him to pop in whenever he deemed it necessary.

From the look on Mason's face, I can tell he had expected an invitation inside, but he doesn't say anything besides, "I'll be here at eight. Allan should have the results of your blood work by then, and we can discuss what he discovers."

My heart sinks at the reminder.

I nod. "All right; I'll see you in the morning then."

I wait until after Mason phases away before turning to slide my key into the front door lock.

"Well," I hear a strange male voice say behind me.

I whirl around to face a man I don't recognize. He's tall with shoulder-length blond hair and a muscular build. From the glow of the streetlights behind him, I can tell he's handsome, with lips spread into a smile most girls would probably swoon over, but I'm not most girls. For the second time that night, I see a glow around someone I have never seen before. The man before me is surrounded by what appears to my eyes as an ominous black glow.

I feel my hand involuntarily lower towards my plasma pistol on my right thigh.

"Can I help you?" I ask.

The man shrugs. "I'm not sure. Can you tell me what you are?"

CHAPTER 4

I feel like pulling my pistol and shooting the stranger for just asking the question.

"I'm afraid I'm going to have to ask you to get off my property. I don't know you, and I don't care to. Now, please, leave, before I call the police."

"I'm sorry; I didn't mean to frighten you," he says. I detect a slight Australian accent in his voice. He makes a move to take a step forward, but I draw my pistol before he gets a chance to lift his foot.

He pulls his hands out of his trench coat pockets and holds them up to show me he isn't carrying anything.

"I'm not here to harm you in any way, Agent," he says. "I just wanted to meet you in person. It's not every day I find someone who can kill a demon without actually doing anything."

I feel my heart start to race faster. How does he know what I did?

"Who are you?" I ask.

"You can call me Lucian. Might I ask what your name is?"

"Agent Riley," I say, not feeling like I should be on a first-name basis with the man standing in front of me.

"Well, Agent Riley, I can assure you that your pistol is not necessary. I'm not here to harm you, just talk."

"What do we have to talk about?"

"Well, I would certainly caution you about the company you keep. Has Mason even told you what he is yet?"

"That's not really any of your concern," I say, realizing he's hit on a sensitive point.

"No, it's not," Lucian agrees, "but it is a concern for you. If I were you, I would find out who it is I'm associating with, Agent Riley. And if he refuses to tell you, well, I guess that speaks for itself, doesn't it?"

As if he sensed we were speaking about him, Mason materializes beside Lucian, holding my Kevlar vest in one of his hands.

As soon as the two men look at each other, it's like the night air is suddenly charged with electricity. Mason's body tenses like he's holding himself back from beating the other man to a pulp.

"Well, speak of the devil," Lucian smiles at Mason, as if he just made a joke. "I was just telling Agent Riley, here, that she should get to know the true you better, Mason. How goes the search by the way? Any luck?"

Mason's jaw muscles tighten. "Do you honestly think I would answer that question?"

Lucian chuckles, but there's no humor in it. It's more like he's laughing at Mason, not Mason's answer.

"And how about you?" Mason asks. "Found what *you're* looking for yet?"

Lucian's smile slowly disappears. "Perhaps; each New Year brings its own small miracle, but I have a feeling this might be my year. I'll just have to see what tonight's reaping has brought to me."

"Well, I would wish you luck, but you know I wouldn't mean it."

"I could say the same, old friend."

"We are not friends," Mason says in a low, menacing voice. "I don't keep traitors as friends."

"Watch your tongue, boy," Lucian's voice booms, "or have you forgotten I can wipe out your existence with one touch?"

"If you're scared of me, by all means do it, and stop talking about it every time we meet," Mason says. "Your bluff has become a bore...what name are you going by now, anyway?"

"Lucian."

"Is that how you choose the bodies? Wasn't there a Lucas once? Why not just go by your real name?"

"Alas, that name has been tainted by the monkeys on this planet; far too obvious and conspicuous now." Lucian turns to look at me. "I must be saying goodnight, Agent Riley. Unfortunately, our time together was cut far too short. Perhaps next time we'll have a chance to get to know one another a little better."

Lucian phases, leaving Mason and me to stare at an empty space.

I slide my pistol into the holster on my thigh.

"Who was he? Another Watcher?" I ask.

"It's a long story," Mason says, looking up at me.

"I have coffee," I tell him, turning back around to my door, silently inviting my very first Watcher into my home.

After I start a pot of coffee brewing in the kitchen, I find Mason in my living room, looking at the Christmas tree set up in front of the large-paned glass window, which faces towards the backyard.

"This doesn't quite look like your taste," Mason says, examining a white crocheted angel, one of many, hanging on the tree.

"That's because it isn't. Mama Lynn put it up for me."

"She's the woman who adopted you, correct?"

"Yes."

"You got lucky to find someone so generous."

"I know. A lot of Tear children ended up on the streets, or worse. I kinda hit the adoption lottery. I'm not sure what would have happened to me if I'd been sent anywhere else."

Mason turns to face me.

"Why do you still live here?" he asks, his gaze travelling around my home. "You're a millionaire. Why not live somewhere else? And why did you choose to become a Watcher agent? You obviously don't need the money. You could do whatever you want."

"I thought I was supposed to be the one digging for answers," I tease, wondering why he's asking me so many personal questions. "Money can't buy back my parents," I say, deciding to answer his questions.

"What if you never get them back?" Mason asks.

I shrug. "Then I don't get them back. But I have to try. If I don't try, I'll always wonder if I could have done more. I don't want doubt following me around for the rest of my life."

"How old were you when the Tear appeared?"

"Seven."

"You seem wiser than most 22-year-olds I've met."

"I think everyone became a little wiser when the Tear appeared. We didn't have much choice. It was, either, learn how to deal with the changes, or go nuts. Crazy doesn't work for me."

I hear the coffee pot buzzer go off, and head towards the kitchen.

"How do you drink your coffee?" I ask.

"Black."

While I'm in the kitchen, Mason asks, "Would you like me to start a fire in the fireplace for you?"

"Sure. Matches are on the mantel in the silver box," I call back.

I've never liked black coffee, so I spend a little time adding in sugar and heavy cream to my cup. By the time I get back to the living room, Mason is still crouched in front of the fireplace, watching the flames. I walk up to him and hand him his cup. After he takes it, he doesn't act like he intends to move, so I sit down on the built-up brick hearth and wait for him to speak.

"So, it's my turn to answer your questions," he finally says, dragging his eyes away from the flames to my face. "What do you want to know?"

"What are the Watchers?" I ask.

It's a question the regular people of the world have been asking for 15 years, but no one has provided an answer.

"You'll need to have an open mind about everything I tell you," he says to me. "And everything I say to you can never be repeated to anyone else. I must have your promise on that, or I can't tell you anything. Can you make that type of promise to me?"

I nod slowly, not sure I like the way this conversation is starting. "I won't tell anyone what you say to me. You have my word."

Mason nods his head, indicating he believes my promise to him.

"The Watchers are angels."

Mason pauses, like he's waiting for his statement to sink into my brain.

"So you're telling me you're an angel? Like from Heaven?"

"Yes."

If anyone else had made such a ridiculous statement, I would have told them to get the hell out of my house. But as I look at Mason, I know what he's telling me is the truth, or at least the truth as he knows it. If I allow myself to believe in angels and demons, I have to allow for the possibility of there being a God, something I'm not willing to believe in as fact just yet.

"So, why are you here?" I ask. "Why are you on Earth and not Heaven?"

"A long time ago, we were sent here by God to teach the human race," Mason explains. "We were supposed to act as your guides and observe your behaviors."

"Supposed to? You make it sound like you failed."

Mason looks back into the fire, either unwilling or unable to meet my eyes.

"We did the one thing God forbade us from doing while we were here. We married human women and attempted to have children with them. We did it because we all yearned to have what human men had, families of our own."

"And I take it your God didn't like you doing what He told you not to?"

"No, He most definitely did not. We were exiled from Heaven because of our sin, and forced to live here."

"Was that so bad?" I ask, not quite seeing that as a punishment. "I mean, you wanted to have families here, right? If you didn't have to go back to Heaven, then you could just stay here and be with them."

"Because of what we did," Mason says, his voice sounding haunted by his memories, "our families were made to pay the price. When our wives became pregnant, the children within them consumed their bodies while they grew in their wombs, killing the mothers. And after the children were born, they were cursed to live a half-life."

"How?"

"I assume you've heard the legend about werewolves."

"They're real?" I ask, not hiding that I'm having a hard time believing everything Mason is saying. However, I know it's the truth. I'm usually good at telling when people are lying to me, Owen being the exception to that rule. Even though everything Mason has said so far sounds outrageous, I know he's telling me what he believes to be true.

"When the moon rises, the children of the Watchers turn into werewolves. It wasn't meant as a punishment for them exactly. It was a punishment for us, their fathers, as a daily reminder that we failed them, and that we shouldn't have gone against God's law."

"So you lost your wives, and your children were cursed to be werewolves. I'm afraid to ask, but did your God do anything else to punish you?"

"We were also cursed with an insatiable hunger for human blood, and designed to produce a pheromone which made it virtually impossible for us to be near human females without them becoming instantly attracted to us."

"So, are you telling me you're a vampire?" I ask, feeling like I should go grab some garlic from the kitchen.

"It's where the legend comes from. Some of us were able to control the urge, and some of us weren't."

"Which side of that fence did you fall on?"

Mason grins grimly. "I was able to control it, but it wasn't easy. I spent a lot of time alone with my son in the beginning. Then, as time went by, it became easier to be around humans again, to live something which resembled a normal life."

"And your child?"

A genuine smile graces Mason's face. "He was freed of the curse when the Tear was made. He and Angela are married now, and they have a family of their own. They were granted human lives, since neither Allan nor I let our children drink human blood during the time they shifted into their werewolf forms."

"How did the Tear break their curse?"

"The Tear didn't do it. God did. The Tear is a result of Lucifer trying to destroy the universe."

"So, you're not just telling me God is real, but that the devil is real too?"

"Yes," Mason pauses before saying his next words, like he wants to make sure I hear them. "You just met him."

I sit there staring at Mason, unwilling to swallow this last bit of information, but knowing I have to.

"Lucian is the devil?" I ask, but already know the answer to my question.

"Lucifer was able to find you," Mason says gravely. "We have to assume he felt your presence, just like I did earlier this evening. Now that he knows where you live, I felt you should know who he is, because you *will* see him again. He's curious about you now, and if there is one thing Lucifer can't stand it's not knowing everything about everything. His presence is what made me decide to tell you the whole truth. I didn't think you would believe he was Lucifer unless you knew the complete story. You did just tell me a couple of hours ago that you don't believe in God, but I'm telling you He is real and Lucifer is real."

Now I feel like I should have paid more attention in all those Bible school classes Mama Lynn made me go to as a child. I feel sorely unprepared to handle what Mason is telling me. My mind is rebelling against the whole 'God is real' thing, even more so than the devil being real. Being a Watcher agent puts me in direct contact with people who seem to be pure evil. Evil I can believe in. A benevolent God? Not so much.

"So how did you stop Lucifer from destroying the universe?"

"I didn't. A woman named Lilly did."

"A human?

"Half human, half archangel."

I feel my eyes narrow on Mason. "Is she the hybrid you were referring to when you asked Allen if he thought I was one? Is that what you think I am?"

"Lilly is the only human who has ever been able to kill like you did tonight. It seems a logical conclusion."

Could that be what my father was? Is that why he always had a golden glow around him? I almost divulge this knowledge to Mason, but decide not to. We will know in the morning if his suspicions are correct. If they are, which I sincerely doubt, I can tell him my secret then.

"Faison would probably call you crazy for thinking there's

anything angelic about me. I'm about as far from an angel as you can get."

Mason's lips form a lopsided grin. "You're more similar to us than you might think. We aren't infallible. And who is Faison?"

"She's my sister. Adopted sister, I guess would be a better term. Mama Lynn had already adopted Faison when I went to live with her. We instantly bonded, which is one reason I think Mama Lynn adopted me too. She didn't want Faison to lose me; and, by that time, I couldn't face losing either one of them."

"I can tell they're important to you. Your face lights up when you talk about them."

"They're my life," I admit. "I can't imagine not seeing them every day, or at least talking to them once a day."

We're silent for a while, mostly because I'm still trying to absorb everything Mason has told me. I feel like he's giving me time to get my thoughts in order so I can make sense of things.

"So Lucifer's the one I need to blame for the Tear," I state, finding a new target for my anger.

"He's the one responsible for its existence. I suppose if you want someone to blame, it would be him."

"How did this Lilly stop him from destroying the universe?"

"Her love for a brother Watcher is what saved us in the end. After she stopped Lucifer, God lifted the curse of hungering for human blood from those of us who never drank it, and made the Watcher children who never drank human blood completely human so they can live out normal lives like they were meant to. He gave us, the Watchers, the task of finding a way to seal the Tear Lucifer's anger made."

I sit up straighter. "So there *is* a way to seal it?"

Mason nods. "We've been searching for it since that day."

"And you haven't found anything in 15 years?"

"Not until today," he says, looking pointedly at me, as if I hold the key to everything.

"I'm no one special," I say shaking my head, not liking the way he's looking at me. I'm no one's savior. "You've got the wrong girl. I'm nothing like this Lilly you've mentioned."

"No, you're not Lilly," Mason agrees, "but there is something about you that's different. You can't deny that. You saw and felt for yourself what you were able to do to that demon tonight."

I take a sip of my coffee as a distraction. I drain the cup and excuse myself, saying I need a refill as a way to gain a moment to myself.

Once in the kitchen, I set my cup on the counter in front of the coffee machine and stare at it absently, not really seeing it. I suddenly realize I've just received too much information at one time. I need a little while to process it all.

Mason walks into the kitchen with his now-empty cup.

I look over at him. "Do you want some more?"

"No; I think I should be leaving."

I feel myself do something I almost never do: panic.

"What if he comes back tonight?" I ask, not sure if my plasma pistol will be enough to fend off the devil.

"I don't think he will. It's not his style; but if it would make you feel better, I could stay here with you for the rest of the evening, just in case."

Now I feel like a chicken. I shake my head.

"No, you don't have to do that. If you say he won't come back tonight, I trust your judgment. If anyone would know his habits, it would probably be you."

"Are you sure?"

"Yeah, I'll be fine."

"Then I'll be here at eight in the morning to pick you up."

I nod. "Okay; see you then."

Mason goes back into the living room, presumably to get his coat. I wait for the distinct pop, which is normally associated with a Watcher's phasing, but never hear it. I walk into the living room to see if anything is wrong. When I get there, Mason's already gone.

CHAPTER 5

When I get up the next morning, I don't feel like I slept at all the night before. It's not far from the truth. The last time I looked at the clock, it was three in the morning. I know I tossed and turned after that, and finally fell into a troubled sleep. The red numbers on the digital clock by my bed say it's seven; time to get up.

I take a quick shower and get ready. I'm not sure what Mason expects me to wear to my new job with him, so I put on my Watcher uniform as a safe bet. I decide to hop in my car and grab some breakfast at Paw Paw's before Mason is due to arrive. As I walk down the steps from my porch, I see my friend and neighbor, George Grady, walking to his white Ford F150 parked in his driveway.

"Hey there, Jess!" he calls out, waving a white-gloved hand.

I can't help but smile at what George is wearing. George is a Tearer who came from a planet where all the men resemble Santa Claus, and all the children look like elves, with pointy ears and rosy cheeks. During this time of year, those Tearers make a killing playing mall Santa or working at private parties for the rich. The planet they come from was dubbed the North Pole by the media, and, unfortunately, it stuck in everyone's minds. I vaguely remember the real name of the planet actually being quite pretty, but can't remember what it is for the life of me. Every time I ask George if his planet is where our Santa Claus stories originated, he just smiles and says everyone should be allowed to believe in magic every once in a while.

"How's the Santa Claus business?" I ask.

George chuckles, making his little round belly shake like a bowl full of jelly.

"Can't complain; I do love seeing all the kids get excited about Christmas on this planet … makes me almost feel like I'm back home."

I try to smile; George and I have had a lot of talks about the family he left behind in his world. I wave goodbye and wish him a good day. When I get into my car, I feel even more determined to find a way to seal the Tear to prevent other families from being ripped apart, but only after I rescue my parents. I know it's completely selfish to think that way, but getting my parents back has been my main goal for most of my life. I'll either get them back or die trying.

Paw Paw's parking lot is crowded when I get there.

Everyone knows Beau makes his special yeast cinnamon rolls on Wednesday mornings. It's almost a sin if you live in the neighborhood and don't get one while they're still fresh from the oven. I find half of my neighbors already standing in line for their share of the rolls when I walk through the door.

I'm sure people who are simply passing through our quaint community and come into the store find Beau unusual. Not a lot of pureblooded Chinese men have a thick southern drawl, but Beau's family was one of the first to settle in Cypress Hollow. After his ancestors worked to construct the railroad system, they remained here and helped build a community with their hard work and perseverance.

Beau is standing behind the counter, carefully putting half a dozen rolls into a white cardboard pastry box for Vern and Sadie Myrick. Vern and Sadie have always reminded me of the couple in the *American Gothic* painting, except I've never actually seen Vern hold a pitchfork.

"Mornin', Jess!" Beau says to me from his position behind the counter, which sets off a cacophony of greetings from the other people present.

Mama Lynn looks up from her phone and motions me over to her position in line.

Mama Lynn was 40 years old when she adopted me. At 55, she's still a looker with her bobbed, slightly-graying red hair and striking green eyes. She's a little plumper than she would like to be around the middle, but when she complains about her weight, I just give her a big hug and tell her she's perfect.

George, aka our friendly neighborhood Santa Claus, has had a crush on Mama Lynn since he was placed in Cypress Hollow by the Watcher Agency. I think the only thing holding George back from asking Mama Lynn out on a real date is the outside chance he might get sent back home through the Tear one of these years. As things are, he said he felt like he would be cheating on his wife back on his planet if he acted on his feelings for Mama Lynn. So, he's kept his feelings for her to himself, never allowing their relationship to go beyond friendship.

"How did things go last night?" Mama Lynn asks, giving me a peck on the cheek when I come to stand by her.

"Everything went fine," I tell her, not feeling like going into a long discussion of what actually happened the night before. "In fact, I got a promotion of sorts."

"Really?" Mama Lynn smiles at me, beaming with pride. "What kind of promotion?"

"I'll be working with a group stationed in Colorado."

"Colorado!" Mama Lynn says in alarm.

"You're not moving, are you, Jess?" Sadie turns around to ask me.

Everyone else in line goes quiet, waiting to hear my answer.

"I'm not moving," I reply to Sadie and anyone else interested. I return my attention to Mama Lynn. "The Watcher in charge is supposed to pick me up and bring me home every day. I'm not going anywhere."

"Phew; you had me worried there for a minute."

We reach the front of the line, and Mama Lynn orders three cinnamon rolls.

"Faison still hasn't made it back from the hospital," Mama Lynn tells me with a shake of her head. "Poor thing will probably be starving by the time she gets back home."

I hear the bell above the front door of the store ring as someone enters behind me. I notice Mama Lynn staring at the newcomer, and turn to see who it is.

Mason is standing in front of the door. I look down at my watch and see that it's exactly eight.

"Can I help you?" Beau asks Mason as he hands Mama Lynn her box of cinnamon rolls.

"He's with me, Beau," I say, walking towards Mason. "Sorry," I tell him. "I just came over to get a roll for breakfast."

"I was worried," he says in a low voice, not saying what he was worried about, because we both know.

I find his concern for my welfare unexpectedly considerate.

"Who's your friend?" Mama Lynn asks, with a welcoming smile as she comes to stand beside me.

"Mama Lynn, this is Mason Collier. He's my new boss."

Mama Lynn holds out her hand to Mason. "Nice to meet you, Mr. Collier."

Mason shakes her hand. "Likewise; and please call me Mason. Jess has told me a lot about you."

Mama Lynn hands me the box of cinnamon rolls, all the

while smiling like sunshine at Mason. "Take these to work with you. I'm sure Mason, here, would like to try one."

"What about you and Faison?" I ask.

"Oh, I'll just grab some more. I know you're late for work."

I kiss Mama Lynn on the cheek. "I'll call you when I get home," I promise her.

When Mason and I step outside, I say, "Sorry for not being at my house when you showed up. I thought I would make it back there before you came."

"It's not a problem. Are you ready to go?"

"Sure, but I need to drive my car back to my house."

"I can move it for you."

Before I can ask what he means, Mason walks over to my car and places his hand on the roof. He and the car both disappear for a fraction of a second before he reappears in the same spot.

"What can you guys *not* phase?" I ask, trying not to freak out that my car just magically dematerialized in front of my eyes.

Mason shrugs; a hint of a smile on his lips. "There isn't much that can't be moved."

"How come I didn't hear that popping noise you guys usually make when you phase?" I ask. It was something I had noticed last night as well.

"We only do it when we phase somewhere public, or we want to make our presence known," Mason tells me. "It's a courtesy, not something which naturally happens when we phase. If we didn't do it, people who weren't looking for our arrival wouldn't be aware we just phased in next to them."

"I'm learning all kinds of secrets about you guys," I say.

Mason shrugs. "We're not as mysterious as most people make us out to be."

He rests a hand on my shoulder, and we're instantly in the basement of his house.

I see Joshua still sitting where he was last night, tapping the touch-screen panel in front of him, with incredible speed and coordination. There's a small garbage can beside his chair, filled with empty Red Bull cans and Snickers wrappers. Nick is nowhere to be seen, for which I'm silently thankful. Allan and Angela see us phase in and walk out of the glass room together to greet us.

"What is that heavenly scent?" Angela asks as she walks towards me.

"Cinnamon rolls," I say, holding out the box to her. "Would you like one?"

Angela takes the box and opens the lid, letting the aroma of Beau's cinnamon and sugar perfections surround her.

"Man," Joshua says, standing up from his chair, "can I have one too? Those smell too good to pass up."

"Sure," I say, secretly hoping Mason and Allan don't want one. There are only three rolls and five people, so two of us will end up being very disappointed.

"Why don't we wait just a minute?" Angela suggests, closing the lid before Joshua can put his hand in the box. "I'm sure Jess would like to know what we found out about her."

I feel my heart sink into my stomach again, but force myself to not let it show.

"What did you discover?" I ask.

"You're human," Allan says.

I wait for him to say more, some grand elaboration, but he doesn't. Allan seems to be a man of very few words, which I can appreciate, but not when it has to do with what makes me different.

"Is there nothing more you can add, Allan?" Mason gently prods, obviously used to Allan's succinct way of speaking.

"No," Allan says. "She's a normal human. No type of angel DNA is present. I couldn't find anything out of the ordinary."

"And trust me," Angela says with a yawn, "we examined every last detail. Jess is just a human."

I hear Mason sigh beside me. "Disappointing, but also interesting."

"Why interesting?" I ask, relief flooding through my system at Allan's discovery, or lack thereof.

"Because, whatever makes you unique is still a mystery; we need to figure out how you were able to kill that demon last night. If you had a hint of something different in your genetic code, we could try to follow up on it, but since you don't, I'm not sure where that leaves us now." Mason looks to Allan. "Is there anything else you can do? Any other tests you can run?"

"No," Angela answers before her father gets a chance to. "Trust me; we ran every test imaginable. Nothing came up abnormal. And you're perfectly healthy, by the way," Angela says to me. "We checked for disease markers and mutations while we were at it, and everything was normal."

"Ok, so now that we know Jess is just a human, can I *please* have a cinnamon roll?" Joshua whines.

Angela opens the lid and lets him pluck one of the over-sized rolls, dripping with white icing, out of the box. For such a skinny kid, I stand in awe of how fast Joshua is able to wolf down the sugary confection. Angela takes her roll out and hands me the box.

"You might want to hide the last one," she suggests, shaking her head at Joshua.

The elevator doors, which seem to be the only way in or out of the basement for regular mortals, open up, and Nick walks into the room with a manila folder in his hands.

"So, did I miss the unveiling?" he asks, coming to stand by us. "Did you find out anything interesting about our newest member?"

"No," Mason answers. "Did you?" he asks, looking pointedly at the folder in Nick's hands.

"No," Nick says, clearly disappointed. "There wasn't anything out of the ordinary about her, but I did find out some things about her parents that were interesting."

Even though I don't like Nick that much, I am instantly intrigued by what his paranoia may have uncovered about my parents' past. I know virtually nothing about them. I didn't even have family photos of them, because we never took pictures.

"What did you find out?" I ask, desperate for any information about where I came from and who exactly my parents are.

"Your mother, Sally Jane Riley, was orphaned when she was five years old. She was shuffled from one foster home to another through the years until she turned 18. After that, she disappeared from public records until she was admitted into the hospital to give birth to you. Your father was a ghost."

I have to assume Nick isn't speaking literally, so I ask, "What do you mean by a ghost?"

"There's absolutely no record of a Peter Riley until your birth. I couldn't even find a marriage certificate for your parents. The only time his name appears on anything official is your birth certificate. Even after that, everything your parents owned was placed in your mother's name. Nothing legally belonged to your father. That's all I was able to uncover. I wasn't able to find photos of them: no driver's license, no passports, no school pictures, nothing. It's like their existence has been completely wiped. I called a few of the people your mother stayed with while she was in the foster care program to see if they could give me any information. For whatever reason, none of them seem to have any recollection of even having your mother in their care. It's like someone went in and deliberately erased your mother's past, even from the minds of the people who knew her."

I stand there, not really knowing what to say. All my life, I wanted to know more about my parents. Now I had to face the fact that there wasn't anything beyond what I already knew myself from just living with them for the first seven years of my life. If there had been anything else to discover about their past, I felt sure Nick would have dug it up. He didn't seem like someone who would be incompetent at his job.

"So, now what?" I ask, not knowing where to go from here, since we seem to have hit dead ends on all fronts where I'm concerned.

"Well, I've found something interesting," Joshua says, licking the last of the white icing from the tips of his fingers.

Joshua returns to his chair in front of the touch-screen panel, and pulls up a video of Lucifer standing outside my house the night before.

"After Mason came back and told us about your visitor last night, Jess, I ran his new face through the facial recognition software to see where he went after he left you. He did his usual scouting of new Tearers, but one thing he did out of the ordinary was meet with one of them twice."

"Twice?" Mason says, obviously hearing this new bit of information for the first time. "Why didn't you tell me this sooner?"

"Because I didn't realize it until after you went to get Jess this morning," Joshua says. "He met the Tearer at the Watcher station in Rochester, NY last night and then again this morning at the temporary housing apartment complex there."

Joshua pulls up a video on the holographic display, showing Lucifer walking out of the apartment complex where the newly-deposited Tearers are sent on their first night on our planet. The man walking beside Lucifer is handsome, in a gritty sort of way. He looks like a man who would play the villain in a movie, with his sharp bone structure and slicked-back brown hair. He's wearing a brown tweed coat with a burnt orange scarf tied around his neck. I watch as Lucifer takes hold of the man's arm, and phases them both out of the picture.

"How long ago did that happen?" Mason asks urgently, like someone watching the last grains of sand drop from the top of an hourglass.

"Maybe 15 minutes ago," Joshua answers.

Mason turns to me. "We need to go before his phase trail disappears."

I look down at the box in my hands and mourn the loss of my breakfast, before shoving it into Nick's hands.

"Merry Christmas," I say to Nick, just before Mason puts his hand on my shoulder and phases us away.

CHAPTER 6

I suddenly find myself standing across the street from where Lucifer was last seen on Joshua's video replay. The apartment building, which houses the Tearers, stands five stories tall and is made out of blue brick with the Watcher logo, a melding of a W on top of an A, on the side, forever marking it as belonging to the Watcher Agency.

Mason quickly walks across the deserted street towards the spot where Lucifer and the Tearer he came to get phased from. I watch as Mason frowns at something only he can see at eye-level.

"Give me your hand," he tells me, holding out one of his. "Let's see how far we can follow them."

I place my hand in Mason's and suddenly find myself standing in the middle of what looks like a Turkish market-place. The warm aroma of mingled spices and sweet meats reminds me just how hungry I am. Colorful stalls surround us, offering a kaleidoscope of edible foods. The late afternoon sun signals to the shoppers around us that suppertime is quickly approaching.

"Where are we?" I ask.

"Istanbul spice market," Mason answers absently, his eyes searching for the trail from Lucifer's phasing.

Not letting go of my hand, Mason phases us, and I instantly find myself on a nondescript street, with strange symbols which look Oriental in origin on the side of buildings and street signs. In quick succession, Mason phases us from one point to another, forcing me to close my eyes in order to stop my empty stomach from churning uncontrollably.

After a few minutes, I hear Mason say, "Jess?"

Cautiously, I open my eyes only to find three Masons swimming in front of me. My legs feel like jelly, and I know I can't prevent my knees from buckling underneath me.

Mason pulls my body in close to his before I am able to fall, acting as my center, since my body has decided to completely betray me.

"Sorry," I say, grabbing the lapels of his wool coat with my hands and resting my forehead against his chest, trying to make my body stop quivering.

"No," Mason says, "I'm the one who's sorry. I shouldn't have phased you so many times in a row. The human body isn't made to withstand travelling like that. I should have known better."

I close my eyes to keep the world from spinning out of

control, and take deep breaths to calm my nerves. Mason's scent, woody, with a hint of cinnamon, fills my senses, and I feel more at ease. One of Mason's hands begins to rub my back in a soothing circular pattern, which coaxes my body into relaxing against him. The heat emanating from Mason's body surrounds me like a warm blanket against my skin, making me feel something I've never felt in the arms of a man before: comfortable.

I pull away, slowly releasing my death grip on his coat, and raise my head off his chest. When I look up at his face, I see confusion in Mason's eyes, and worry creasing his brow, giving him a brooding look. I slowly push away from him, finding my legs are once again able to support me on their own.

"Thanks," I say, feeling embarrassed for needing his help in the first place. Needing or asking for help from other people is something I don't do very often. After the disappearance of my parents, I quickly developed the philosophy that if you couldn't do something yourself, perhaps it was something you shouldn't be doing. You couldn't always count on other people to be there when you needed them. The more you let yourself rely on others, the more dependent you became on their help. It was just a fact of life.

I look around and notice we are standing in an open field, with nothing but grass and trees surrounding us.

"Where are we?" I ask.

"In the middle of nowhere, basically," Mason says, clearly disappointed. "Lucifer had his people help him cover his phase trail. There were too many trails to follow, so I chose some at random on the off chance we would hit the right one."

"What do you mean by, his people?"

"The angels who rebelled with him; they were all sent here with Lucifer after the war in Heaven. I believe my father hoped that forcing them to live among humans would teach them why humanity is so important to Him. Unfortunately, I only know of one rebellion angel who actually learned that lesson."

"How was he able to learn not to hate us anymore?"

"He fell in love with a human, and made close bonds with others."

"Where is he?" I ask. "Do you think he can help us?"

"No. Will was allowed back into Heaven after he sacrificed himself in the last battle with Lucifer. He gave up his life to give Lilly a chance to live."

"This Lilly must be special to have someone else willingly die for her."

Mason's eyes light up with joy, telling me Lilly is someone important to him too.

"She's special to all of the Watchers. We watch over her, and would lay down our lives to protect her and her family if it came to that. I doubt Lucifer will try to harm them, since he knows Lilly is in direct contact with God, but sometimes Lucifer doesn't think very clearly, and lets his pride and jealousy rule his actions."

"So what do you guys do? Take turns being with her?"

"Not exactly; there is only one of us who stays with her

constantly. His name is Malcolm. Malcolm's family life allows him to be more naturally integrated into Lilly's. He's part of her family, so his presence is expected by her and Brand's children. He's almost like a second father to them."

"Will I ever be able to meet her?"

"I don't know yet. We don't allow many people to bother her." The protective tone in Mason's voice tells me it might be easier to get into Heaven than be granted an audience with Lilly.

"You almost make her sound like someone you worship."

"No, we don't worship her," Mason says, "but she is precious to us. She helped bring all of the Watchers back together, and allowed us to earn forgiveness from our father for not only us but our children as well. She keeps our hopes up when we feel like we'll never find a way to seal the Tear. I guess you could say she's like our little sister, mother, and counselor, all wrapped up into one person."

I look around at the empty field, not seeing much of anything significant.

"How exactly were you following Lucifer? You said something about a phase trail."

"Each time an angel phases, they leave a connecting trail to the spot they travelled to. It can only be seen by another angel."

"What does it look like?"

"It's like looking at a hole in space. I can see the place they travel to through it."

"So, you said Lucifer had some help in hiding his phase trail. How many trails do you see in this one spot?"

Mason looks around, like he's doing a mental count. "Forty-four," he finally answers. "There are too many. We'll never be able to pick the right one. Let's go back to headquarters. Maybe they've been able to find out something useful since we've been gone."

When we phase back to headquarters, I'm faced with watching Nick lick the last bit of icing off his fingers. It instantly reminds me I still haven't eaten breakfast yet, causing my stomach to grumble its discontent.

"We couldn't find him," Mason tells the others. "Have you been able to discover anything else which might be helpful, Joshua?"

"Maybe," Joshua says, scratching his head like he's confused. "I noticed it last night when I was scanning the area where Jess lives. I didn't think too much of it, until I started looking through the file Nick brought in this morning about Jess' parents."

Joshua turns back around to his touch-screen control panel and brings up a satellite image of my parents' house. After a few more waves of his hand on the control panel, the picture takes on a blue hue, with a red pulsating dot directly over the house.

"What is that?" I ask.

"Gamma radiation, but sometimes you see that just from normal underground mineral deposits. That's why I didn't pay it much mind last night," Joshua tells me. "But when I went back and took a closer look at it this morning," he says, zooming in on the circle of red, "I noticed it doing this."

As we watch, the dot blinks on and off in a pattern.

"Is that an SOS signal?" Nick asks, sounding completely sure he has to be wrong.

"Yeah, weird, huh?" Joshua says.

"We should go there to see if we can find the source," Mason tells me.

"Take me back to my house," I say. "I'll drive us there."

In no time at all, Mason and I are in my car heading to my parents' home. I make a quick stop at Beau's store on the way out and find one cinnamon roll left, like destiny took pity on me. When I get back into the car, I open the box and turn to Mason.

"This is a onetime offer to share the best cinnamon roll you'll ever eat in your life," I say to him. "I'm willing to split it with you if you would like to try it."

Mason smiles, and I feel my heart make an involuntary lurch in my chest at how it transforms his usually austere expression, strangely finding myself wanting to make him smile more often.

"No; I couldn't deprive you of something you've obviously been wanting for a while now, but I do appreciate the offer."

I pick the roll up.

"You don't know what you're missing," I say as I take my first bite of the soft yeasty goodness in my hands. The silky texture of the melted sugar coats my tongue, making me feel like I've taken a bite out of Heaven itself. In no time at all, I have the roll eaten, and the growling monster living in the pit of my stomach finally seems satisfied.

"Do you feel better now?" Mason asks me, a hint of amusement in his voice as he watches me devour my breakfast.

I lick the last sweet traces of frosting from the tips of my fingers and nod, "You have no idea. I'll probably be on a sugar high for the rest of the day."

I hop out of the car and place the now-empty box in the trash.

As we're driving down Hwy 1, I turn the radio on to a station which only plays Christmas music this time of year. One of my favorite songs comes on: Mannheim Steamroller's *The Holly and The Ivy.*

"Do you have any plans for Christmas?" Mason asks me.

"Faison and I usually stay over at Mama Lynn's on Christmas Eve. Then we do what we've always done and wake up early Christmas morning to open gifts and eat Mama Lynn's sausage-egg-cheese casserole. This will probably be the last Christmas we get to do that, though."

"Why is that?"

"Faison is getting married next April. I'm sure she and John Austin will want to start their own family traditions."

"Do you have someone special in your life? Any plans to get married?"

I shake my head. "No; I don't date."

A pregnant silence hangs in the air before Mason says, "Mind if I ask why?"

I glance over at Mason and see that he's seriously interested in my answer.

"I guess I've just been too focused on finding a way to get my parents back. Most of the guys my age are only interested in having a good time, and that's not for me. Faison's been trying to set me up with John Austin's brother for forever, but I keep finding ways to put her off."

"Why?"

"I have a hard time letting people in," I confess, not exactly knowing why I'm telling Mason something I haven't actually verbalized to either Faison or Mama Lynn, though I have a feeling they already know what I'm about to tell Mason. "I don't think I could handle falling in love and having him sucked up through a wormhole like my parents. I can't afford to lose someone I care about like that again. It's just not worth the risk to me."

"But don't you want to have a family of your own one day?"

"Not until the Tear is sealed," I say with finality. "The fewer people I care about, the less risk there is of losing someone else I love."

"We'll find a way to seal it," Mason says like a promise. "I have a feeling we're getting closer to solving the problem. I was meant to find you, Jess. There's no doubt in my mind you're the clue I've been waiting for."

"But why now?" I ask. "Why 15 years after the Tear

appeared? Why weren't you allowed to find me back then, when it could have helped so many people?"

"I'm not sure," Mason answers. "It's hard to know exactly what God's plans are for us, but I trust Him to guide me in the right direction when it's the right time."

I almost envy Mason's faith in his God. It's something I've never been able to do so blindly. However, if Mason is *actually* an angel, his faith isn't based on blind trust. He knew his God personally, something I was still having a problem wrapping my brain around. Mason's God had borne the brunt of my hate for creating the Tear and allowing it to destroy so many lives. It was easier to just believe that type of God didn't exist than believe He did, and simply didn't care enough to help us when we needed Him the most. A God like that, I could do without.

I turn off Hwy 1 onto Cloverdale Road. The house my parents and I lived in is close to the levee. The property is surrounded by a five-foot-high barbed wire fence and the entrance blocked by an electronic padlocked gate. In no time at all, we are parked in front of the two-story farm house my parents left me.

We get out of the car and walk up the creaky wooden steps to the front porch and door. The wood swing hanging on the porch squeaks as the winter wind pushes it back and forth.

"So, how are we supposed to figure out where the radiation signal is coming from?" I ask, finding the key to the house on my key ring. I know it's old-school to use physical keys instead of a fingerprint lock but, like I told Mason, I don't trust computers.

Mason pulls out his cell phone, which is one of the new clear models.

"There's an app to detect radiation levels," he tells me.

I smile. "Are you serious? Who thinks up some of these apps?"

"I don't know, but every once in a while you find one which fits the occasion perfectly."

After I open the front door, I let Mason step in first, holding his cell phone in front of him, watching the read-out on his screen to see if his app will lead him in the right direction.

The inside of my parents' home is what you would expect to find in such a house. The furnishings are simple and rustic. Nothing too modern exists in the space, except for the new appliances I had installed in the kitchen last year. The artificial Christmas tree we set up the year they were taken still stands in the corner of the living room, with all of its lights and ornaments hanging from the limbs. Every week, Ms. Mona, the cleaning lady, comes over and tidies up the house for me, which mostly just consists of dusting and vacuuming. But she keeps the house looking the same way it did when my parents were taken. I just hope one day I will be able to give them back their home just the way they left it.

"Do you stay here sometimes?" Mason asks, scanning the living room area with his phone.

"Every once in a while," I say, walking over to the Christmas tree to straighten a wayward Cinderella.

Mason comes to stand beside me, looking at the tree.

"These decorations look more like you," he comments.

When I look at the tree, I have to admit he's right. An array of Disney characters, Santas, and homemade ornaments adorns the tree. My parents always let me pick out new ornaments every Christmas, slowly building up our collection to fit what was important to me each year.

"I still believed in Santa Claus the year they were taken," I hear myself say. "I asked the mall Santa to bring me an American Girl doll named Rebecca, and I wanted a dress to match hers, because that's what the company used to do. But Santa never came to the foster care center I spent that Christmas in. I thought maybe that was why my parents had been taken, because he thought I was a bad girl that year. If Santa didn't think I was worthy enough to have my doll, maybe he took my parents as a way to punish me."

"I'm sorry you had to go through that," Mason says, and I hear the sincerity in his voice. "That must have been a hard time for you."

"It was a hard time for a lot of people," I reply, turning my back to the tree, no longer wishing to linger on my memories. "What does your phone say?"

Mason looks down at the read-out on his display. "It doesn't seem to be down here. I think we should look upstairs."

I lead the way to the second floor by way of the staircase in the foyer.

"There are three bedrooms up here, plus my father's study," I tell Mason.

He points his phone in each direction, and finally gets a spike on the display.

"That room," he tells me, pointing to the door that leads to the study.

Of all the rooms in the house, my father's study is the one I haven't been in since my parents disappeared. It's haunted by too many fond memories from my childhood. As a little girl, I would go in there and curl up on my daddy's lap as we sat together in his leather recliner. He would read all the classics to me like I was a grown up. Huck Finn and Peter Pan were my heroes, whisking me off to strange new worlds, with my father steadfastly by my side to share the experiences with me.

I walk to the door and take a deep breath before turning the brass knob. I let the door swing inward. It creaks, as if finding its voice to welcome me back after such a long time away.

Mason follows behind me, sweeping his phone over everything, from my father's desk to the shelves of books and cabinets lining the walls. Finally, I see another spike show up on Mason's display, indicating the source of the radiation is coming from the brick fireplace. Mason walks to the fireplace, trying to pinpoint the exact location of the radiation, and finds that the signal is strongest within the chimney itself.

Mason quickly drops his phone back into his coat pocket

and shrugs his coat from his shoulders. Before I know it, he has most of his body up the flue of the chimney.

"Do you see anything?" I ask, curious to know why something of any importance would be hidden inside my father's fireplace.

"Hold on," Mason says with a grimace as I see his body stretch, like he's trying to grab something almost too high to reach.

When he comes back out, he's holding a medium-sized metal box in one hand.

He walks over to my father's desk and sets it down. There is no lock, so he simply releases the catch and lifts the lid. Sitting inside the box is a pristinely-polished silver crown with strange, fluid, circular rune marks decorating its surface. I find myself mesmerized by its beauty, and begin to wonder how my father came to be in possession of such a thing.

I hear Mason gasp, dragging my attention away from the crown, to his face. It's apparent he recognizes the crown, and is as surprised to see it stashed away in my father's study as I am.

"What is it?" I ask. "I mean, I can see it's a crown, but do you know where it came from?"

I see Mason's Adam's apple bob up and down as he swallows hard before telling me what he knows.

"It's one of the seven archangel crowns," he says with reverence.

"Why would something like that be stashed away in my father's fireplace?" I ask.

"I don't know, Jess." Mason says looking up at me. "Can you tell me?"

Mason's penetrating gaze makes me feel uncomfortable, because I feel like he thinks I'm keeping a vital piece of information from him. I can't deny that I'm not, but my father's voice reverberates in my head, telling me to keep my secret to myself.

"I've never seen it before," I say honestly.

Mason stares at me, apparently expecting me to say more. I avert my eyes from his probing gaze, and stare at the crown instead.

Finally, Mason reaches inside the box to pull out the crown. Just as he's about to wrap his fingers around it, he stops, but it's not as if he does it intentionally. I see him strain to move his fingers inward to grasp the crown, but it's like there's an invisible force-field around it, preventing him from performing such an action. Finally, with a grunt, not out of frustration but from strain, he gives up and withdraws his hand from the box.

"You try to pick it up," Mason suggests to me.

"If it won't let an angel pick it up, I seriously doubt it will let me," I say.

"Just try, Jess," Mason encourages, his voice asking me to trust him on this.

I shake my head, completely confident I won't be any more successful than Mason was. When I place my hand over the crown, I feel something like static electricity dance across my palm, and quickly yank my hand back to my side.

"What's wrong?" Mason asks, concern in his voice.

"I felt something," I say. "Did you feel a tingling sensation when you tried to pick it up?"

"No; I felt nothing."

With my heart hammering inside my chest, I place my hand inside the box once again, ignoring the electricity the crown seems to be pulsing with, like a living creature against my flesh. With no problem at all, I wrap my fingers around the base of the crown and pull it out of the box. I stare at it, not knowing exactly what to do with it now that I have it. Before I can ask Mason what I should do next, the iron box on the desk disintegrates into a pile of ash.

"Interesting," I hear Mason say, like magic happens in front of him every day.

Maybe it does, and I'm just a hapless human who is caught up in things I don't quite understand.

"What do we do now?" I ask.

"I don't know," Mason says shaking his head. "I'm not even sure why the crown is on Earth."

"You said it was an archangel crown?" I ask, just to verify I heard him correctly the first time.

"Yes. The archangel it belongs to should be wearing it right now; that's why I don't understand why it's here. It should be in Heaven, not on Earth. It must have been sent here to help in some way. I just don't understand how."

"Why can I hold it?" I ask. "Why couldn't you pick it up?"

"I don't know," Mason answers, "but it was obviously made to only respond to your touch."

"So, what do I do with it?"

"See if it will fit on your head," Mason suggests.

His idea sounds ridiculous, but I try it anyway. I place the crown on top of my head, but nothing happens. I don't suddenly have some grand epiphany and the Earth doesn't quake beneath my feet. The only thing I notice is how light-weight it is.

Feeling slightly ridiculous standing there with a crown on my head, I ask, "See anything? Any kind of divine inspiration hitting you? Anything at all?"

"Only that you would look beautiful as a queen," Mason tells me, not joking at my expense; just making an observation.

I lower my eyes, no longer able to meet Mason's gaze, and pull the crown off my head, smoothing down my hair where it was perched.

"So, what do we do with it now?" I ask, chancing a glance in Mason's direction.

"I need to speak with some fellow Watchers about it. Maybe together we can figure out what needs to be done next."

"Do you want me to come with you?" I ask.

"No, not yet; I need to speak with them alone first and tell them what we know so far. When I know what our next move should be, I will come to you."

"So, what, you just want me to go home for now?"

"I think that would be best. I'll contact you later this afternoon. Maybe by then we'll have a better understanding about what the crown's being here means."

In no time at all, Mason has me and my car sitting in my driveway.

"Try to get some rest," Mason tells me. "I'll let you know what our next move is as soon as I know what it should be."

Mason phases.

I sit in my car, staring at the crown of an archangel in my hands, wondering what the hell I've gotten myself into.

CHAPTER 7

When I finally decide to stop staring at the crown, I get out of my car and walk up to my porch.

Just as I'm about to open the door, I hear, "What's that you have in your hand?"

Startled, I place my other hand on my plasma pistol and swiftly turn around to face Lucifer.

"You have seriously got to stop sneaking up on me like that," I tell him irritably, my hand itching to pull my pistol from its holster.

He looks amused by my rebuke. "I'm sorry, Jessica. I didn't mean to scare you."

"How do you know my name?" I ask, distinctly remembering not telling the devil my first name the night before, because I didn't want to be on a first-name basis with him, even before I knew his true identity.

"I know everything there is to know about you," he says, a twinkle of mischief in his eyes. "You didn't think I wouldn't do my research on your past, did you? Someone as special as you is worth getting to know all about."

"I'm no one special."

He smiles indulgently. "Yes, you are. You simply don't realize it yet."

"Do you know what's different about me?" I ask, wondering if the devil might actually be helpful in solving the mystery in which I find myself.

"No," he admits reluctantly. I can see admitting it bothers him, "not yet, but *that's* certainly a clue." He looks pointedly at the crown in my hands. "I'm sure Mason told you what it is."

"Yes." I say, not offering any more information.

"I wonder why it's here," he ponders, and I instantly know he's as clueless as the rest of us as to its purpose. "It really shouldn't be, you know."

"Was there a reason you came back here...what should I call you; Lucian or Lucifer?"

"Lucian would be less conspicuous, in case any of your neighbors see us talking, but it's up to you; either name is fine with me. Sadly, there aren't any children named Lucifer these days. And, to answer your question, I had a yearning to see you again, Jessica."

"Should I be scared you just said that?" I ask, not wanting Lucifer to yearn for my company in any way, shape, or form.

"I'm not here to harm you," he tells me, and I believe him for some strange reason. He seems earnest in his statement.

"Then why are you here?" I ask.

"To be honest, I'm not completely sure." He smiles at me, letting me see he's as confused as anyone about his actions. "There's something familiar about you, something I can't quite put my finger on, to tell you the truth. It's made me rather determined to figure it out."

"Does that mean I should expect more visits from you?"

"Most certainly."

"And if I asked you to stay away from me, would you do it?"

"I'm afraid I can't," he answers. "I'm inexplicably drawn to you, Jessica."

"Uh, what kind of drawn, exactly?"

"It's not in a romantic sense, if that's what you're worried about," he chuckles. "Though," Lucifer looks down at his body, "I can't see why you would object to having this form in your bed. Women seem to like it quite well."

"So do you change into whatever form you want?" I ask, since no one else has bothered to explain that part to me yet.

"No, but I can take over any human body of my choosing."

"What happens to the person whose body you use?"

"Their soul is pushed out, and mine takes its place."

"So you kill them."

"Yes." There's no malice in his statement; just fact.

"You still haven't explained this yearning you say you feel to be with me," I point out.

"I'm not sure I can explain it sufficiently, but rest assured, it's not sexual in nature; more friendly than anything."

"Can the devil have friends?"

The smile on Lucifer's face fades. "I had a best friend once. He and I did everything together, until he sided with our father instead of me during the war."

"Who was he?"

Lucifer's brow lowers, and he looks at me like I should already know the answer to my own question. "Don't all people in this part of the world go to church and learn these stories on Sunday morning?"

"I have a hard time believing in something I can't see," I tell him.

Lucifer cocks his head. "Are you telling me you don't believe in God?"

"Honestly, I'm not sure what I believe anymore. You and Mason seem to think He's real. I've just never had a good enough reason to believe in Him."

"Well, aren't you just full of surprises?" Lucifer smiles again. "Far be it for me to try to convince you otherwise. He seems to have plenty of people fooled into believing He's all-knowing and benevolent. It's refreshing to find someone who isn't so gullible."

Being praised by the devil doesn't seem right, but I won't lie and say I believe in or trust in God wholeheartedly. He might exist, but that didn't mean I had to agree with every-thing He did.

"So are you telling me you want to be my friend?" I ask.

"I haven't quite decided," Lucifer says, "but when I figure it out, I'll let you know."

Lucifer disappears.

When I walk into my house, my cell phone rings; it's Mama Lynn.

"I saw you out my window, talking to a handsome stranger," she says to me. "Is he someone you're dating?"

"No!" I say a bit too emphatically. "He's just someone I have to deal with in my new job; no one important."

"Well, are you already home from work this early, or do you have to go back?"

"I might have to go back later. Mason had to go talk to some people about some evidence we found today."

"Then why don't you come to my house? Faison and I are making sugar cookies. It would be more fun if all three of us made them together. Then you girls can take me to the hospital to see Uncle Dan."

I cringe inwardly. With everything that has happened since I made that promise to her, I had completely wiped it from my mind.

"Ok, let me put something up first, and I'll be right down."

I go to my bedroom and hide the crown underneath my pillow. I suddenly realize it's not exactly Fort Knox, but basically anywhere in the house is easily accessible if someone really wanted to steal it.

I spend the next three hours with Faison and Mama Lynn, trying to forget about the crown and Lucifer. We make cookies, which will be delivered to all our friends as Christmas gifts, and eat lunch together. It reminds me of when Faison and I were kids around this time of year. We would bug Mama Lynn to make her famous iced sugar cookies just so we could snack on the ones she deemed unworthy of giving as a gift.

The conversation at lunch eventually turns to my work. I learn that Mama Lynn has told Faison about meeting Mason that morning.

"So, is he cute?" Faison asks me excitedly.

"He's a Watcher," I say in response. "What do you think?"

"Then he's drop-dead gorgeous," Faison sighs. "If that were the reason you wanted to be around Watchers all the time, I could fully understand and support your chosen profession."

"Why does he have that scar on his face?" Mama Lynn asks. "I've never seen a Watcher with something like that."

"A scar?" Faison asks, becoming even more excited. "That must mean he has a tortured past."

I roll my eyes at Faison and her fanciful notions. "I don't know where the scar came from. We haven't exactly gotten to be bosom buddies in less than a day. He hasn't shared all his deepest, darkest secrets with me."

"Not yet," Faison adds.

"He doesn't seem like someone who shares his thoughts easily with a lot of people," I say.

"Well," Mama Lynn sits back in her chair at the dining table, "that certainly sounds a lot like someone Faison and I know."

"I share," I say in my own defense, knowing she's talking about me. "I tell you and Faison everything."

"You tell us about your day," Mama Lynn says, "but you rarely share what you're feeling. There's a difference."

I don't respond, which just seems to verify what Mama Lynn has said about me.

I get a call on my cell phone, and thank whatever higher power there might be for the temporary save.

"Hello?" I ask, not recognizing the number.

"Where are you?" Mason asks.

"I'm at Mama Lynn's house. Where are you?"

"Your house, but I'm walking to you now."

I stand up and walk away from the dining table to go to the front door. After I open it, I see Mason walking along the sidewalk, heading my way. I wave to him, and he waves back. I end our call and wait for him to walk over.

I soon find Faison and Mama Lynn standing on either side of me, peering out the door to watch Mason's approach.

"Wow," Faison says. "I think that scar just makes him look hot; kinda rough and not as perfect as the other Watchers."

"It does lend him a manly ruggedness," Mama Lynn agrees with a nod. "Now, you invite him in," she tells me. "I want to give him some of the cookies we just baked."

"I'm not sure he's a sweets kinda person," I tell her, remembering his ability to withstand the offer of sharing Beau's cinnamon roll just that morning.

"Oh, everyone likes something a little sweet every once in a while," Mama Lynn says, heading back to the kitchen.

"Yes, they do," Faison says suggestively beside me. "And I think he's just the sweet you need right now."

I feel my cheeks flush. "Faison, I swear to God if you try to play matchmaker I'm gonna strangle you. He's my boss. Don't try to make something out of nothing."

"Your mouth may say that, but your flaming red cheeks are telling me a different story," she says with a knowing smile. "I've never seen you blush when I tease you about other boys. Is there something going on between the two of you I should know about?"

"We just met last night!" I say a bit too loudly. I glance at Mason, who's only a few yards away now, hoping he can't hear a word we are saying.

"I fell in love with John Austin the moment I saw him," Faison says, a faraway look in her eyes as she remembers the day.

"You were in second grade," I remind her, bringing her out of the clouds and back to reality. "I don't think a seven-year-old is able to comprehend what true love is."

"It doesn't matter how old you are. True love finds you at some point in your life whether you're seven or a hundred. Thankfully, you're not an old maid yet. There's still hope."

I stick my tongue out at Faison, which just makes her giggle.

Mason finally arrives at the front door.

"You better come on in," I say to him. "Mama Lynn wants to give you some of the sugar cookies we made," I forewarn.

"Hi," Faison says, holding out her hand to Mason. "Faison

Mills. And you're Mason...." she says, fishing for his last name.

"Collier," Mason provides. "It's a pleasure to meet you. Jess has spoken very highly of you."

Faison beams her beauty queen smile as she looks up at Mason with her big doe eyes. I can read her face like a book and know she's about to do something that will no doubt embarrass me.

"Have you told Mason about the party yet?" Faison asks me.

I suddenly feel like getting a roll of duct tape to bind Faison's lips together, ensuring she is unable to speak her next words.

"Jess, here, has refused to let me set her up on a date, but I was thinking maybe you could be her escort; that way we could all get to know you a little better, since we'll probably be seeing a lot of one another from now on."

Faison's ability to use her southern wiles on the male population is legendary in Cypress Hollow. With one bat of her long eyelashes, she's been known to make even the most ornery man melt to her will. I look at Mason and realize it's the first time I've seen him utterly speechless. I instantly want to go hide in a closet until the whole disastrous encounter is over with.

"Well?" Faison says, trying to coax an answer from Mason.

"I'm sorry," Mason says. "Was there a question in what you just said?"

"I was asking," Faison says slowly, so Mason hears her words clearly, "if you would like to escort Jess to a Christmas party at our friend's house tomorrow night."

Mason looks over at me, and I can see he doesn't quite know how to respond.

"I suppose I could act as Jess's escort, if she really needs one," he says haltingly.

"Good; then that's settled," Faison says, smiling at her accomplishment of finding me a date on such short notice, even though she never actually asked me if it was what I wanted.

Mama Lynn appears in the arched entryway to the kitchen from the living room.

"Come on in, Mason," she says, ever the epitome of southern hospitality. "I've got something for you." She waves him over, indicating he should follow her into the kitchen.

Mason walks into the house, and I close the door behind him.

Faison leans into my ear and whispers, "I think he likes you."

I look at her like she's lost her mind.

"You practically bushwhacked him into taking me to that stupid party; a party I wasn't even intending to go to," I whisper back heatedly.

"But he likes you," Faison says, full of excitement because she's always been a hopeless romantic.

I just shake my head and walk to the kitchen, completely

unsure how I will ever recover from my Faison-induced morti-
fication.

Mama Lynn is just handing Mason a snowman tin-full of
cookies when I reach the kitchen.

"Now, you share these with the people you and Jess work
with," Mama Lynn instructs. "I only make them once a year,
so you'd better enjoy them while you can."

"I'll be sure everyone gets a chance to taste your
wonderful baking," Mason tells her. "Thank you for your
thoughtfulness."

I see Mama Lynn blush slightly as she waves her hand.
"Oh, they're just a little something we give to all our friends at
Christmas."

"Then thank you for including me in such a special group
of people."

Mama Lynn smiles. As Mason turns around to find me, I
see Mama Lynn point to Mason and make the 'ok' sign with
her hand, telling me she approves of him. It makes me wonder
if Mama Lynn had been the mastermind all along behind
Faison's ambush of Mason. Had she been secretly orches-
trating a way to get Mason and me on a date since she met him
that morning? It's then I realize how desperate the two most
important people in my life are to see me go on a date. Poor
Mason is fixed in their crosshairs now, a fact which almost
makes me pity him.

When Mason faces me, I know there is only one thing to
do: get him out of Mama Lynn's house before she has us
married off.

"I need to speak with you in private," I say to Mason, tilting my head to indicate that we should go outside.

Mason turns to look at Mama Lynn.

"I'll make sure the people we work with in Colorado get these," he tells her. "Thank you again."

"Anytime," Mama Lynn smiles.

Mason turns to Faison. "Nice to have met you, Faison; I suppose I will see you at the party tomorrow night."

Faison smiles, "Oh, you can count on it."

Once we step outside, I start to walk down the sidewalk to my house, not wanting curious ears to hear what I have to tell Mason.

"Lucifer came to see me," I say.

Mason scowls. "What did he want?"

"He seems to think he and I can be friends," I say, shaking my head at the absurdity of the string of words I just uttered.

"I don't think he knows the true meaning of that concept," Mason comments dryly. "Did he say why he thought the two of you could be friends, or, more importantly, why he wants to be friends with you?"

I shrug. "Just that he sensed something familiar about me. He didn't elaborate much on the subject." I pause for a moment, not sure how Mason will take my next revelation. "He saw the crown."

Mason stops walking, forcing me to stop and turn to face him.

"What did he say about it?"

"Not much, just that it shouldn't be here. More or less the same thing you said to me when you first saw it."

"Did he try to take it from you?"

I shake my head. "No. He didn't seem interested in trying to take it."

Mason's eyes narrow in on me. "You don't seem scared of him."

I suddenly realize Mason is right. "No, I guess I'm not. He hasn't really done anything to make me scared of him."

"But you know who and what he is," Mason points out. "That in itself would scare most humans."

"I can't really explain it to you," I tell him. "I don't understand it myself. If anything, I guess I feel pity for him."

"Pity?" Mason questions, like it's the most illogical thing I could have said. "Why?"

"From what I know of his story, he lost everything because of his pride and his hatred of humans. I can't imagine living with a hate that eats you up like that. He let it control him, and he lost everything. He doesn't seem to have anything to live for now, except revenge. I guess I pity him because I can't imagine living like that."

"He made his own decisions," Mason says, not arguing with my statement, but reminding me Lucifer wasn't forced into anything.

"I know," I reply, suddenly feeling a need to change the subject. "By the way, you really don't have to go to that party with me tomorrow night. Like I told you earlier, Faison is always trying to set me up with people, and you were just her latest victim."

A small smile stretches Mason's lips. "No, I would like to go. It's probably a good idea for me to get to know some more of your friends. If anything were to ever happen to you, I would know who else to contact besides just Faison and Lynn."

"I guess that makes sense," I say, feeling my heart deflate a little with his sensible logic. "What did the Watchers you went to speak with have to say about the crown? What's our next move?"

"None of them seem to know why it's here either, but we've decided you should take the crown to Lilly. Since you are the only one who can even touch the crown, you have to be the one who takes it to her. Maybe she will sense something about it we can't. We've arranged for you to meet with her tomorrow morning. Can you be ready by nine, or should I plan on coming a little later?"

"No, I'll be home this time. I promise. I know how hard it must have been for you to arrange this meeting."

"You'll have to meet with her guardian first," Mason tells me, a warning in his voice. "He doesn't let anyone near her until he's met them."

"Will I be meeting him tomorrow morning too?"

"No, I showed Malcolm where you live. He'll be back sometime this evening. He had a few errands to run first. When he does come, just be yourself, and he won't have any problems allowing you to meet with Lilly. Give me a call at the number I just called you from after he leaves. I would like to know how the meeting goes."

"Okay," I say. "Is there any reason he would disapprove of me?"

"I don't think so," Mason says, not sounding completely sure, "but like I said, Malcolm is very protective of Lilly and her family. If he senses any kind of threat from you, he won't let you near her no matter how much I ask him to. Don't worry, though. You'll do fine."

"You might want to let him know I won't be home until late this evening. I have to take Mama Lynn to Baptist Memorial to see her brother."

"I'm sorry to hear he's sick," Mason says sympathetically.

"He's not expected to make it too much longer, so she wants us to say our goodbyes."

"And how are you handling this?"

I shrug my shoulders.

"Death is a part of life," I say unemotionally.

Mason's eyebrows lower, and I can tell he's concerned by my answer. Before he tries to dig any deeper into my feelings, I say, "I'll call you as soon as Malcolm leaves and let you know how it goes."

Mason nods, seeing I don't want to talk about my uncle anymore.

"All right; I'll be waiting to hear from you."

Staying true to my word, Faison and I take Mama Lynn to Memphis so she can visit with Uncle Dan.

"Ever since he had that accident and became paralyzed

back when you girls were teenagers, his health has just been deteriorating," Mama Lynn says on the drive up. "I swear it was like he just didn't have anything to live for anymore. Then this year, when they found cancer in his lungs, and saw that it had spread to his bones, it's like he just completely gave up and is waiting for God to call him home."

Both Faison and I remain silent.

I remembered Uncle Dan's accident clearly. I was the one who caused it.

It happened the day I confronted him with what he had done to me as a child. I was a spunky 13-year-old and wanted him to say he was sorry for doing the things he did. But all he did was smirk and tell me I should stop trying to deny I didn't enjoy it as much as he did. In that moment, all I saw was red. I completely lost my temper and kicked him so hard in the groin that he fell to his knees. With him in such a compromising position, I couldn't prevent myself from kicking him under the chin, causing him to fall back and hit his head on the brick steps leading up to his front door. Blood had poured from the wound on the back of his skull.

To this day, I can remember just standing there, watching his dark red blood pool around him. I can't say for sure if it was due to shock or just a morbid need to watch him suffer, but I didn't run for help immediately. I think I stood there for a good 15 minutes before I ran to find Mama Lynn. I didn't tell her what happened. I just said that I found Uncle Dan that way when I went over to see him. She immediately called an ambulance, and they arrived just in time to save his life but not his ability to walk.

When he awoke, he didn't seem to remember that I was the cause of his fall. Shortly after that, we found out his spinal cord had been damaged, and that he would forever be paralyzed from the waist down; a fitting sentence for a pedophile, if you ask me.

When we reach Baptist Memorial, I allow Faison and Mama Lynn to walk ahead of me. I don't want to be here. I don't want to be near a man who took so much away from me. Not only did I lose my parents, but I was also placed in a position where my childhood innocence was snatched away from me.

Uncle Dan is in the hospice ward, since there's no hope for him to recover. We're basically just waiting for him to die. I stand at the entrance to his room as Mama Lynn goes into caretaker mode. She walks over to what remains of the man who terrorized me as a child more often than I allow myself to think about. I can hear his ragged breathing from where I stand. I watch as the living skeleton in the bed turns his head to look at his sister. Uncle Dan once weighed a good 270 pounds, but the person lying in the bed is nothing more than skin covering bones. His once-thick brown hair is now reduced to small patches scattered randomly on his scalp, like a mangy dog. His eyes are hollow, and I'm not even sure he knows who Mama Lynn is, much less Faison and me.

I watch as Mama Lynn takes her brother's hand and kisses it tenderly. I know seeing Uncle Dan in such a state is killing her, and it's that knowledge more than anything else that makes me turn away from the scene and walk down the hallway to a window overlooking the Memphis skyline. I lean against the wall as I look out the window, and feel my heart burn with a mixture of sorrow for Mama Lynn's pain and righteousness for a death I feel is long overdue. I've always hated Uncle Dan for the things he did to me, but a small part of my soul cries for the agony being suffered by the creature I see, wasting away to nothingness. I soon find myself crying for someone I have hated most of my life, and can't seem to make my heart stop aching for the pain Mama Lynn is enduring.

"Jess?"

"Jessica?"

I look at the window and see the reflections of both Mason and Lucifer. They're standing side by side, directly behind me.

I turn to face them, wiping the tears from my eyes.

"What are you both doing here?" I ask, embarrassed for having been caught in such a vulnerable position.

"I felt you," they say in unison.

"I felt your pain," Lucifer says, narrowing his eyes at me. "What's wrong? Why are you crying?"

I shake my head, not wanting to have to explain anything. "It's nothing."

"You're lying," Lucifer says knowingly. "I don't believe you are one to cry very often." Lucifer looks at his surroundings. "Is one of your family members sick?"

"Our uncle," Faison says walking towards us from Uncle Dan's room.

Lucifer turns to Faison, and all I want to do is tell her to run. My only solace is that Mason is there with me and can help protect Faison if Lucifer attempts to harm her.

"And, pray tell," Lucifer says in a voice which sounds beguiling, "why is his death affecting Jessica so deeply?"

Faison looks at me, and I shake my head at her, warning her not to say anything.

"That's Jess's business. If she wanted you to know, she would tell you herself."

Lucifer turns to look at me. His gaze makes me feel like he's digging into the deepest recesses of my mind. I try to make my expression impassive, revealing nothing, yet Lucifer's expression turns dark, and I feel like I've just revealed everything to him.

"He abused you in some way, didn't he?"

I remain silent and still, but Faison gasps at Lucifer's spot-on deduction.

Returning his attention to an easier target, Lucifer says to Faison, "Did he beat her?"

Faison looks at me and shakes her head.

"Faison," I say as a warning not to do or say anything else.

"Then he sexually abused her, did he?" Lucifer says in a voice that doesn't need confirmation. He knows it's true.

I watch as Mason's eyes grow dark at this news. When he looks at me, I can see pity; something I don't want.

Lucifer turns to me again. "Why feel sorrow for such a person? You should be ready to dance on his grave."

I look down, not knowing how to explain how I feel. Finally, I shake my head and say, "I don't know. I shouldn't care, but I don't like seeing anyone in that much pain."

Lucifer smiles and it sends shivers down my spine.

"I can promise you he won't know true pain until after he dies."

I watch Lucifer turn on his heels and stroll down the hallway towards Uncle Dan's room.

"What does he plan to do?" I ask Mason.

"I'm not sure, but we should probably go see."

The three of us quickly walk down to the entrance of the room. When we get there, I'm thankful to see Mama Lynn is nowhere to be seen. I basically force Faison to stay behind me and Mason as we block the doorway to watch Lucifer. Lucifer leans over and whispers something into Uncle Dan's ear. Uncle Dan's body begins to tremble uncontrollably, causing the metal bed to rattle as Lucifer straightens up again.

"There's a special place for you in my world," I hear Lucifer tell him. "I can appreciate evil deeds when done right, but those of you who prey on children who are unable to defend themselves will find no quarter of safety. I look forward to your time in my realm. If you think you're suffering now, you have no idea what suffering truly is. I can promise you, any pain you inflicted on your victims will be revisited on you a million fold."

As Lucifer pulls away, I'm able to see Uncle Dan's face. It's a mask etched in terror as he stares at Lucifer.

I hear the toilet in the bathroom flush, and Mama Lynn steps back into the room.

"Who are you?" she asks Lucifer, and then I see recognition dawn on her face. "Oh, you're one of Jess's new friends. I saw you earlier today at her house. Hi," she says holding out her hand. "I'm Jess's mom."

Lucifer shakes Mama Lynn's hand, and I quake inside.

"Pleased to make your acquaintance," Lucifer says smoothly. "I am truly sorry for what you must be going through right now, but I'm sure your brother will be going exactly where he needs to be when all is said and done here."

Mama Lynn nods, thinking Lucifer's words are meant as a comfort. When she looks over at Uncle Dan, it's only then that she notices how terrified he looks.

"Dan?" Mama Lynn says, walking over to his bedside. I hear Uncle Dan whimper like a child.

Lucifer saunters over to me.

"If you need me for anything else," he says, "please let me know. I'm always around."

Mason and I watch him walk past us out of the room and continue to stroll down the hallway.

Faison looks up at Mason.

"Jess might like a walk outside to get some fresh air," she suggests, giving me an excuse to leave.

Mason holds his arm out to me. I stare at it for a second, not sure if I want to leave or stay. I hear another whimper of despair come from Uncle Dan, and my dilemma is quickly resolved. Without taking Mason's arm, I turn and head toward the door leading to the stairs. Mason follows close behind. Once inside the stairwell, I take a seat on the top step, and Mason sits down beside me.

He doesn't say anything or even attempt to look my way. He simply sits with me. I appreciate his silence because I really don't want to talk about Uncle Dan, or what just happened between him and Lucifer. A small part of me rejoices at the fear I saw on Uncle Dan's face from Lucifer's promise, and another part of me pities what awaits him when he dies.

"Is there really a Hell?" I ask Mason, turning my head to look at him, awaiting his response.

He looks at me and says, "Yes."

It's all the confirmation I need. I look away from Mason and stare down the well of stairs in front of us. I feel Mason's worried gaze still on me, and silently wish he would just look away.

"Is there anything I can do for you?" he asks.

"I appreciate you coming," I tell him, truly meaning it, "but I would really just like to sit here for a little while without talking. I don't want to be alone, but I don't want to talk either."

"I understand," he says and looks away.

We sit there in silence. I close my eyes, and when I do, all I can see is the terror Lucifer's promise stamped on Uncle Dan's face. A part of me rejoices at what Lucifer has done to him, and another part of me pities a man who never showed any pity for me. Mama Lynn has always chalked up my refusal to date because of my determination to find my parents. How could I tell her that it was her brother's fault I was so emotionally backwards when it came to relationships with the opposite sex? The guilt she would feel from such an admission would tear her apart at the seams.

"Would you allow me to take you somewhere for a few minutes?" Mason suddenly asks me. "I would like to show you something. I promise to have you back before you're missed."

I nod my head, not trusting my voice to be strong enough, because I desperately do want to be somewhere else right now.

Mason rests his hand on the step between us, palm up, letting me be in control of when we leave.

I take a deep breath and place my hand in his. His fingers close around my hand gently.

"Here we go," he says, warning me we're about to phase.

I smile at the thoughtfulness, remembering all too well how aggravated I was at him the night before when he phased me without warning.

I suddenly find us sitting outdoors on a grassy plain, large rectangular stones looming all around us in a circle. I instantly know where we are… Stonehenge.

Mason stands up and helps me to my feet, since he's still holding my hand. He keeps holding my hand as he says, "I like to come here when I need to think about things. I find it peaceful. I thought you might like it too."

"You know," I say, looking around the ancient structure, "I think I've seen more of the world in the past 24 hours than I have my whole entire life."

"Hopefully, you'll allow me to show you more of it," Mason says before letting go of my hand.

I walk up to one of the stones and glide the palm of my right hand against its cold, rough surface. It's nighttime in England, and I'm thankful I still have my leather jacket on. The full moon is high in the clear night sky, decorated with a multitude of pinpoint stars. I lean my back against the stone and close my eyes, cleansing not only my lungs but my mind by breathing the clean night air. Its crisp coolness helps ease the pain inside my chest, forcing the invisible hand gripping my heart to relax and fade away.

Being in a foreign part of the world makes me realize how sheltered my life has been thus far. I open my eyes and look around me, marveling at the magnificence of a place that has existed for thousands of years, but is completely new to me. It makes me wonder how many firsts I will have with Mason acting as my guide.

I look back at where Mason stands, and notice him watching me.

"How often do you come here?" I ask, needing to fill the silence between us.

"Not as often as I would like," he admits. "I used to come here quite a bit before the Tear, but since the Tear, I haven't had much time." Mason seems hesitant to speak further but eventually asks, "Would you like to talk about it?"

I shrug, feeling the withdrawn child within me try to shy away from the question.

"I seriously doubt you want to hear the sordid details," I tell him.

"I'm sorry you had to endure something like that as a child, especially after losing your parents so suddenly."

I'm touched by Mason's sincerity, but I honestly just want to forget about it. I don't need to delve headlong into any type of psychoanalysis of how my screwed up childhood made me into the touchy, withdrawn adult I am today.

"You said you felt me," I say. "Was it like the time I killed Owen? You said you felt me then too."

Mason's head tilts down, like he's trying to find the words to describe what he experienced. "I don't know why Lucifer and I can feel when you are in pain. It doesn't make a lot of sense, but, for some reason, we're connected to you by your emotions."

"Do you think it's only my pain you can feel?"

"I don't know," Mason shrugs. "I suppose we'll have to wait and see."

I push my body away from the stone at my back and walk towards Mason.

"Thank you for bringing me here," I tell him. "I needed it."

"I hope it helped in some small way," he says, holding his hand out. "Ready to go back?"

No, not really, I say to myself. But I know I need to go back. I can't hide from my life forever.

When Mason phases me back, we're standing outside the hospital entrance.

"I wasn't sure if you wanted to go inside or not," he explains.

"This is perfect," I reassure him. "I really don't want to go back in there. I'll just call Faison and tell her to come out."

"Do you want me to stay with you until she arrives?" he asks.

"No, I'll be fine."

"Ok, well, don't forget to call me after Malcolm's visit," he gently reminds me.

I silently curse to myself. I had completely forgotten about Lilly's guardian coming to see me.

I nod my head. "I will."

Mason seems reluctant to leave, and I have to admit I'm a bit reluctant to see him go. His presence comforts me for some reason.

"I'll be waiting for your call," he says.

I nod. "Okay."

He phases, and I'm left alone, something I'm used to. However, for one of the first times in my life, I don't want to be.

CHAPTER 8

We make it back home at around six that evening. Close to seven is when I hear my doorbell ring. I turn the TV off and steel myself for what I assume will be an interrogation of sorts from Lilly's guardian, Malcolm.

When I open the door, I come face to face with one of the largest men I've ever seen. He reminds me of the men who adorn the covers of Mama Lynn's historical romance novels. With his rugged good looks and long black hair falling to frame his face, I can only imagine he gains a lot of attention from the fairer sex quite easily. He's wearing a blood-red silk shirt opened at the front to reveal a quite impressively muscular chest. The shirt is tucked into a pair of tight-fitting black jeans with a black leather duster completing the ensemble.

"Hi," I say. "Are you Malcolm?"

He grins at me in a friendly-enough manner, but his eyes tell me he's not someone whose trust I will earn instantly.

"And you must be Jess Riley. Or would you prefer I call you Agent Riley?"

"Jess is fine."

"I assume Mason told you why I'm here."

"Yes. He said I couldn't meet Lilly unless you approved of me first."

"Exactly right," he says. "May I come in so we can speak?"

I step out onto the porch, forcing Malcolm to take a step back.

"I would rather we spoke out here, if you don't mind."

Letting another Watcher have free reign to come and go inside my house wasn't something I was willing to do.

A lopsided grin appears on Malcolm's face, and I realize he knows exactly why I'm refusing him entry.

"Good," he says, nodding his head. "You understand the importance of privacy. Most people would have done the polite thing, not the smart thing. Now," he crosses his arms in front of his chest and takes a defensive stance. "Can you tell me exactly how you have been able to accomplish these amazing feats I've heard about from Mason? Do you honestly not know what makes you different?"

"No," I say, without having to lie, "I don't know why I've been able to do the things I have."

"You must have some sort of clue," Malcolm prods.

Like everyone else, I know Malcolm is fishing for the

information I've kept to myself about my father. Since I have no intention of telling Mason until I absolutely have to, I certainly don't intend to tell Malcolm.

"I really don't know," I say.

Malcolm's eyes darken slightly, indicating he doesn't believe me in the slightest.

"I'm not sure I can let you meet with Lilly," Malcolm says. "Honesty is an important trait to her. If she senses you aren't being completely open, I'm afraid the two of you won't be starting off on the right foot. She doesn't put up with liars."

A cell phone in Malcolm's jacket begins to buzz.

"Excuse me," he says, turning his back to me and fishing the phone out of his pocket.

"Yes, dearest?" he asks, his tone immediately softening. "No, I haven't forgotten to go get the chocolate croissants for Tara." He pauses as whoever is on the other end of the line says something. "I don't think so. She's lying to me about something." I know he's talking about me and I cringe a little inside. I don't like being called a liar, but I can't deny that's what I'm doing. "I don't think that's wise, dearest. Trust me on this." Another long pause before Malcolm sighs in resignation. "If you're sure that's what you want, then I will do it. I don't like it, and I will be watching closely. You can at least give me that much to ensure your safety." It's then I realize he's speaking to Lilly. "All right, I'll tell her. And tell Tara to have a little patience. I know she's eating for two now. She doesn't have to keep reminding me." Malcolm laughs at something Lilly says. It's a nice sound, and something I never would have expected to hear from someone as formidable as he. "Okay, I'll keep that in mind. I'll be home soon."

After Malcolm ends the call, he turns around to face me. His demeanor is back to hard-as-nails interrogator, and I wonder how Lilly found a way to make the man in front of me melt to her will just with a simple phone call. It's then I realize she must be a miracle-worker.

"Lilly says she wants to meet you, even though I disagree," Malcolm tells me; not trying to hide the fact that he doesn't trust me around Lilly. "I'm warning you," he says, taking a step forward, looming over me, "I will be watching."

"I understand," I say, knowing without a shadow of a doubt that Malcolm will rip my head from my shoulders if I even so much as look at Lilly the wrong way. I have to admit I'm even more intrigued to meet with Lilly now. Mason and Malcolm are two of the most intimidating men I've ever met, yet their concern over Lilly's safety seems to touch a soft spot in each of them. It makes me wonder what my reaction to her will be.

After Malcolm leaves, I call Mason to tell him what happened.

"Lilly must have known Malcolm would find something to use as an excuse to prevent you from seeing her," Mason sounds amused over the phone, like he expected Malcolm to disapprove of the meeting even before he came to see me. "Be ready by nine in the morning," Mason tells me. "We'll go see Lilly together. Oh, and dress warmly. It snows in the mountains." Mason pauses before asking, "Are you all right, Jess?"

With his simple question, I know he's still worried about me and what happened earlier at the hospital. His concern for my welfare warms my heart, making me wonder why he seems to care so much.

"I'm fine," I tell him. "Thank you for asking."

"All right," he doesn't sound convinced but doesn't push me for anything else either. "I'll see you in the morning."

When I get off the phone, I suddenly realize my stomach is tied up in knots over my upcoming meeting with Lilly. What if Lilly uses whatever special powers she possesses on me too? What if she doesn't allow me to keep my secret from her? I realize I'm biting the side of my bottom lip in worry, and wonder what new revelations the next day will bring.

There is a knock on my door at exactly nine the next morning. When I answer it, I find Mason standing on the porch, dressed in a dark brown suede coat over a dark grey wool button-down cardigan and white collared shirt. A pair of tan jeans and sturdy- looking brown leather boots completes his winter wardrobe. In his left hand is something which resembles a Christmas present. By its rectangular shape and exposed corners, I can tell it's a book of some sort. The only thing holding the red crinkly paper around it is the silky white ribbon tied in a crosswise bow.

I decided to dress as warmly as I could, since snow wasn't exactly something I had to contend with every day. I have on an eggshell-colored cable turtleneck sweater and slim-fitting black jeans tucked into a pair of shearling- cuffed black suede UGG boots.

I grab my eggplant-colored fox-fur-trimmed coat from the chair by the door and quickly put it on as Mason asks, "Are you ready?"

"Yeah, just give me a minute to get the crown," I say, quickly tying the belt of my coat around my waist as I head to my bedroom and drag the crown out from under the super-secret hiding spot beneath my pillow. I make a vow to myself to find a better hidey-hole for it when I get back home.

When I make it back to the front door, I see that Mason isn't alone anymore.

"As I said last night," Malcolm tells me, looking similarly dressed as the last time I saw him, except that the shirt he's wearing is emerald green, "I'll be watching."

I feel myself swallow involuntarily and wonder if I made the right decision in leaving my plasma pistol at home. I miss its weight against my thigh, especially when I find myself in a hostile situation.

"Malcolm," Mason says, in a tone that makes Malcolm's stance not as stiff, "Jess is no threat to Lilly. If I thought she was do you honestly think I would have suggested this meeting?"

Malcolm scowls at me.

"She's lying about something," he says to Mason, but keeps his eyes on me, as if he's watching for my reaction to what he has to say. "Even I can tell that. *You* have to know it's true."

"I know," Mason says, making me look at him in surprise. I had a feeling Mason knew I was withholding information from him, but this is the first time he's said anything in front of me to verify my suspicions.

"Then how are we supposed to trust her if she doesn't trust us?" Malcolm questions.

"Trust is earned," Mason replies, looking at me, "not given."

I find it hard to meet Mason's eyes and start to wonder if it's time to reveal my secret to someone. When I look back at Mason, I feel an intense, inexplicable urge to tell him everything. I decide to wait and see how my meeting with Lilly goes first. If she's able to tell me exactly what's different about me, maybe then I won't feel like I'm betraying my promise to my father to keep my special gift a secret.

Mason holds his hand out to me. "Are you ready?"

"I'm not sure," I say honestly.

Mason tries to give me a reassuring smile of encouragement, which only makes my knees feel weak, because the expression makes him look so handsome. I mentally try to shake off the effect his smile is having on me and focus my thoughts on the day to come.

"Don't worry," he says, stretching his arm out further, urging me to take hold of his hand. "Trust me."

I take a deep breath and slide my hand into Mason's.

I find myself standing inside the foyer of a home festooned to the hilt with tasteful Christmas garland wrapped in glittery red ribbon and other festive decorations. The spicy scent of pumpkin pie fills the air inside the house, instantly putting me at ease. To the right, I see a large living room with a fire blazing in a river rock fireplace, keeping the house toasty warm. To the left is a dining room where I see a man sitting at the table, concentrating on something written in an old spiral notebook lying in front of him.

"Seriously, Brand," I hear Malcolm say beside me. "Don't you think it's time you gave up on trying to write that poem? It's been 15 years. If the words haven't come to you by now, they never will."

The man Malcolm addressed as Brand leans back in his chair and looks over at us.

"My wife wants it done," he says simply. "Maybe one day I'll find the right combination of words to describe how wonderful she is."

Brand stands from his chair and walks towards us.

"Jess Riley," Mason says, as Brand comes to stand in front of me. "This is Lilly's husband, Brand Cole."

I remember Mason telling me Lilly's love for a brother Watcher was what saved the universe from being destroyed by Lucifer. Yet the man in front of me is older than any Watcher I've seen. If I just based his Watcher status on looks alone, I have no doubt he could be a Watcher. His facial features are model-perfect with the exception of small laugh lines at the corners of his eyes. He has short, wavy brown hair and grey eyes, which seem lit with a light all their own. A few, almost unnoticeable, strands of grey are just starting to appear at his temples, marking his age at somewhere around 40.

Brand holds out his hand, and I shake it. His easy smile almost eliminates the fear Malcolm has instilled in me about meeting Lilly. I can't imagine anyone married to the man standing in front of me not being just as open and welcoming as him.

"It's nice to meet you, Jess," Brand says, his voice lilting with a cultured British accent. Unlike some people you meet for the first time, I know he means what he says and that politeness isn't dictating his words. "Lilly has been looking forward to meeting you and seeing the crown." Brand's eyes drop to the silver crown clasped tightly in my left hand. "It's been a very long time since I saw one myself," he admits.

A beautiful girl, around the age of 14 or 15, bounds down the wooden staircase leading from the second floor. She comes to stand by Brand, and I immediately know she's his daughter because they share the same extraordinary eye color. Her long auburn hair flows over her left shoulder like the fall of water and reaches down to her waist. Her features are exquisite and almost make me jealous of her beauty, but the sweet soul I see before me is not someone to be envied; only cherished.

"This is my daughter, Caylin," Brand says, putting his arm around the girl's shoulders so naturally I know their relationship is a close one. For a fleeting moment, I do envy Caylin. I envy her having her father by her side.

"I have something for you from Joshua," Mason says, handing Caylin the ill- wrapped present I noticed earlier in his hands.

"Do I need to have another talk with that boy?" Malcolm asks, his eyebrows knitting together in a scowl.

"It's just a gift, Malcolm," Brand says. "Not a proposal of marriage."

"Hmm," Malcolm sounds less sure about that than Brand. "Nonetheless, I'll speak with him again just to make sure things stay innocent."

"Uncle Malcolm," Caylin says, smiling up at the man standing beside me. Her eyes beam at him so lovingly I know there has to be more to Malcolm than what he's shown me thus far. "Please leave Joshua alone. We're just friends. Plus, you can't chase off every boy who might like me."

"Who says I can't?" Malcolm grunts. "Besides, boys Joshua's age only think about two things constantly. One of them is food and the other…"

"Enough, Malcolm," Brand says, effectively cutting Malcolm off before he can embarrass us all. "I don't think our guest came here to listen to our family squabbling." Brand returns his attention to me. "Lilly is in the nursery with Mae. It's right up the stairs, first room to the left."

I look to Mason, and he gives me an encouraging nod to go on up. Just as I walk to the foot of the stairs, I feel the massive presence of Malcolm close behind me.

"Lilly said she wanted to meet with Jess alone," Brand tells Malcolm.

"And I told her I wouldn't allow that," Malcolm responds in a clipped voice.

Brand shrugs. "Suit yourself, but don't come crying to me after Lilly tears into you. You know she doesn't like to be ignored. It's not like she would let Jess do anything to her anyway. She can take care of herself almost better than you can take care of her."

I hear Malcolm sigh before he takes a step back from me.

"Fine, but I want to go on record that I don't like it."

"Duly noted," Brands says and tilts his head to me, indicating I should probably hurry up the stairs before Malcolm changes his mind.

CHAPTER 9

When I reach the top of the stairs, I see a door to my left painted with a mural of jewel-colored dragons floating on a background of white fluffy clouds. Hanging on the door by a pink-and-white-polka-dot ribbon is the name 'Mae' in a curly-cue font.

I knock on the door and hear a woman beckon from the other side to come in.

When I walk in, I feel my breath catch in my throat at the beauty of the room. I feel as though I have just stepped into a magical wonderland with fantastical creatures walking and flying in a garden-scape so gorgeous it could only have been conjured up by someone who loves the meaning of life to its smallest detail. Adorning the ceiling are puffy clouds that look three-dimensional and are home to a multitude of chubby angelic creatures with white wings, looking down as silent protectors to those below them.

A woman in her early 30s stands by a crib which looks like an open version of Cinderella's carriage, draped with glittery white material gathered at the top by a golden crown attached to the ceiling. The woman has the same color hair and facial features as Caylin, leaving no doubt that I am finally face to face with Lilly.

"Hi," she says in a whisper. "Come on in. I just got Mae to go to sleep, so we should have a little while together. Close the door behind you. Brand has a baby monitor downstairs."

I'm not sure why it matters that her husband has a monitor, but soon learn the answer. Lilly walks to a white rocking chair in the room and picks up a heavy brown quilted coat lying across it. After she buttons it up, she walks over to me and holds out her hand.

"Ready?" she asks.

I look at her offered hand, not knowing exactly what is going on.

"Ready for what?" I ask, not trying to conceal my confusion.

"I seriously doubt even my husband will be able to keep Malcolm from coming up here to check on me. I thought perhaps we would go somewhere more private." She holds her hand out to me again, and it's only then I understand what she intends. I suppose it really shouldn't be a surprise to me that she can phase just like the Watchers. She is, after all, half archangel.

I place my hand in hers and suddenly find myself standing outside a quaint log cabin. The front door to the home opens and a black woman, around the same age as Lilly, steps out. From the protrusion of her belly, I assume she's close to giving birth.

"Well, don't just stand there," the woman says, waving us towards her. "Get in her before that big lug has a chance to follow you."

Lilly squeezes my hand reassuringly, and tugs me forward towards the house before releasing me.

After we step inside the cabin, Lilly turns to the other woman.

"Tara, I would like to introduce you to Jess. Jess, this is my best friend in the world, Tara."

Tara holds out her hand to me, and I shake it.

"Nice to meet you, hon," she says. "Now, get going before he figures out what we're up to. I'll keep him at bay for as long as I can, but you know he has leverage over me."

"I know," Lilly says, rolling her eyes at her best friend. "He's your chocolate croissant dealer."

"I can't have him too mad at me," Tara sighs. Her thoughts seem to drift off, and I'm pretty sure she's envisioning these chocolate croissants.

Lilly laughs and gives her best friend a peck on the cheek. "Stand firm for as long as you can," she tells Tara.

Lilly holds her hand out to me again. Without hesitation this time, I place my hand into hers and find myself standing in the middle of a trail on the side of a mountain. When I look across the great expanse, I see a lake and a large house far in the distance.

"That's my home," Lilly tells me. "Malcolm built it for me years ago. We spend most of our time here when the kids don't have to be in school."

"Malcolm built that for you?" I question, wondering for a second time that day what type of man lay behind the rough and tough exterior of Lilly's protector. The house has a delicate quality to it that seems to match Lilly's personality exactly. Only someone who truly cared about her could have expressed it in architectural form.

"Don't let him fool you," Lilly says to me, a smile in her voice. "He's not just the person he shows to others. There's more to him than that."

This I have figured out on my own.

"Anyway," Lilly says, taking a seat in a hollow cut-out in the rock face behind us, "come tell me about yourself, Jess."

I walk over to the naturally-made bench, snow crunching beneath my feet, and sit beside her.

"Not a whole lot to tell, really," I say. "My parents were taken through the Tear when I was seven. I was adopted a year later by my foster parent, worked hard to get my bachelor's degree in three years instead of four, and joined the Watcher Agency as soon as I got out. Now, I'm working for Mason, and have never been so confused about who or what I am in my life."

Lilly smiles in a way that tells me she understands exactly what I'm going through. "It can be hard to find out you aren't who you thought you were," she tells me, "but it can also be an exciting adventure if you let it. Sometimes information is kept from us until we're ready to hear it. I know it's scary to discover you're more than you could have ever imagined, but now is the time for you to face certain truths about yourself and be open to accepting them. Your life so far has made you strong enough to handle what needs to be done from this point on." I see Lilly look down at the crown still clutched in my hand. She holds out her hand to me. "May I see it?"

I try to hand the crown to Lilly, but I see the same thing that happened to Mason the day before happen now. She's unable grab hold of it, like there's an invisible force field no one but me can break through.

"Well," Lilly says, and I hear the surprise in her voice, "that's interesting." She puts her hand back in her lap. "Would you mind holding it up so I can see the writing better?"

I hold the crown up to her eye level. She points her index finger up and spins it, indicating I should rotate the crown so she can see all sides of it.

"Hmm," she says. "Have you been able to read the writing?"

I shake my head. "No, I thought all the engravings were just there for decoration." My heart begins to beat wildly in my chest. "Mason didn't say it was writing. Can you read it? Do you know what it says?"

"It's a name," Lilly looks up from the crown and meets my eyes. "It's the name of one of the archangels. I think that crown belongs to Jophiel."

This information doesn't help me at all.

"I'm afraid my knowledge of things in the Bible is limited," I confess. "Who was Jophiel? Was it an archangel responsible for anything special?"

"It's the archangel who guarded the Tree of Life in Eden. I've read that Jophiel once used a flaming sword to prevent humans from reentering the garden. That's about as far as my knowledge goes on the subject, though. We'll have to ask the men the rest of the story."

I sigh. "I really wish I had paid more attention in those Sunday school classes now."

Lilly laughs. "Don't worry," she reassures, "Mason will make sure you know everything you need to." Lilly cocks her head at me. "In fact, he seems to think rather highly of you, which says quite a bit about the type of person you are."

"What makes you say that?" I ask.

"Just the way he talked about you when he first came to see me to ask for this meeting. He admires your strength…and beauty, if I'm reading him right."

I feel my cheeks flush under Lilly's scrutiny. Of the two of us, she's far more beautiful than I am. Just from being around her the short time I have, I understand why all the Watchers feel a need to keep her out of harm's way, because I feel it too. If it came to it, I knew I would lay down my life for the woman sitting beside me, without even thinking twice about it. She holds an ethereal glow that instantly makes you feel warm and loved, yet there is also an incredible strength within her too. Lilly is someone I hope to be able to call friend one day, but know I will have to earn such an honor.

"I'm not sure what Mason thinks about me," I say. "He can be hard to read sometimes."

Lilly sighs. "Out of all the Watchers, Mason holds the most guilt over their fall from Heaven. I've tried my best to make him see he shouldn't feel guilty over what happened back then, especially since God provided him a way to redeem himself."

"Why can't his God just forgive him?"

"He has," Lilly tells me, smiling wanly, "but Mason can't seem to forgive himself just yet. My hope is that, once the Tear is sealed, he'll feel as though he's done enough to deserve forgiveness." Lilly looks at me and says, "I hope you can help him see what a good man he is."

"How am I supposed to do that?"

Lilly's lips part into a smile, as if she knows something I don't yet.

"When the time is right, you'll know. You'll feel it in your heart. Oh," Lilly says, like she just remembered something, "I have a message for you."

"A message? From who?"

"God asked me to tell you that there will come a time soon when you should share your secret with Mason. He said it was something you've kept hidden from everyone, even those closest to you. Do you know what He's talking about?"

Slowly, I nod. "Did He tell you what my secret was?"

"Oh, no; He doesn't do that. In fact, His message to you is

probably one of the more direct ones He's ever had me give to someone else. He speaks obtusely most of the time, and it takes me a while to figure out what He's actually saying," Lilly laughs.

"Lilly!"

We turn our heads, and see Malcolm standing in the same spot we phased to just a little while ago.

"I wondered how long it would take you to sweet-talk Tara into letting you into her house," Lilly says, like the cloak and dagger method we used to have some time alone had just been a game of cat and mouse.

Malcolm shakes his head. "Why do you insist on driving me crazy with worry?"

He walks up to us and holds a hand out to Lilly to help her stand.

"There was never anything to worry about," Lilly tells him, placing a hand on Malcolm's chest, which seems to instantly soothe his ire. She looks up at him. "You should know by now I always get what I want."

Malcolm tries to scowl his disapproval of Lilly's methods, but I see a hint of a smile play across his lips, and this time the smile makes it to his eyes. Malcolm leans down and kisses Lilly on the forehead gently, and I know the action means more than just a friendly peck. It's then I understand why Malcolm is so overprotective of Lilly. He's in love with her.

"Next time," he says, a playful admonishment in his voice, "at least pick somewhere warm to go. You might catch a cold out here, dearest."

"Next time," Lilly answers back, "don't make me go to extremes when I have an opportunity to make a new friend."

"I will try," Malcolm says, but I can see it will be an impossible task for him.

"Ok, let's get back before my husband starts to worry." Lilly holds her hand out to me. "Maybe Brand and Mason can figure out why Jophiel's crown was hidden in your father's fireplace."

Unfortunately, when we tell Brand, Mason, and Malcolm which archangel the crown belongs to, none of them has a grand epiphany.

"It's definitely a mystery to me," Brand says as he and Lilly sit on the leather couch in the living room together, holding hands. "By all rights, that crown shouldn't be on Earth at all."

"That's what Lucifer said too," I say absently, which seems to be the wrong thing to say in the wrong place.

Malcolm comes at me so quickly I don't completely register the pain from him slamming me up against the wall at my back, until I'm pinned there by one of his large hands squeezing my neck.

"How do you know Lucifer?" he demands.

I instantly feel Malcolm's hold around my throat disappear as Mason hits him with an open palm from the side, sending Malcolm flying across the room to crash into a wooden table by a picture window.

"Enough, Malcolm," Mason thunders, and even I flinch at the authority in his voice. "I've tried to put up with your behavior for Lilly's sake, but you have gone too far this time. From this point forward, you are to leave Jess alone unless I say otherwise. You are not allowed to touch her unless her life is in danger, or she allows it. Am I making myself clear, or do we need to step outside to finish this conversation?"

Malcolm picks himself up off the floor.

"No," he says, rubbing the arm Mason just slammed, "you made yourself plenty clear. But how does she know Lucifer? We weren't told about that part."

"No," Mason admits, "I purposely left that information out. I didn't want to cause Lilly any undue worry."

"It's not like I thought he simply disappeared," Lilly says. "I know he's still around." Lilly looks at me. "But how do you know him, if you don't mind me asking?"

"It wasn't by choice," I assure her, rubbing my neck to take away some of the sting from Malcolm's attack. "He came to see me the same night I met Mason for the first time. And he's seen me carrying the crown."

"What does he want with you?" Brand questions, his face a picture of worry, and I know it's not worry over where my loyalties lie, but for my safety.

"I think," I start to say, realizing the rest of my sentence sounds ludicrous inside my own head before I say it out loud, "he wants to be my friend."

"Friend?" Malcolm scoffs. "He hasn't had a friend since the war, and even before then he was so egotistical only Michael could bear to be around him."

"Did he say why he wants to be friends?" Brand asks.

"Just that he felt a strange yearning to be with me."

"Does he want to have sex with you?" Malcolm asks bluntly.

"Malcolm!" Lilly and Mason say at the same time, with totally different inflections. Lilly's is admonishing, while Mason's voice holds a note of warning.

"What?" Malcolm asks. "It's an honest question. You know how Lucifer can be."

"I did ask him about the sex thing," I admit, feeling my face grow hot with everyone staring at me. "He said his yearnings weren't sexual in nature. Even the friend thing he wasn't completely sure about. He just said he feels some sort of connection with me."

"Maybe we can use his feelings for you to our advantage," Mason says. "He might unintentionally let his guard down around you and tell you things he shouldn't. If anything, Lucifer is vain, and likes for people to think he's the smartest person in the room."

"Just be careful if you intend to play that sort of game with him," Brand tells me. "And don't be fooled if he tries to play on your sympathies. He'll use whatever knowledge he has about you to gain your trust. Don't let him. He only cares about himself and his own agenda."

"And we still don't know what that is yet, right?" I ask.

"No," Mason admits. "But we can count on one thing; whatever it is won't be pleasant for anyone."

"Should I try to lead my conversations with him to get the information we want?" I ask.

"No," Malcolm answers. "He likes to feel in control of things. Simply follow wherever he leads, and eventually he'll end up telling you what you want to know without you having to do anything but listen. Just be patient and let him feel like you're someone with whom he can let his guard down."

"How do I do that?" I ask, not sure how you gain the trust of the devil.

"Be yourself," Lilly advises. "You're someone he naturally wants to confide in, from what you've said so far. If you try to act the way you think he wants you to, he'll know, and leave his guard up when he's around you. It may be difficult, but try to relax when you're with him. I don't think he has any intention of harming you. If he did, he would have done it by now. You're a mystery to him, and he revels in the fact that he knows everything. Be his enigma. That in itself is probably part of the reason he feels attracted to you. You may be the only thing on Earth or in Heaven that he doesn't understand."

"So," Brand says, "what about the crown? There must be a reason it sent out that homing beacon so you could find it when you did, but what triggered it to activate?"

"It had to be when Jess killed the changeling," Mason says. "Like I told you before, I felt a disturbance when it happened. It seems logical the crown was meant to activate when Jess showed the first sign of her powers."

"Why do I have powers?" I ask. "All of Allan's tests proved that I'm an ordinary human. There's nothing special about me."

"You are special," Lilly tells me. "We just haven't figured out why yet. But, rest assured, we will."

"How can you be so confident about that?" I ask.

"Because it's your destiny."

"God tell you that too?" I ask jokingly.

Lilly smiles. "Yes; in His own obtuse, roundabout way, He did."

"I don't suppose He would just flat out tell you what's going on?" I ask hopefully.

"Uh, no," Lilly tells me with a smile and shake of her head. "Unfortunately, He doesn't help like that. Sometimes He forces you to find the answers for yourself in order to reveal another piece of the puzzle."

"Sounds incredibly annoying," I say, causing smiles all around, even from Malcolm.

"Annoying is a good word," Mason says, his eyes twinkling at me in amusement.

I feel my heart tighten in my chest from the way he's looking at me, and instantly find myself wondering how I can make him look at me like that more often.

I glance in Lilly's direction and see her eyes travel from Mason to me. A knowing smile spreads her lips, and I quickly look away.

"Mom!" I hear Caylin yell in agitation as she chases a boy of about 10 or 11 into the living room.

Brand catches the brown-haired boy around the waist as he attempts to run by him. The boy laughs as Brand pulls him onto his lap.

"Will won't give me back my book," Caylin complains, slightly out of breath as she stands in front of her parents.

"Will," Lilly says, a motherly warning in her voice, "that was a Christmas gift to your sister, not you. Give it back to her."

"But I just wanted to read it. It's not really a book anyway. It's a comic."

Caylin quickly pulls the book out of her brother's hands while her father has him trapped.

"It's a first-edition copy of *Calvin and Hobbes*, you dork. It's a collector's item, not something you play with."

"Is that what Joshua gave you?" I ask, coming to take a closer look. If there was one thing Faison and I could agree on, it was reading Calvin and Hobbes before we went to sleep as children. Calvin's imagination was fodder for many dreams in my youth.

Caylin holds it out to me, and I see that it's not only a first edition, but also a signed copy.

"Wow, that *is* a collectable. It must have made a dent in Joshua's savings."

"You think?" Caylin asks, her face lighting up.

"He must think a lot about you," I tell her as she smiles shyly at the news.

"Hmm," I hear Malcolm say, "I'm sure he does."

I immediately decide to make sure Joshua gets his chance at an innocent romance with Caylin. If left up to Malcolm, Joshua wouldn't be able to see her until she was 80. We

Calvin and Hobbes fans had to stick together to fight the injustices of the world, or at least their overprotective uncles.

"Speaking of Joshua," Mason says, "we should probably go back to headquarters to tell the others what we've learned."

"Remind Allan and Angela about coming over for dinner Christmas Eve," Lilly tells Mason. "And you had better be here this year too. No more excuses about work. The world will continue to rotate for the few hours you spend with us."

"I promise I'll be here," Mason says, like he's talking to a nagging mom.

"Good," Lilly looks at me. "You're more than welcome to come with Mason," she suggests. "There will be a lot of other Watchers present you might like to get to know."

"Thank you," I tell her, "but I have a family obligation of my own that night."

"Family comes first," she says, looking at her husband and kids. "But know that you have an open invitation to our home, which ever one we might be occupying at the time."

"Thank you," I tell her, knowing she means it and isn't just saying it to be polite.

"We will contact you if we figure anything else out," Mason tells them all, holding out his hand to me.

As soon as my skin touches Mason's, I find myself standing in headquarters, staring at a video feed of Lucifer talking to Faison outside my house.

CHAPTER 10

"When did he arrive?" I hear Mason ask Nick and Joshua, who are sitting in front of the control panel, watching the scene as it unfolds.

"Not too long ago," Nick answers. "I don't think they've been talking for more than a couple of minutes."

"Take me home," I say to Mason, not caring that it sounds more like an order than a request.

Without argument, Mason grabs my arm and phases us to my house.

"I'm sorry we didn't get to talk more at the hospital last night," I hear Lucifer say to Faison.

"Faison!" I call out sharply as we come to stand with them.

Faison jumps slightly and holds a hand to her heart, obviously not aware that Mason and I just phased in.

"Jess," Faison smiles at me, not having a clue how much danger she's in, "I just came over to see if you wanted to go out to lunch, and found your friend waiting here for you, to ask the same thing."

Lucifer turns to me with an enigmatic smile on his face.

"I wanted to check on you after what happened last night," Lucifer says to me, his eyes sliding over to Mason. "Mason," he says in a greeting that lacks any warmth.

"I'm fine," I tell Lucifer, desperately wanting to get Faison out of his presence.

"Why don't you and Faison go on to lunch?" Mason suggests, coming to stand between Lucifer and me in a protective manner. "I would like to speak with Lucian about a private matter since he's here."

I grab Faison by the arm and say, "Let's go," silently thanking Mason for giving me a good excuse to get Faison out of harm's way

As I'm dragging a bewildered Faison to my car, I chance a glance over my shoulder, and see Mason and Lucifer engaged in a staring contest, which looks anything but friendly. Once safely inside my car, I crank it up and drive quickly away from the possible nuclear explosion of wills about to happen in my front yard.

"Who is that Lucian guy, anyway?" Faison says. "You never said anything else about him after what happened at the hospital. Is he a Watcher too?"

"Listen to me carefully," I say. "If you ever see Lucian again, you walk in the opposite direction, ok?"

"Is he dangerous?" Faison asks, sounding fascinated.

"Yes, and not in a good way; he's the most dangerous man I know," I tell her, not having to exaggerate in the slightest. "Please, don't talk to him again if you can help it, and for goodness' sake, don't let him inside Mama Lynn's house. Ok?"

Sobered by my words, Faison nods.

"I'm sorry, Jess. I didn't know. He seemed okay the way he took up for you at the hospital. He certainly put the fear of God into Uncle Dan when he spoke to him. And he looks so nice. I thought he was someone you trusted."

"Like they say, don't judge a book by its cover."

Faison is silent for a while as I drive us over to the Holly-wood Café for lunch.

"So, Mason seemed awfully protective of you back there," she says.

"Don't read anything into it. Mason isn't interested in me like that," I reply, even though I feel a small part of me wish he were. "Besides, you know my rule."

"Ugh, that stupid rule again?" Faison looks up to the heavens. "Why can't you make her act like a normal human being for once?"

"Who are you talking to?"

"God," Faison says, closing her eyes. "I'm sending up a silent prayer to ask that He make you give up your rule about not getting serious with someone until the Tear is closed. Amen."

"It's a good rule," I say defensively. "If you'd ever lost someone to that thing, you would understand."

Faison looks over at me, and I see fire in her eyes. I silently wait for the explosion.

"I understand just fine," she says in a controlled voice. "Who was the one who held you when you used to cry yourself to sleep because you missed your parents?"

"You."

"Who beat up Wendy Shea when she picked on you for being an orphan?"

"You."

"And who goes out to that field by your folks' house every year to see if they'll be returned or not?"

"You."

"So don't sit there and tell me I don't understand what you're going through, Jessica Michelle Riley, because I've pretty much been through it all with you since the day we met."

Faison crosses her arms over her chest and looks out the window.

"Faison," I say, trying to draw her attention, but she refuses to look at me, "you know I love you. I wouldn't have made it all these years without you by my side. Please don't be mad at me. I've got too much going on right now to be in any condition to handle that kind of added stress."

Faison's arms slowly uncross as she turns her head to look at me. "Just promise me one thing," she says, "and I won't be mad at you."

"Anything."

"If things go well tonight at the party with Mason, I want you to ask him out on a real date, not just one I set up for you. And I mean a *real*, honest-to-God date, where you get all gussied up and go out to dinner somewhere nice."

"Why is it so important to you that I date?"

"Because everyone needs somebody, Jess; you've been hiding from the world since we were kids, never letting a boy kiss you or even give you a proper hug from what I know. You're 22 years old, and you've never been kissed by a man you care about. That's just not natural, Jess. Stop hiding behind the Tear and what Uncle Dan did to you. Let yourself feel something for another person."

"I love you and Mama Lynn," I say in my own defense.

"That's because you didn't have much choice in the matter. We wouldn't have let you hide from us, no matter how hard you might have tried."

"So my asking Mason out is contingent upon us having a good time together tonight, right?"

"Yes."

"What if we make each other completely miserable? Am I still bound to this promise?"

"No, you can wiggle your way out of it, but only if I see that the two of you don't have a lick of chemistry."

I nod my head. "Okay, I agree to your terms. Now stop being mad at me. You know I can't stand it when we fight."

"I don't like it either," Faison admits.

Suddenly, I do something I almost never do; sneeze.

"Are you coming down with a cold?" Faison asks.

I shake my head.

"You know I hardly ever get sick," I say, just as I sneeze a second time.

"No getting sick," Faison firmly orders. "You are not going to find a way out of this date tonight."

I sneeze again and cough for good measure. I groan inwardly because I know I'm coming down with something. Whether I want to admit it or not, I actually was looking forward to taking Mason to the party that evening. As I pull into the gravel parking lot of the Hollywood Café, I suddenly have a coughing fit, and begin to resign myself to the fact that my plans for the evening will most likely not be happening.

By the time we make it back to my house, I know I'm running a fever. Faison makes me get into my comfy red Santa Claus flannel pajamas, take some medicine, and crawl into bed.

"Rest is the best thing for you," she says, placing a glass of water and a box of tissues on my nightstand.

"I need my phone," I tell her, barely able to keep my eyes open I feel so tired. "I should call Mason and let him know I'm sick. I'm not making it to that party tonight."

"I'll handle that for you," Faison reassures me. "You just get some rest."

I close my eyes and drift off into a dreamless sleep.

In the distance, I hear the ringing of bells, and begin to wonder if I am hallucinating. Slowly, the noise pulls me out of my sickness-induced slumber, and I realize it's my doorbell ringing. I groan into my pillow and drag myself out of bed to see who it is. When I look through the peephole, I feel my heart begin to race.

"Jess?" Mason says on the other side of the door. "Are you okay in there?"

I rest my hot forehead against the cool wood of my front door, and curse softly. I run my hands hastily through my hair, knowing I must look a mess, but lacking the energy to care too much. I open the door and find myself just staring at Mason in all his perfection. He's dressed in a well-tailored dark blue suit, white shirt, and blue silk tie. I watch as his eyes take in my disheveled appearance in one sweep, and suddenly feel a little nauseated at what he must think.

"I take it we're not going to the party," he says, looking pointedly at my Santa Claus flannel pajamas.

"I'm sorry. I thought Faison was going to call and tell you that I'm sick."

Mason shakes his head slowly. "No, I never received a phone call from her. And you need to be in bed; you look dead on your feet."

"Thanks," I say, trying not to take offense. I was pretty sure I looked like death warmed over, and Mason just confirmed it.

"May I come in?"

"I don't want to make you sick too."

"I can't get sick, Jess. Even if you had the bubonic plague, it wouldn't affect me."

"Come on in then," I say, not sure why he wants to be with me in my current state.

After he closes the door, we just stare at each other as we stand in the foyer. I get the distinct feeling he's not sure why he's there either.

"Have you had anything to eat for supper?" he finally asks.

"No," I say, sneezing into the crook of my elbow, as lady-like as I can.

"Come on." He gently puts his hands on my shoulders and turns me in the direction of my bedroom. "Let's get you settled in bed, and I'll go get something for you to eat."

Mason escorts me to my room and tucks me underneath the white down comforter on my bed. He turns the nightstand light on, which gives the room a soft glow.

"Would you like me to turn your TV on so you can watch something while I go get some food for us to eat?"

"Sure, just start the DVD that's already in there."

Mason goes to the TV mounted on the wall over my dresser and presses the necessary buttons. Before I know it, I hear the comforting sound of the 20th Century Fox trumpets blowing. Mason turns to face me just as the original *Star Wars* movie begins to play.

"I've never seen this one," he tells me.

"Hand me the remote," I quickly say as I prop pillows behind my back to sit up more comfortably in bed. "It's sitting on top of the dresser."

Mason finds it and hands it to me. I press pause to stop the movie.

"I can't, in good conscience, let you leave my house tonight without at least seeing the first *Star Wars* movie," I tell him, feeling that it's my duty as a sci-fi geek to at least make him watch the very first Jedi adventure ever made. "I'll wait until you get back to start it."

Mason grins. "Okay, be right back."

He phases, and I wonder what he plans to bring for me to eat. In less than ten minutes, he reappears with a nondescript brown paper bag in his hands.

"You do like Chinese takeout, right?" he asks.

I nod. "Especially if you thought to bring back some egg drop soup."

"Got it handled. Let me put it in a proper bowl for you, though."

He heads out of the room, and I soon hear the rattling of dishes in the kitchen. A few minutes later, Mason reappears with one of the fold out trays Mama Lynn gave me last Christmas. She gifted me with two of the trays, and I always wondered who the second one was supposed to be for. I assumed it was her subtle way of hinting I should find myself a man.

Mason stands the tray across my lap. The egg drop soup instantly calls my name, begging me to eat it.

"That smells really good," I say, inhaling the warm vapors rising from the bowl.

"It's the best I could get on short notice," Mason says. "If you're still sick tomorrow, I'll make you my famous chicken soup."

"You cook?" I ask, finding it hard to imagine Mason spending time in the kitchen with such a delicate endeavor.

"When you've lived as long as I have, you become a master of all trades," he shrugs. "There isn't much I don't know how to do if the occasion calls for it."

Mason walks out of the room and comes back with one of those white takeout boxes and a pair of chopsticks. He takes off his jacket, tie, and shoes, before lying on the other side of the bed with me to watch the movie.

"Why did you dress up for the party?" I ask him.

Mason's forehead crinkles. "It's what I always wear to parties. Why? Would it have been inappropriate?"

"Obviously you've never been to a get-together in the South," I say. "Jeans and a t-shirt would have been fine. The only time men wear suits down here is if they're going to a wedding or a funeral."

"Thanks for the tip," Mason grins. "I'll remember that next time."

Mason grabs one of the takeout boxes and opens it. Inside I see what looks like shrimp lo-mein.

I point the remote towards the TV.

"Ready?" I ask before pressing play.

"Ready when you are," he says, dipping his chopsticks into his noodles and watching the TV screen intently.

And thus began Mason's indoctrination into the Star Wars universe. Watching it with someone who has never seen it before is like watching it for the first time. Covertly, I observe his reaction to certain scenes, and more often than not end up finding myself just outright staring at the man in my bed. It suddenly dawns on me that he is the first man who has ever been granted the privilege.

By the end of the movie, just as Princess Leia is hanging the medals around our heroes' necks, Mason turns to me and asks, "So who is your favorite character?"

I shake my head. "He's not in this first movie. He doesn't show up until the second one."

Mason's interest seems piqued. "Do you have it?"

"Silly man," I tease. "Of course I have that movie; no respectable Star Wars fan would be caught dead without a copy. Would you like to watch it?"

Mason stands up. "Point me in the direction of where it is."

I send Mason to the living room and instruct him to look for the *Empire Strikes Back* DVD in the large entertainment center there. When he comes back in, he exchanges the DVDs in the player. Then he comes over to my side of the bed and puts the palm of his hand against my forehead.

"Hmm, you still seem to be running a fever," he assesses. "Can you wait a minute before starting the movie? I may have access to something that will make you feel better more quickly than conventional medicine."

"Ok," I say, not knowing exactly what type of unconventional medicine he might be referring to.

"Be right back," he promises, and phases away.

Within five minutes, Mason reappears with a bottle of

purple liquid in his hands. He sets the bottle on the nightstand and says, "One second; I need to get a spoon."

He goes to my kitchen and returns quickly with said spoon.

"So, what is that stuff?" I ask, feeling my left eyebrow rise of its own accord as Mason fills the spoon with the purple elixir.

"Angela and my son give it to their children when they have colds. It's made by a fairy friend of ours."

"Fairy?" I question, sure I've heard him wrong. "Like a Tinkerbelle kind of fairy?"

Mason chuckles, and I find the sound makes me feel better than any medicine I've taken so far.

"No, Malik is not that type of fairy. He knows a lot about herbal remedies, things modern science hasn't even discovered yet. He and Tara started an herbal remedies business that has done quite well, from what I've heard. Brand invested in it a few years back, and they've done a lot of online business so far."

"Tara? Is that Lilly's best friend? I met her today."

"Oh, is that where Lilly took you? Tara's cabin?"

"It was the first place. We went inside and then phased to a spot on the side of the mountain her house faces."

"That's probably where you caught this cold," Mason says, shaking his head. "Lilly should have taken you somewhere warmer. Your body isn't used to cold mountain air."

"I don't normally get sick," I tell him. "I've probably only caught five colds in my whole entire life."

"But when you go into a new environment, you're faced with not only a difference in the weather, but different pollens from plants that you're not normally around." Mason holds the spoon up to my mouth, and I let him pour the liquid against my tongue.

It's the best-tasting medicine I've ever had, a mixture of sweet berry flavors, with a hint of tartness.

"Are you sure that's medicine?" I say. "It tastes more like candy."

Mason smiles, instantly making me smile. "I'll give you their website if you would like to buy some of their products. They don't only sell medicine, though. They have a line of soaps, which I buy, and beauty products as well."

"Is that a hint?" I ask jokingly, acutely aware I'm not looking my best at the moment.

"No," Mason says. His serious tone makes me look into his eyes as he gazes down at me. "It's not a hint. You're quite beautiful without needing any help."

I quickly look down at my hands in my lap, not knowing what to say to his heartfelt compliment.

Mason sets the bottle of medicine on the nightstand and takes the spoon back into the kitchen. When he returns, he hits play on the DVD player and resumes his position on my bed.

"So," he says, "who is your favorite character?"

"Yoda," I tell him, snuggling up with my pillow as the movie begins.

"Little green creature with pointy ears, right?"

I look over at Mason and see him looking down at me. "Right."

"And here I assumed the dashing Han Solo would be your favorite character."

"Looks aren't everything," I say to him. "Han's funny and dashing, I guess. But Yoda is wise. He's lived a long time and knows just what to tell Luke to make him strive to be a better person."

"Well, if you prefer wisdom over looks, maybe there's hope."

"Hope for what?" I ask, not understanding what he's implying.

Mason is silent as he looks down at me. He quickly looks away and gets comfortable as the movie begins.

"Nothing," he finally says. "It's not important."

I want to push him to tell me what he meant, but know such a move might make him leave, and that's the last thing I want to do. As I lay there watching Mason instead of the movie, I feel an uncontrollable need to reach out and pull him closer to me but force myself to resist the urge. My tried and true warning siren sounds off in my head, telling me to keep my distance from Mason, but I mentally tell it to shut the hell up because all I want to do is let myself imagine what it might feel like to have him hold me.

I feel my eyelids get heavier and finally close, just as Mason pulls the comforter up over my shoulders. A cool hand rests against my forehead, and I know he's checking my temperature again. Just as I'm about to float into the ether of dreams, I faintly feel the soft touch of his fingertips glide down my exposed cheek.

"Sweet dreams, Jess," I hear him whisper before I fall off the cliff into the realm of dreams.

When I wake up the next morning, I'm faintly aware that I have my body draped across my pillow. I tighten my arms around its warmth and instantly feel it start to move beneath me. Even half asleep, I know that's not supposed to happen. When I open my eyes, I find myself not looking at the white sheet of my pillowcase, but a white button- down shirt filled with Mason.

I tilt my head up and find Mason looking down at me, a twinkle of amusement in his eyes.

"Good morning," he says before giving me a small smile.

Fully awake now, I realize that not only is my arm completely around his chest but one of my legs is sandwiched in between his intimately. Apparently, during my fever-induced sleep, I had unintentionally made him into my own personal teddy bear.

I slowly extricate myself from his body, trying to maintain what small amount of dignity I have left and say, "I'm so sorry."

"You don't have to apologize," he says gently, and I know he means it.

"How long did I have you trapped like that?" I ask.

"Most of the night," he reveals.

"You should have just rolled me over," I say.

"I did," he replies, his smile growing wider, "but you just rolled back over and assumed the same position."

I groan and drop my head in my pillow face-down, completely mortified that my subconscious had assumed control of my body while I slept.

"I'm so sorry," I say again, but this time into my pillow, unable to face him just yet.

"What did you say?" Mason says, and I hear the smile in his voice. "I didn't quite catch that with half your pillow in your mouth."

I turn my head on my pillow and look back over at him sheepishly. "I said I'm sorry."

He's silent for a moment. His gaze caresses my face with an intense look, as if searching for something before asking, "Are you?" His tone almost sounds like my incessant need to apologize has hurt him in some way.

I sit there staring at him, not sure if I should tell him how I really feel; that I'm not sorry in the slightest that I cuddled with him all night, even if I can't remember it. Or, if I should do what I always do when I feel myself getting too close to someone else, and say something sarcastic, which will push him away for good.

Before I get a chance to make a choice, Mason swings his legs off the bed to the floor, and stands, running his fingers agitatedly through his short hair before turning to look back down at me. His crisp white shirt is now wrinkled, as are his pants. His normally-smooth face now has a trace of stubble, which only makes him look more ruggedly handsome than usual to me.

"Your fever seemed to break during the night. Are you feeling better?" he asks, apparently taking my silence to his previous question in stride, and not pushing for an answer.

I lay there and realize I do feel better. I nod.

"I feel a lot better; whatever is in that medicine you gave me seems to have worked."

Mason nods. "Good. Why don't you take a bath? You were sweating a lot last night. I'll go make you some breakfast."

"You don't have to do that."

"I know I don't, Jess," he says almost harshly, "but you need to eat to build your strength back up." He starts to walk out of the bedroom. "I'll see what you have to cook in the kitchen."

And then he's gone.

I lay there wondering what I did wrong to change him from the almost-happy Mason I woke up with to the taciturn Mason now banging around in my kitchen. All I can think is that he took my silence at his question as meaning I *was* sorry I used him like my very own body-length pillow. Even if I had been truly sorry, why was he reacting so badly? Did I wound his male ego? Did the women he normally slept with treat him like a god the next morning?

I felt my stomach muscles tighten at the thought of Mason in bed with other women. Before I can linger on why it upsets me so much, I jump out of bed and go straight to my private bathroom to take a shower. I had hoped the warm water would rinse away the mental images I was having of Mason sharing the same bed with someone else.

If only hoping had worked....

After my shower, I invest a good 15 minutes in making myself presentable. I've never been one to put on a lot of makeup. I figure if it takes you more than 10 minutes to apply it, you probably have more problems than makeup can fix. I blow my hair dry and pull it back into a simple ponytail at the nape of my neck for ease.

I dress in a pair of comfortable jeans and a red sweater with sparkly silver filament interwoven into the thread. Since it is Christmas Eve, I know Mama Lynn will make me and Faison go out on our annual cookie delivery and caroling visits. So, I strive to at least look a little festive. I find a red-white-and-pink-striped sweater scarf to complete the ensemble.

I hear the doorbell ring just as I slip on my favorite black suede Uggs. When I reach the foyer, I soon find I'm already too late to be the first one to the door.

Mason stands in the foyer with the door open wide, holding a spatula in one hand, and shaking my neighbor George's hand with the other.

"Glad to meet any friend of Jess's," George tells Mason. George is dressed casually today in a red and green plaid flannel shirt, jeans, and black tennis shoes. Being that it's Christmas Eve, his work as a mall Santa is complete since everyone knows Santa should be back at the North Pole, preparing for his nightly flight around the world.

"Mason Collier," Mason introduces himself.

"George Grady."

"Hey, George," I say, coming to stand by Mason.

I see a Tupperware bowl in George's hands and instantly know what he's brought me.

"Is that what I think it is?" I ask, my stomach suddenly jumping up and down in anticipation.

George hands me the bowl.

"Shrimp and grits," he confirms. "Lynn told me you were home all night sick. Thought you might like something to eat this morning. You're looking good for someone who was running a fever last night," he comments with a smile, "happier than I've seen you in a long time in fact. Has something happened?"

I involuntarily glance in Mason's direction before taking the bowl out of George's hands.

"No," I say, "nothing too unusual." Even I can hear I'm holding something back.

George looks at Mason and me without saying a word, but I see a knowing glint appear in his eyes.

"Well, I'll let the two of you have your breakfast," George says, before holding out his hand to Mason again. "Good to meet you, son; I hope to see you around more often. You seem to have a good effect on our Jess."

I instantly feel my cheeks begin to burn. I chance a look in Mason's direction, and see that he just looks confused by what George has said to him.

"It was a pleasure to meet you too," Mason replies,

choosing not to comment on George's last statement, which only makes me want to go back to bed to bury my head in my pillow again, avoiding any more embarrassment.

"See you tonight, Jess; you know Lynn'll make us all go caroling later."

"Ok, George, see you then. And thanks for the food."

George smiles, "Anytime."

As Mason closes the door, I turn back towards the kitchen to give my cheeks an opportunity to cool down. When I get there, I see that Mason has been busy and pretty much plundered what little food I had stored in my refrigerator. Sitting on a plate is a beautifully-made fluffy omelet with bits of ham, cheese, and green onion. I see bacon still sizzling in a pan on the stove, and watch as Mason walks over to take the three strips out and blot the excess grease off them with paper towels. He sets them on the plate with the omelet, and grabs a glass filled with what looks like freshly-squeezed orange juice.

"Sit," he directs, nodding his head to the breakfast table in the room.

I do as instructed without complaint, and let Mason serve me the breakfast he worked so hard on.

"I don't remember having oranges," I say, as he slides the glass of orange juice in front of me.

"You didn't. I went over to my son's house and borrowed some from their fridge."

"Where does your son live?" I ask, taking a sip of the juice.

"Near London; he and Angela live with Allan there."

"Why do they live with him? I would have thought they would have a home of their own."

Mason sighs. "It's an old story. Allan has trouble relating to the outside world, as you might have guessed when you first met him."

"You mean his staying in the glass room when I first arrived?"

"Allan has a compulsive disorder. He's deathly afraid of germs. You might not know it from looking at him, but he's gotten a lot better than he used to be. Lilly's helped him overcome a lot of his phobias, but he's been that way for so long I fear it will take years more for him to ever be completely normal again."

"After he ran all those tests on my blood, he didn't try to hide away from me when I saw him again. He actually did come out of his glass room."

"He knew you weren't a threat anymore. Those tests were for his peace of mind, as well as gaining more information about you."

"It must be terrible living like that, afraid to touch anything or anyone."

"It's one reason Jonathan and Angela live with him. It seems to help him gain more control over his problem, since he has to deal with their kids too. You know how messy kids can be."

"It seems like that would be a nightmare for him."

"You would think, but he seems to enjoy having them around. Plus, Angela was his caretaker for so long, I'm not sure she really wants to be away from him anyway. They all seem to get along, so the arrangement works for them."

Mason walks back to the kitchen and opens a drawer. He's soon back with a fork for me to eat with.

"So, you go caroling with your mother, Faison, and George every Christmas Eve?"

"Yes; unfortunately."

Mason grins. "Why unfortunately?"

"Faison thinks she can sing, when she really can't. She gets quite loud, which only compounds the effect her voice has on others."

Mason chuckles. "Have you ever thought about telling her the truth?"

"Oh, God, no," I say, shaking my head. "She gets really touchy on the subject. We just let her keep thinking she's the best singer in the world. It's easier than trying to reason with her. Plus, it's one of my guilty pleasures, because her singing always makes me smile, and cringe, but mostly smile. I know it's probably wrong not to say something to her so she doesn't keep embarrassing herself, especially when we go out to karaoke, but I just can't bring myself to tell her. It would completely break her heart."

"Karaoke? Do you get up and sing?"

"Only when Faison forces me to," I laugh. "I'm not much of a singer either."

Mason looks down at my plate. "You should probably eat that before it gets too cold."

I do as he advises, and he walks out of the room. A minute later he reappears, shrugging back into his suit jacket.

"I should leave now," he tells me. "I usually spend Christmas Eve and Christmas with Jonathan and Angela. We're all supposed to go to Lilly and Brand's tonight too."

I swallow the bit of egg in my mouth and ask, "So what do you want me to do with the crown?"

"Just keep it for now. It's safer with you than anyone else. Maybe one of us will receive divine inspiration as to what we're supposed to do with it next."

I feel a need to think of something, anything, to make Mason stay a little while longer, but my mind is a complete blank.

"We normally take off work for Christmas," he tells me, "so I won't be back to pick you up for work until next Monday, unless something important comes up between now and then."

I feel an unfamiliar ache inside my chest, as I realize I won't be seeing Mason again for almost another three days.

"Well, let me know if anything happens," I say, "anything at all. Don't hesitate to call. I'll have my phone with me at all times."

I force myself to stop talking. The more I talk, the more I sound like a teenage girl trying to give a boy she's interested in non-subtle hints that she wants him to call her.

Mason narrows his eyes at me, as if he's trying to figure something out about me.

"I'll call if anything pops up," he promises, "otherwise,

just try to enjoy your time with your family. I left the bottle of medicine by your bed just in case. If you start to feel bad again, let me know." A roguish grin appears on his face. "I don't mind playing doctor."

I smile. "Thanks for that, by the way. I'm sure I wouldn't be feeling this good if you hadn't."

"Glad I could help."

We stare at each other for a moment, me not wanting him to go so soon, and him not seeming in a hurry to phase over to his son's home.

"I'd better get going," he finally says. "Jonathan will start to wonder where I am."

"Okay."

He hesitates, and my body aches to reach out and find a way to make him stay a little while longer.

"Merry Christmas," he says.

"Merry Christmas," I say.

And he phases away, leaving me alone in a house that seems silent and empty now without him in it.

CHAPTER 11

I quickly eat my breakfast, not wanting to stay inside my empty home any longer than I have to. After I wash the dirty dishes, I head over to Mama Lynn's house. I see Faison and John Austin making out in his truck, parked in front of Mama Lynn's home and rap the side of his charcoal-grey Dodge Ram with my fist. I see them both jump apart guiltily, which makes me laugh.

John Austin steps out of the truck and rushes me like a linebacker, picking me up in the air and twirling me around.

"Merry Christmas, almost-sister-in-law!"

"John Austin, put me down!" I say as authoritatively as I can through my laughter.

John Austin does as requested, but plants a peck on my cheek before letting me go. His tousled brown hair and happy brown eyes tell me he and Faison have been out here for a while, necking in his truck. If anyone is like a brother to me, it's John Austin. He and Faison have been joined at the hip since we were all seven-years-old, so it was either learn to love him, or forever feel like a third wheel when around the two of them.

I had picked on Faison for saying she knew John Austin was the one for her when she first saw him in second grade, but a part of that was due to jealousy. She was right. He *was* the one for her, and to have found him at such an early age was a small miracle. I knew that within our circle of friends, their marriage would stand the test of time no matter what happened. Plus, he knew if he ever hurt her I'd shoot him and bury his body where no one would ever think to look for it. I was a highly-trained Watcher agent, after all.

"Be here at seven tonight," I tell him. "You know Mama Lynn likes to go caroling no later than that."

Faison walks around the truck and is quickly enveloped in John Austin's loving embrace.

"I wouldn't miss my baby's singing for anything," he says, giving me a conspiratorial wink before nibbling the side of Faison's neck, making her giggle.

I just smile, because John Austin and I made a pact long ago to never openly discuss Faison's lack of singing ability to one another in front of her or behind her back; though we do allow ourselves to give each other meaningful glances on the subject every once in a while.

I lean forward and grab one of Faison's hands. "Come on; we gotta go deliver those cookies to people."

Faison quickly gives John Austin one more lingering kiss on the lips before allowing me to drag her into Mama Lynn's house.

"Mason came to my house last night," I tell her as we make our way up the sidewalk. "I thought you were going to call to let him know I was sick."

"Oh, I'm sorry! I completely forgot to do that," Faison's tone tells me she's anything but sorry. "So, what happened?"

I tell her.

"Oh, my God, he stayed the night? Yep, it's definite. He likes you."

I shake my head. "I had him trapped. He didn't have much choice about staying."

"You weigh about 120 pounds, Jess. If Mason had wanted to leave, he could have. Stop trying to rationalize things. Now we know for sure he likes you. The only question is do you like him?"

I didn't answer Faison. I was pretty sure the grin on my face said it all.

It ends up taking most of the day to deliver all the tins of cookies we have. It wasn't a matter of how many cookies we had to deliver, as much as it was the time we spent visiting with each of our friends in the neighborhood. In the South, if you didn't come in and sit for at least a cup of coffee or some-thing sweet to eat, you were considered rude. Many of the people in our community are old, and don't have much family left to visit with them during the holidays. Making sure those people feel like they are still important to us is the best gift we can give them.

It isn't until almost five that evening that we reach our final destination, Vern and Sadie's farm. Vern is outside, placing the harness around their mule's neck to pull the old doctor-buggy-style carriage they own.

"Hey there, Vern," Mama Lynn calls out as we walk into their yard.

Vern and Sadie live on the outskirts of town, which allows them to keep their farm animals in their front yard if they so choose. They do have a rusty old tin barn in the backyard, but they were never ones to force their animals to stay in it if they didn't want to.

"Hey, now, Lynn, girls; I hope those are your cookies in that tin," Vern says with a gap-toothed grin.

"You know it is," Mama Lynn replies. "You takin' Odalie to the cemetery?"

Vern pats Odalie's neck. "Yep; it's that time again."

I hear the screen door of their old farmhouse squeak, and see Sadie walk out, wrapping a red knitted scarf around her neck.

She smiles when she sees us, and I notice a small brown paper bag in the shape of a bottle peeking out of her coat pocket.

"Hey, there," she says, coming to stand with us.

"Merry Christmas, Sadie." Mama Lynn hands Sadie the Santa Claus tin. "Maybe you can share one with Jamie."

Sadie smiles sadly and nods her head. I see her eyes glaze with unshed tears before she hugs Mama Lynn tightly.

"You know how much he used to love them," Sadie says. "Thank you."

"Well, we'll let you two go say hi to him. Ya'll have a good Christmas."

As we wave good-bye and walk back to the car, I see Vern wipe tears from the corners of his eyes.

Almost ten years ago, Vern and Sadie lost their one and only child, Jamie, to cancer. He'd struggled with it all his life and his body simply gave out one Christmas morning. Now, every year, Vern and Sadie ride over to the cemetery to say Merry Christmas to their son, allowing Odalie to carry them over. By not driving a motorized vehicle, they give themselves the freedom to imbibe in the liquid courage sitting comfortably in Sadie's pocket.

At a little before seven that evening, George and John Austin make it over to Mama Lynn's for our annual caroling extravaganza. Each year, Mama Lynn chooses a theme for us, and this year she chose to make us all wear light-up reindeer antlers. Only, poor George is forced into wearing a flashing red nose too. We all knew that it was only our undying love for Mama Lynn that made us willingly debase ourselves in front of our friends and neighbors.

As we walk around the neighborhood, singing Christmas

carols and carrying our flashlights, people come out of their homes to thank us for stopping by and wish us a Merry Christmas. When we reach Beau's home, I almost bust out in laughter because his whole family is wearing Santa Claus earmuffs. Since it's not that cold outside, I can only assume Beau bought them to muffle the high-pitched screech of Faison's falsetto singing voice. Beau winks at me in a conspiratorial manner when we turn to leave, and I force myself not to laugh.

When we get back to Mama Lynn's house, we all drink some spiked eggnog and eat the snacks Mama Lynn prepared for us, a tradition we were all used to and one we wouldn't let her get away with not doing. We play Pictionary until almost midnight before sleep calls our names. When I lay down in my old bedroom, my thoughts drift of their own accord to Mason. I lay there wondering what he is doing at that exact moment. I hug the pillow on the other side of the bed close to my body and drift off to sleep.

The next morning I'm rudely woken up by a crazy woman shaking me half to death. I open one eye and see Faison standing over me.

"Stop," I tell her, my voice deadly serious.

"Get up!" Faison says, continuing to shake me. "Santa Claus came to see you last night!"

I turn my head away from her, hoping she gets the hint. "There is no Santa Claus, Faison. But there *is* something called sleep."

I suddenly find myself without any covers, which makes me sit up in bed so I can glare at Faison.

With a sheepish grin, knowing she might have gone too far, she drops the sheet and comforter to the floor.

"Please, Jess. I'm not joking. Santa Claus came to see you last night. Come on!"

Before I know it, she's pulling on my arm to get me out of bed.

"Okay, okay, okay," I say. "I'm up. You don't have to pull my arm out of its socket."

Like an excited four-year-old, Faison rushes out of the room ahead of me and bounds down the stairs. I stifle a yawn as I slowly make my way to the first floor. Half way down the stairs, my gaze is drawn to a large mound of silky material, landing somewhere in the color spectrum between royal purple and periwinkle. It's one of the most gorgeous colors I've ever seen.

As I make it to the bottom of the stairs, I see Mama Lynn sipping a cup of coffee, staring at the dress and Faison emphatically waving me over.

"Come on," she urges me. "Read the note!"

I walk over and see that the mound of silk I saw from up the stairs is a stunningly beautiful dress, something you would only see on TV in a fancy party sequence. The ruching of the organza skirt would be enough to give the gown a rich design, but when added to the thicker silk comprising the inner front skirt and bejeweled bodice, I feel my breath taken away by its beauty.

"Read the note!" Faison almost screams at me.

I look at the small table beside the chair where the dress lays, and see a delicate masquerade ball mask. Its base color is silver, but it has gold accents around the eyes. A light coat of a deep red glitter accentuates the curves and crevices of the mask, and glittering crystal clear jewels matching those found on the dress dance in the light of the morning sun streaming through the window.

A folded white note stands behind the mask. On the front of it is my name, written out in curvy gold filigree writing. I reach for the note and look inside it.

I know I'm a little late but hope you will forgive me. The dress doesn't match exactly, but I hope you like it and have somewhere to wear it soon.

Love,

Santa Claus

"So, what does it say?" Faison asks excitedly.

I hand her the note as I look back at the dress.

Faison reads the note quickly. "Maybe you should open the gift too," she suggests, handing me the note. "That must be what he's talking about with the matching thing."

"What gift?" I ask.

"The one sitting under the tree," Mama Lynn points to a

box with her pinky finger as she takes another sip of her coffee, watching me carefully.

I look under the tree and see a glittery gold box a little bigger than a shoebox, with a silky white ribbon wrapped around it, tied in an intricate bow.

I pull the present out and stare at it for a moment. I slowly pull one end of the bow, and it collapses easily, away from the box and onto the floor. When I lift the lid, I feel the sting of tears burn my eyes before they fall freely down my cheeks.

Faison and Mama Lynn come to stand beside me and peer inside the box.

"Oh, my God," Mama Lynn says, "is that what I think it is?"

"How did he even find one?" Faison asks. "They stopped making those things years ago."

Gently, I pull out the Rebecca American Girl doll I wanted the Christmas my parents were taken through the Tear. She's dressed in a pink and blue masquerade ball gown, complete with mask, gloves, and fairy wings.

"He's Santa Claus," I answer, even though we all know who brought the gifts. Besides Faison and Mama Lynn, there was only one other person who knew what I asked Santa to bring me 15 years ago.

I hug the doll to me, and let myself bask in Mason's thoughtfulness.

A little while later, I find myself staring at the phone in my hands, chewing on my bottom lip, and debating for the hundredth time that morning if I should hit send.

"Just send it already," Faison urges me, rolling her eyes. "Stop thinking so much."

We have just finished eating Mama Lynn's famous egg-sausage-cheese breakfast casserole and are sitting around the dining table.

"It's the polite thing to do, considering all the trouble he went to," Mama Lynn says, placing her elbows on the table and leaning in towards me.

"But he signed it Santa Claus," I say. "Maybe he didn't want me to know they were from him."

Faison snatches the phone out of my hands, and, before I can grab it back, I see her hit the send button.

"There. It's done. Now let's go play with the dress!"

I sit in stunned silence, letting myself realize what just happened.

"I can't believe you did that," I say, resting my forehead on the table and banging it softly three times.

"You were going to send it anyway," Faison reasons. "I just made sure you did it this year instead of next."

The phone buzzes in Faison's hands. Surprisingly, she hands it back to me without trying to read the text first.

I open the message and read what I wrote, plus the response.

Dear Santa, thank you for my gifts. I love them all. Jess

. . .

Dear Jess, I'm glad you like the gifts. I was told you have been a very good girl this year. Santa

"Oooh," I hear Faison say over my shoulder, "maybe he's into role-playing. You should tell him you want to be a naughty girl next year and ask if he wants to help you with that."

I feel my cheeks flush.

"Faison," Mama Lynn says standing up, a warning in her voice, "help me clear the table while Jess texts him back."

"What do I say?" I ask her, not knowing how to respond to his text.

Mama Lynn smiles. "That's up to you, sweetie."

I look down at Mason's response and decide what to write back.

Mason, your thoughtfulness has touched me deeply. I really don't know what to say but thank you. I'm not sure where I will wear the dress, but it's gorgeous. I've never owned anything to match its beauty.

I send the message and find myself waiting breathlessly for his reply. It takes almost five minutes for him to send something back.

. . .

Angela hosts a masquerade ball every New Year's Eve in her London home. I thought you might like to attend and wear the dress there...

I stare at the text, not sure who is inviting me: Angela or Mason. I decide it doesn't matter. Any excuse to wear the dress and have Mason see me in it is fine with me.

I would love to come to Angela's ball. The dress is too beautiful not to be seen.

I wait for the reply and get one almost instantly.

Angela and Jonathan both say they can't wait to see you there. Merry Christmas, Jess. See you Monday.

I sigh; slightly disappointed he's cut our conversation off so succinctly.

The phone vibrates in my hand and I quickly look at the text.

. . .

P.S. I can't wait to see you in the dress

Another text appears.

P.P.S. I know you will look beautiful in it

I smile down at the last message.

"So I guess you found the right thing to say?" Mama Lynn asks, coming to sit down beside me at the table.

"He sort of invited me to a masquerade ball on New Year's Eve," I tell her. "But I can't tell if he plans to take me himself or if I'm just supposed to go there stag."

"Jess," Mama Lynn says, as if I should know better, "no man buys a dress like that for a woman he doesn't intend to go out with himself."

"You know… he stayed with me the night I was sick."

"Yes, I know."

I look up at her in surprise.

"George told me all about meeting him yesterday morning," she tells me. "He said he never saw you look so happy."

I feel my heart tighten in my chest.

"It scares me," I tell her in a whisper, not even sure if I'm ready to admit my feelings to myself, much less to her.

"Jess, you've been hiding from the world for a long time now. I haven't said anything because I know what you've been through, but you need to take a chance and let yourself fall in love with someone. Stop being scared of what might happen. There's no one on this Earth who knows what the future holds for any of us. You are too good a person to only let yourself love Faison and me. There's a whole world out there you've not let yourself experience because you've been too scared of being hurt again. I don't think your parents would approve. I feel confident in saying they would tell you to live every day of your life like you're living your last day on Earth. Life's too short to worry about being hurt all the time. The only way you'll ever find happiness is by letting other people in."

"I know you're right," I say, but a small part of me still wants to hold back and shield my heart.

Mama Lynn puts one of her hands over mine still holding the phone, resting on the table.

"Take a chance, Jess. For once in your life, let your heart tell you what to do instead of your brain. If you don't, you might miss out on something special."

I nod, letting her know I've heard what she has to say.

Mama Lynn stands up, and I look down at my phone, intent on sending one more message.

And I'm sure you will look handsome in a tuxedo. Look forward to seeing you Monday.

. . .

I wait to see if I get a response, and smile when it appears almost instantly.

Until Monday...

I don't know if it's wishful thinking on my part or not, but the dot, dot, dots make me want to believe he'll be as miserable as I will be for the next two days.

CHAPTER 12

By the time Monday morning rolls around, I'm a nervous wreck. I pace in my living room, occasionally resting my hand on the butt of my plasma pistol just for added comfort. I look up at the clock on the mantel and see that it's a minute before eight. Knowing how punctual Mason always is, I feel my heart hammer against the wall of my chest because I know he'll be here soon.

I don't know what I'm going to say to him or how our relationship will change after everything that's happened between us since the night I got sick. Fortunately, I don't have time to worry about it much because the doorbell rings. I grab my leather jacket from the couch and hurry to the door.

Mason is standing there, dressed in what must be his favorite grey wool coat, since he's always wearing it.

"Good morning, Jess," he says, a hint of a smile on his face.

"Morning," I reply, putting on my jacket.

I walk out the door and lock it behind me. Mason places his hand on my arm, and I instantly find myself back at headquarters.

Joshua is in his usual spot at the control panel, watching holographic images of Lucifer and his new best friend.

"So they're not hiding anymore?" I ask.

"No," I hear Nick say behind me, causing me to jump slightly. I hate it that I let him sneak up on me. "They've been doing some traveling since Christmas."

"Are they looking for something?" I ask.

"That's what we're trying to figure out," Mason tells me, taking off his coat and draping it over a chair next to Joshua.

Joshua spins around in his chair and holds out a small cardboard box to me.

"Merry Christmas, Jess," he says. "I figured I would save you the trouble of having to rip through the paper."

I take the small box and open it up. Inside lays a pewter Christmas ornament of Yoda, hanging from a red ribbon.

"Someone told me you like Yoda," Joshua says. "I thought you might like that for your tree."

I smile. "Thank you, Joshua," I say, feeling my heart warm towards the boy. "That was very thoughtful of you."

"No prob," he replies, before spinning back around to continue his work.

I look at the ornament and know exactly who told Joshua I

like Yoda, but I have no idea how I ended up being the topic of a conversation between Joshua and Mason.

I put the ornament back in the box and set it on a nearby table.

"Do you know who the Tearer is yet?" I ask.

"I haven't been able to get close enough to tell," Mason says.

"When did they show back up?" I ask confused.

"Yesterday afternoon," Mason tells me. "I've been trying to catch up with them, but they're good at covering their tracks."

Why didn't he come get me?

"I would have helped," I tell him, wondering why he didn't use the opportunity as an excuse to be around me yesterday.

"We weren't sure what was going on," he explains, "and I didn't want to disrupt your time with your family."

"You brought me in to help you," I say. "Let me try to do my job. So far, I haven't been allowed to do much."

"If I had thought you could help," Mason says, "I would have brought you in; but, like I said, we haven't been able to tell what they're doing yet. It would have been pointless to have you phasing around the world with me. Plus, your body isn't designed to handle that much phasing at one time. You've already experienced that for yourself. It was just easier for me to go alone, Jess. I didn't need your help."

I bristle at his words and decide to drop the subject. Perhaps I was wrong; maybe Mason really wasn't interested in me as anything more than someone under his command. I stick to that idea and grab onto the excuse to latch the lid over my heart instantly, before it has time to decide otherwise.

"So we don't know what Lucifer is doing, and we have no idea what the crown means. Is that about the gist of our situation?" I ask, not hiding my new-found irritation from my voice.

"That about sums it up," Nick says from his spot beside me.

"Not quite."

I turn to Mason, waiting for him to say more.

"Would you like to share with the class, Mr. Collier?" I ask.

"I've been thinking about the crown, trying to figure out why you would be given Jophiel's. I would like to try something, but I'm not sure if it will work. Only angels are allowed into the place I would like to take you, so I'm not sure how dangerous trying to phase you in there might be."

"Phase into where, exactly?" I ask, not sure I want to go somewhere which seems to make Mason so uneasy.

"Eden."

I feel my face scrunch up involuntarily. "You're not going to tell me the Garden of Eden is a real place too, are you?"

"It's very real," Mason says, completely serious, "but it can only be accessed by angels, because it's an inner realm."

I assume I look as confused as I feel, because he explains further.

"An inner realm is a pocket of space which doesn't exist in

this dimension. Eden was moved by Jophiel and Michael when the Tree of Life needed to be protected. Jophiel used to have to guard it with his sword, but they decided the Tree would be just as safe, if not more so, if they moved it from this reality to an inner realm."

"But we've already tested me, and I'm apparently as human as a human can get," I say. "What makes you think I'll be allowed into Eden?"

"I would like to try it with you holding the crown. It may be your ticket in there, and that might be why only you can hold it. I don't think it is coincidence that you were chosen to find Jophiel's crown. It's almost like a written invitation to go to the one place he was in charge of. We need to at least try it. If it doesn't work, it doesn't work. There's no harm in testing out my theory."

"Man," Joshua exclaims. "Do you think a camera would work in there if I gave you one? I'd give my left arm to see that place."

Mason raises a dubious eyebrow in Joshua's direction. "Absolutely not; we're not going to desecrate holy ground with modern technology."

Joshua shrugs, "Can't blame me for trying."

I grab the cardboard box with my Christmas ornament.

"Ready when you are, boss," I say.

Mason looks at me, like what I've said and how I've said it surprises him.

"Is everything all right?" he asks me in a low voice, a question meant for my ears only.

"Everything is fine," I reply, holding my hand out to him. "Better take me home so I can get the crown."

Mason takes hold of my hand, and I find myself standing in my bedroom.

"How did you know this is where I kept it?" I ask.

"I saw it the other night beneath your pillow," he answers, apparently amused that I would keep such a priceless artifact in a place so accessible.

I set the box on my nightstand and reach under my pillow to retrieve the crown.

"You should leave your pistol and phone here too," Mason advises.

I pull the pistol from my thigh holster and dig my phone out of my pants pocket, setting them both down next to the box.

"Okay; ready to go," I say, holding out my hand.

Mason looks at my hand and then looks back up at me.

"Did I do something wrong?" he asks. "I get the distinct feeling you're upset with me about something."

"It's nothing," I say, pushing my hand out further for him to take.

He takes my hand, but, instead of just grabbing it as usual, he spreads his fingers, forcing mine to intertwine with his.

"Why are you angry with me, Jess?"

The hurt way he asks this question forces me to look up at him and see the worry in his eyes. I feel the lock around my heart strain to be released, but choose to ignore its cry.

"Let's just go," I say, looking away from him.

He's silent for a moment, and I can feel him looking at me, waiting to see if I will change my mind and answer his question.

"Phasing to an inner realm is different from phasing on this dimensional plane," he finally says, giving up on my answering him.

"Why does that sound like a warning?" I ask, forcing myself to look back at him.

"Because it is; the travel affects angels differently. I'm not sure what it will do to a human. Phasing to Eden is almost like entering Heaven. I just want you to be aware that you might feel differently there. If you do, don't worry; it's natural."

I nod my head, now completely worried, even though Mason seems to think his little pep talk should have calmed my nerves instead.

"I'm ready," I tell him, tightening my hold on his hand.

He tightens his in return and phases us to where it all began.

I find myself standing on the greenest grass I've ever seen in my life. When I look up at the azure-blue sky, I feel my breath catch at the sight of jewel-colored dragons flying through the air. It instantly reminds me of the nursery in Brand and Lilly's house. I know then that one of them must have painted it, because the place I'm standing in looks just like the murals in their daughter's room.

I take a deep breath, and my mind feels instantly cleansed by the sweet smell of the air.

"It almost smells like cotton candy," I tell Mason.

The multicolored leaves of the tall trees around us rustle in the wind, making them sound like they're singing. I let go of Mason's hand and bend down to touch the grass at my feet. The blades don't feel coarse and waxy like they do on Earth, but silky to the touch, almost like velvet. I have an instant urge to strip all my clothes off and lay in the grass to watch the flight of the dragons overhead.

"Uh, Jess?" I distantly hear Mason say, only then realizing my jacket and shirt are lying on the ground at my feet, and my hands are positioned to unbutton my pants.

I look at Mason, confused.

"What am I doing?" I ask, not having even realized I was stripping in front of him. I quickly reach down to retrieve my shirt, slipping it back on.

"I did warn you that this place might affect the way you think," Mason says.

I scowl at the amusement on his face.

"And you couldn't have said something to bring me back to reality before I took my shirt off?" I ask accusingly.

"I just thought you were warm," Mason says, holding back his laughter behind a smile. "I didn't think you were going to perform a striptease act in the middle of paradise; though who am I to complain about something like that?"

I feel my mouth gape open as I stare at him in complete shock. "That's so...." I can't think of anything but, "That's such a man thing to say!"

"I am a man," he reminds me.

"But you're an angel too," I remind him. "You should have a higher set of standards than a regular man."

"A fallen angel," he reminds me, turning serious. "It was because of our love for women like you that we fell from grace."

"You all made your own choices," I say. "Don't blame my sex for your transgressions."

"I didn't mean it like that," Mason is quick to say. "You're right. We made our own choices. And we paid for the consequences of our actions."

After I have my jacket back on, I say, "So what is it exactly that you think I'm supposed to do here?"

"I'm not sure," Mason says, looking around us, "but we should probably go to the Tree of Life to see if Jophiel left another clue for you there."

As we walk through the garden, I see a myriad of creatures I never would have thought actually existed. I wouldn't even know how to explain them because they don't have counterparts in the real world. I do, however, see creatures that look like tiny fairies, but I feel sure they aren't. If Lilly's friend is married to a fairy, I seriously doubt he looks like a little multi-colored butterfly about as big as the palm of my hand.

Mason doesn't have to tell me when we reach the Tree of Life. It's hard to miss. Not only is it the largest, most beautiful tree in the garden, but it has a fiery sword, blazing brightly with orange flames, embedded in its trunk.

"I don't understand why it's there," Mason says, his

eyebrows lowered in confusion. "Why would Jophiel leave it stuck inside the tree?"

I seriously hope Mason doesn't think I have an answer to his question, because I feel sure I am far more clueless than he.

We walk up to the Tree, and Mason grabs the hilt of the sword. He gives one swift tug, but the sword remains steadfastly embedded in the trunk, not giving an inch. He steps back and motions me forward.

"Why don't you give it a try?"

I don't know what to do with the crown, so I stick it on my head. I grab the sword's hilt with both my hands, intent on yanking with all my might, but soon find that I don't need to strain so hard. The sword, in all its fiery magnificence, comes out like the trunk is made of butter and not wood.

I feel the crown on my head begin to grow warm against my scalp. When I look up at Mason, his eyes are large, and he's breathing so hard I fear for his health.

"What's happening?" I ask him.

"The crown is glowing," he says. "It's glowing like it normally would on the head of an archangel."

"But I'm human," I remind him.

"Jessica..."

"Did you hear that?" I ask, looking around me, trying to find the owner of the voice.

"Hear what?" Mason asks.

"Jessica, it's time we had a talk..."

I look at Mason, completely frightened now because I suddenly realize the voice is coming from inside my head.

Before I can stop it from happening, the world around me grows dark. I faintly hear Mason scream my name, but that's the last thing I remember before falling unconscious.

CHAPTER 13

I don't remember even opening my eyes. I just suddenly find myself standing in the middle of my mother's flower garden in the backyard of my childhood home. It's springtime and a warm breeze caresses my skin, bringing with it the scent of freshly-cut grass and morning dew. My mother's rose bushes are just beginning to bud, and the tulips, daffodils, and azaleas are in full bloom, surrounding me with pinks, yellows, and warm whites. I sense movement from the direction of the white-painted Victorian-style gazebo in the middle of the garden, and notice an angel standing there. I know he's an angel because he has white wings attached to his back, which are flaring slightly as he watches me.

"Who are you?" I ask, refusing to move an inch until I get an answer.

"Come speak with me, Jessica. We have a lot to talk about."

Before I know it, I'm standing inside the gazebo, staring into the bluest eyes I've ever seen. The man is handsome, with wavy jet-black hair that just touches his shoulders, and a face I find both kind and stern at the same time. He's dressed in something that looks similar to a black Roman soldier's uniform, complete with shredded leather skirt and hard leather breastplate.

"Who are you?" I ask again, feeling my heart rate increase.

The man flexes the wings on his back, as if they annoy him.

"You know, I've never quite understood why you humans always think of us with bird wings on our backs," he sounds almost amused. "They're quite uncomfortable."

"I don't understand," I admit. "You *are* an angel, right?"

He looks at me and smiles. For some reason, his expression puts me at ease.

"I look the way you think I should look," he tells me. "Don't suppose you could think of angels without the wings," he looks down at what he's wearing, "and without the gladiator costume?"

"How can I change how you look?"

"We're in your conscious right now, Jessica. You can change anything and everything you see. I believe you chose this place because it's where you were the happiest as a child."

I decide to test his theory and imagine him without the wings.

To my surprise, the wings disappear.

"Ahh, thank you," he says, rolling his shoulders.

Then I imagine him without a stitch of clothing on.

He looks down at himself, completely exposed, but doesn't try to cover up.

"Well," he says, placing his hands on his hips, "it's an improvement, but I'm not sure how well you'll be able to concentrate on what I need to tell you if I remain naked, Jessica."

I imagine him in a bunny costume. I laugh.

He smirks at me. "Not really an improvement."

I dress him in a faded pair of jeans and a white T-shirt, with black angel wings embossed on the front.

"Thanks," he says, sitting down on one of the two benches in the gazebo.

I sit on the opposite bench, watching him warily.

"Are you going to tell me who you are, and why we're here?" I ask.

The man smiles at me and leans forward by resting his elbows on his thighs. He clasps his hands together and begins to tell me about my destiny.

"My name is Michael."

"The Archangel Michael?" I ask. He nods once. "So why are you inside my head, Michael?"

"I've always been a part of you," he tells me. "I've remained hidden within you until now."

"What do you mean you've *always* been a part of me?"

"When you were conceived, my essence or, you could say,

my soul, attached itself to yours. We were drawn to one another, Jessica, for whatever reason."

"How did that happen?"

"It happened the night the Tear appeared."

"But I was seven years old when that happened. How could you have become a part of me when I was conceived? You're not making any sense."

"I know Mason has already told you what happened on Earth when Lucifer made the Tear, but let me tell you what happened in Heaven when it happened."

I feel myself involuntarily lean forward, intrigued by the oration of such a tale.

"When it happened, God came to us, the seven archangels, and told us what the results of Lucifer's actions would be. He said that, although Lucifer wouldn't accomplish destroying the universe, he would break it, Tear it into a thousand different pieces that might never match up again. He said we were the only ones who could stop Lucifer's next plan. And, before you ask, because I know you will, He didn't tell us what that next plan was, exactly, just that we were the only ones who would be able to stop him when the time came."

"That's interesting," I say, not being facetious in the slightest, "but that doesn't answer my original question. I was seven when the Tear appeared. How are you a part of me?"

"Time moves differently in Heaven," Michael says. "Here, time moves linearly. You have your past, present, and future, and they happen in that order. In Heaven, it's not linear because we need to be able to step into all three timelines to cause changes when needed. So, when we were asked to come here, we all chose a particular point in time to jump into. Most of us came in the past, and I believe one of us chose that exact night or what was the present."

"How did you choose me?"

"I didn't choose you. You chose me."

"I chose you? Baby me chose to attach itself to the soul of an archangel?" I ask dubiously.

"All of the archangels went to the Guf to find suitable souls to meld with."

"The Guf?"

"It's the Treasury of Souls. We went there and explained to the souls present what our mission was. The only way the melding could work is if the human souls chose us, not the other way around. Seven of you volunteered to become our vessels. You knew what you were getting into, and chose to fight the good fight, I guess you could say. You're a lot stronger than you've given yourself credit for. Even then, you understood the risk you were taking, but you still chose to take me with you and fight for what was right. It's the rarest of souls who chooses that type of path, Jessica."

"What, one who's a glutton for punishment?" I retort, trying to make light of his praise.

"One who knows what's worth fighting for."

I sit there, trying to absorb what he's just told me, and decide I should try to find out as much information while I can.

"So all seven of you are here, on this Earth?"

"Yes."

"Where are the others?"

"That I can't tell you, because I don't know. You're the one who will have to find them."

"And how exactly am I supposed to do that?"

"We are all connected to one another; at least our souls are. When you finally find the first vessel, you'll understand what I'm talking about more clearly. The first one will be the hardest, though. You'll have to find the place within yourself that connects you to them. If you can concentrate on that small part of them, you will be able to visualize who and where they are, but the first one may be hard for you to find."

"Thanks for the words of encouragement."

Michael smiles. "You can do it, Jessica; I know you can. Let Mason help you. I believe he holds the key to your success."

"Why would you think that?"

"He makes you want to bring down the walls you've built around yourself since the disappearance of your parents. If you don't let yourself connect with someone you actually care about, I'm afraid there might not be any hope of you finding the others."

"Well, can't you help me? Isn't that why you hitched a ride with my soul? You're an archangel, right? Shouldn't you have some sort of superpowers? Aren't you the reason I see that people who don't belong on Earth glow different colors?"

"Yes, I'm the reason you see certain people's auras. It is a power that was given to me, so I could know where certain legions of angels were during the fight with Lucifer in Heaven. You see the Tearers as having red auras because they simply don't belong on this Earth, and their natural auras are corrupted, but you only have access to some of my powers at the moment. I can only help you so much, until all seven of us are brought back together. Until then, you and the other vessels will each need to find the crown that was placed here on Earth for you, plus your corresponding talisman."

"Talisman?"

"The flaming sword is your talisman, Jessica. The others will have their own holy relics that they will need to find."

"Why do we need these talismans?"

"The objects are meant to help you focus the powers you will develop as you grow in number. It's easier for humans to have a physical object they can project upon. Having something you can hold tends to help you concentrate. Once the others have found their crowns and talismans, they will be able to communicate with their archangel just like you and I are now."

"Why do I have Jophiel's crown and not yours?"

"Not all of you will get the crown that corresponds to your archangel. Things don't have to be that literal all the time. You were given Jophiel's crown because it was the clue you needed, or, in your case, Mason needed, in order to lead you to the sword. Like I've said, you're a fighter, and the sword best complimented that quality in you."

"If we are all meant to fight against Lucifer, does that

mean Lilly will be helping us to stop him? She did it once before; surely she can do it again."

"Lilly is my child. I would rather not involve her in this matter," Michael says, taking on a protective tone. "She's found her happy ending, and I want it to stay that way. Besides, she can't take on all the princes of Hell by herself. Only the combined power of the seven of us will be enough to stop them."

"Princes of Hell? Where are they?"

"They were scattered across the universe when the Tear opened. It was something Lucifer hadn't counted on happening. Usually it would be simple enough for him to call the other six to his side, by summoning them through the rings he made them from his own crown, but they don't have the rings anymore."

"Where are the rings?"

"I don't know."

"So is that what Lucifer meant when he told Mason each new year brings its own small miracle? He's waiting for the others to come through the Tear?"

"Lucifer saves up his power every year in order to open the Tear," Michael says. "He's found at least one of the other princes. All he needs now are the other five."

I sit there in silence, absorbing what Michael has just said.

"He's responsible for it opening every year?"

"Yes. He's not powerful enough to cause any real damage, just opening it to search for the others."

"Not cause any real damage?" I exclaim, on the verge of

hysteria. "You've seen what that thing does to people's lives! How can you sit there and say it doesn't cause any real damage?"

"That's not what I meant, and you know it, Jessica. Yes, I know it rips people's lives apart, but the universe remains intact. Lives continue, just differently."

"Spoken like someone who's never truly lost someone they love." I hear the harshness of my voice, but don't care; it's what I believe.

"I've suffered loss," Michael says, and I see the evidence of pain in his eyes. "I lost my best friend to his own greed. I had to abandon the woman I loved because I was ordered to. I never had a chance to know my one and only child because my involvement in her life would have diverted her from her true path, the path she was born to take. I've known loss just as painful as yours, Jessica. Don't think you're the only one who holds a monopoly on heartache, because you're not."

I suddenly feel like I've just been put in my place, and look away, unable to look Michael in the eye anymore.

"I didn't mean to make you feel bad," he says gently, "but you must remember we've all had to make sacrifices; some of them harder than others, but just as painful."

"I'm sorry. I didn't think about what you've been through. I was just being selfish."

I'm silent for a moment before I ask him another question.

"So after I find the other six and get them their crowns and talismans," I say, "what do we do?"

"Let's concentrate on the most important thing first ...

finding the first vessel. When you're finally together, your powers will combine, and you'll be able to find the next archangel vessel a little easier. Each time you add another member, finding the next will become far simpler. The first one will be the hardest if you don't allow yourself to connect with people; I hate to add to your burden, but that responsibility rests solely on your shoulders."

"No pressure there," I say, taking a deep breath and letting it out slowly.

"You can do it," Michael says, so sure of his statement it makes me look back up at him.

The look of confidence on his face instills me with the courage I need to face the task he has laid out before me.

"Will this be the last time I see you?" I ask.

Michael smiles. "No, you've awoken me now. If you need to speak with me, just call out to me in your dreams, and I will come to you."

"Okay," I say, standing up. "How do I get out of here so I can start looking for the other vessels?"

"Wake up."

I open my eyes and find myself in a strange bedroom. A painting of a woman in a red dress is on the wall across from the bed I'm in. Her hand is propped against her cheek as she leans to the side, staring down at me. A lacquered dresser sits beneath her. On its surface is a bouquet of white roses in a crystal vase. The sword is still grasped firmly in my right hand, and the crown is lying in the crevice between my pillow and the other pillow on the bed.

Streams of sunlight enter the room through a pair of paned glass doors, on the wall facing the outside of the building I'm in. Gauzy white drapes hang from hooks above the doors, scattering the light across the red tiles on the floor. I push the thin white quilt covering me off my body, and swing my legs over the side of the bed.

I'm still wearing my Watcher uniform, but find that my shoes, socks, and thigh holster are missing. I stand up and walk over to the lacquered dresser to place the sword and the crown on its surface. Then I walk over to the glass doors to discover where I am.

Outside is a grey stone terrace that looks out over an immaculately-kept formal garden, its shrubbery trimmed in various complementary geometric designs. Past the garden are acres of rolling hills, covered in what appears to be grapevines.

I hear the door to the room open behind me, and turn to see who it is.

I watch as Mason's eyes travel from the bed, where he obviously thinks I should be, to where I'm standing.

He smiles, and I feel my heart sing as the look of concern on his face turns to relief, relaxing his features and making him more handsome than any man, or angel, has a right to look.

"How are you feeling?" he asks, coming to stand by my side.

"I'm fine. How long have I been asleep?"

"Two days."

I'm silent; sure I've heard him wrong. "Did you just say two days?"

He nods. "Two days."

I feel my tummy grumble, as if confirming for a fact that what he's saying is true.

"Do you have something I can eat?" I ask, now feeling the full emptiness of my stomach gnawing at my backbone.

Mason holds his hand out to me, and I assume we're about to phase somewhere to find me food, but he simply laces his fingers between mine and tugs on my hand, urging me to follow him. We walk out of the room, holding hands as if it's the most natural thing in the world for us to be doing. I smile, finding the intimate contact unexpected.

As Mason leads me down the hallway, I instantly know we have to be in a mansion. The hallway is as long as my street back home, with various rooms branching off it.

"Where are we?" I ask, observing the distinctly European furniture and old-style oil paintings hanging on the walls.

"My villa in Tuscany," he answers. "I wanted to keep you somewhere safe. Not many people know about this place." He turns to face me and smiles. "It's where I come to hide from the rest of the world."

"So, are we hiding?" I ask, amused by the idea of Mason trying to hide me.

"In a way," he replies. "I wasn't sure what was happening to you. I didn't want to take the chance of you falling into the wrong hands while you were defenseless."

"So you were my bodyguard?" I ask.

Mason looks back at me, his eyes travelling the whole length of me.

"It's a body worth guarding."

Thankfully, he turns his head before he can witness a completely girly moment of me blushing. I feel like I should fan my cheeks they're so hot, but instead I just concentrate on my breathing so I don't forget how.

When we reach the first floor, Mason quickly escorts me through a light, airy room with a large built-in stone fireplace on the far wall. Three white sofas with coral-colored throw pillows surround an oversized wood coffee table. A large antique chandelier hangs in the center of it all, softly illuminating the exposed cherry-wood beam ceiling.

We descend another set of stairs and walk a short distance down a hallway to the kitchen area. The kitchen is a lot smaller and cozier than I would have imagined for a house so large. The appliances in the kitchen are the most modern things I've seen in the house thus far. Apparently, Mason does like to cook because I can tell he has spared no expense in this room. Antiqued white cabinets line the walls, with black marble counter tops. A wood table with white painted legs and chairs sit in the middle of the room. Mason lets go of my hand so he can pull out one of the chairs at the table for me, a courtesy no one has ever bestowed upon me before.

After I sit down, he walks to a large industrial-sized refrigerator and pulls out a large silver platter filled with various cheeses, fruits, sliced meats and vegetables. After depositing the feast on the table in front of me, he takes out a loaf of

French bread from one of the cabinets, and begins to slice it up while I nibble on a piece of aged cheddar cheese.

I can't stop myself from watching Mason as he slices the bread. The way his muscles move beneath the electric-blue button-down shirt he's wearing as he works the knife in and out of the bread mesmerizes me. I grant myself permission to let my eyes travel down the length of him. I find myself smiling. Thankfully, he decided to tuck his shirt into the pair of form-fitting jeans he's wearing. It's a side of Mason I had never paid much attention to before, and am appreciative for the opportunity.

"Jess?"

I quickly lift my gaze from the inappropriate spot I have been staring and find Mason's head turned in my direction, catching me in the act of ogling him.

"Yes?" I ask as innocently as I can, hoping beyond hope that he didn't just see me staring at his butt.

A lopsided grin appears on Mason's face, and I know I'm totally busted.

"I was asking," he says, a hint of amusement in his voice, "if you would like me to make you something else to eat. I have a fully-stocked kitchen. I can make you anything you want… if it's food you want, that is."

I feel like crawling underneath the table and staying there until the end of time. Not brave enough to address the elephant in the room, I shake my head.

"No, I'm fine with what's here," I say looking at the tray of food in front of me before I cautiously look back at Mason.

He turns around to face me and leans against the counter, arms crossed over his chest.

"So you're sure there's nothing else you might want to have instead?"

It's then I experience my first ever Freudian slip as my eyes, and I swear they do this on if their own accord, drop down to Mason's hips. I quickly look away and find a piece of dust on the wall to my left extremely interesting to stare at.

"No," I say, shaking my head sagely, "I'm fine."

I don't dare look in Mason's direction until he turns back around to arrange the bread on a plate. When I do let my eyes travel back to where he stands, I notice that his shoulders are shaking slightly, and I know he's quietly laughing.

Normally, I would feel appalled by my behavior, but if it made Mason laugh, I can live with a little embarrassment. He doesn't seem to be the type of person who relaxes enough to laugh very often, and I feel a strange sort of pride that my blatant leering of his person brought him a small amount of joy.

When he does turn back around to face me, his smile is so bright I find it utterly impossible not to smile too.

"Is there anything in particular you would like to….*drink?*" he asks, emphasizing the last word in a way that makes it sound naughty.

"Water?" I ask, completely ignoring his suggestive tone.

He nods his head and grabs a glass from the cabinet, filling it with water from the tap.

"I have an artesian well on the property," he tells me,

sitting the crystal-clear water in front of me. "It's probably the purest water you'll ever drink."

He sits down across from me, and I take a sip of the water.

"Wow, that really is good water," I say.

I grab a couple of slices of bread, sliced meat, and cheese to make a sandwich. Just as I'm about to take a bite, I notice Mason staring at me, and stop.

"I feel funny with you looking at me while I'm eating," I tell him.

"Would you rather I stood and turned my back to you?" he asks, smiling knowingly.

"No," I say, not even pretending that we both don't know what he is implying, "but is there something else you could be doing in here while I eat?"

Mason stands and goes to the refrigerator, pulling out what looks like cut up chicken.

"I was planning to make you some of my famous chicken soup. Would you like some for supper?"

"Yes, that sounds good," I say, taking a bite of my sandwich and instantly feeling my hunger begin to ebb.

While Mason goes about cooking his soup, I end up eating three sandwiches in a row, and begin to wonder if I will have room for the soup later. After the last sandwich, I completely drain my glass of water and get up to get another.

"What are you doing?" Mason asks, seeing me rise as he's dropping diced carrots into his pot of soup

"I need some more water," I say. The words end up

sounding like a question instead of a statement, because I'm not sure why he's questioning me.

"I'll get that for you," he tells me. "You just sit down and rest."

He takes the glass out of my hand and fills it from the sink. I sit back down and tell him, "Thank you."

Once Mason sets his soup to boil, he returns to the table and sits down across from me.

"Now, can you tell me what happened?"

I tell Mason everything Michael told me, and finally decide to reveal my secret of *'seeing the truth of things'* to another living soul.

"So that's all you were keeping from me?" he asks, somewhat relieved.

"How did you know I wasn't telling you the complete truth?" I ask. "That first night we met, I could tell you and Isaiah knew I was holding something back."

"The Watchers who have never tasted human blood were able to retain the power of being able to tell if someone is lying. We knew you weren't exactly lying to us, but we also knew you weren't telling us the complete truth either."

"I didn't know you guys could do that," I say, not sure how I feel about being around a walking lie-detector.

"It's not something we normally tell others about," Mason says. "It can make some people uncomfortable to be around us."

Mason rests his elbows on the table and leans in towards me. "You know, all this time we thought the answer to sealing the Tear was an object of some sort. It never even occurred to me we should have been looking for people, and now we know what, or I guess who, Lucifer has been looking for all these years. Did Michael give you any advice as to how you should connect with the other archangel vessels? Is there something in particular that you need to do? Some sort of ritual?"

I look down at my hands, not quite sure how to tell Mason that he might be the key to me finding the others. Voicing that fact to him will also force me to admit I'm developing feelings for him. I'm not ready for that just yet.

"He seems to think you might know of a way to help me concentrate enough to find the first one," I say instead.

"Me?" Mason doesn't sound too sure about that. "Did he happen to say what it is I can do to help you?"

"Not specifically," I say, wondering if Mason can tell I'm holding a piece of important information back from him with his super Watcher lie-detector.

If he does, he doesn't let it show. He sits back in his chair, and it's almost like I can see the gears shift from one idea to another. Finally, he just shrugs his shoulders and says, "I guess we'll just have to try everything."

Mason gets up and walks over to pull back my chair, to make it easier for me to stand.

"You really don't have to do that," I tell him. "I can move a chair on my own."

"I'm old-fashioned," he explains. "If I'm with a lady, I like to do things for her."

He gently takes one of my hands, which makes me wonder if he considers this a natural thing for us to be doing now, and leads me out of the kitchen back to the living room we passed through earlier. The fire blazing in the hearth lends the room warmth, which is at once calming and relaxing.

"Sit down on this sofa," Mason instructs, leading me to the one facing the fireplace.

I do as he says, waiting for further instructions.

He lets go of my hand and sits down in front of me on the coffee table.

"Now close your eyes and try to relax," he tells me, his voice taking on a soothing tone.

I close my eyes.

"Listen to the crackling of the fire," he says in a low voice. "Can you hear the heat popping the wood?"

"Yes," I say in a low voice of my own, not wanting to break the mood Mason is trying to create.

"Keep listening," he instructs, "and try to find that part of yourself where you never go; somewhere deep down that you keep hidden away from everyone, even yourself."

Mason remains silent while I try to do what he asks.

I hear him move, and try to keep concentrating to find that part of me that I keep locked way. I feel the spot on the sofa beside me dip as he sits closer to me, and I smell the scent of him.

"Keep concentrating," he whispers so close to my ear I feel the small hairs on the back of my neck stand to attention.

"Block out everything around you, and stretch out your feelings to find the others."

I begin to wonder how he thinks I can do that. He's sitting so close to me that I can feel the heat from his body mingle with mine. His warm breath tickles my cheek, and I'm finding it incredibly hard to breathe, much less concentrate on my inner id.

"Do you feel anything, Jess?" he asks, breathlessly.

I quickly open my eyes and stand up.

"Did it work?" he asks, surprise in his voice.

I bury my face in my hands, and rub up and down in slight frustration.

"No, it did *not* work," I say, taking my hands away and looking down at him. "How am I supposed to concentrate with you whispering in my ear like that?"

Mason looks bemused.

"I'm sorry," he says. "I thought if you could concentrate on my voice that maybe it would help you focus better."

"It's more difficult for me to concentrate with you so close," I confess. "You're just too distracting."

I see the first signs of a pleased smile tug at the corners of his mouth.

"Is that a bad thing?"

I stare at Mason and see the same expression I saw the morning I woke up in his arms and he asked me if I really was sorry I had slept with my body draped across him the entire night. Michael's words to me about allowing myself to care for someone else reverberate in my head:

"If you don't let yourself connect with someone you actually care about, I'm afraid there might not be any hope of you finding the others."

"No," I hear myself tell him. "It's not a bad thing. But you're just…" I didn't know how to put it without sounding like a complete idiot, "you're just too…distracting!"

Mason allows the little sprites tugging at his mouth to form his lips into a complete smile. He stands up. "So how can I be less distracting and still be helpful to you?"

I take a deep breath and let it out. "I have no idea. Could you grow ugly or smell bad or try to not be so damn perfect somehow?"

I see Mason's cheeks grow red at my request.

"Why are *you* embarrassed?" I ask in complete exasperation. "I'm the one who should be completely mortified."

I bury my face in my hands for the second time in less than five minutes, intent on hiding that way for all eternity.

I feel Mason grasp my shoulders and gently force me to turn and face him.

"Jess, look at me."

"Why? Did you spontaneously grow a pair of horns out of the top of your head, or grow warts all over your face in the last few seconds?"

I hear him chuckle softly. "No, but look at me."

I force myself to lower my hands, but have a hard time lifting my eyes to meet his.

"Jess…" he gently coaxes.

Hesitantly, I look up at him and meet his gaze.

Through the unfathomable depths of his bright blue eyes, I see his longing for me to truly see all of him.

I sigh inside at his perfection and slowly lift my hands to cover my face again.

"How was that supposed to be helpful?" I ask, my voice sounding accusing.

I hear Mason chuckle louder at my predicament.

"Jess, I am not perfect," he says, and I know he believes his own words. "Just look at me."

Confused by why he would believe such a thing about himself, I drop my hands from my face and look straight at him.

"What about you *isn't* perfect?" I ask, completely dumbfounded by why he thinks so little of himself.

He turns his head so I can fully see his scar.

"See," he says, "not perfect."

The pain I hear in his last words makes my heart ache for him.

Tentatively, I lift my right hand towards his face. He seems to know what I'm about to do and doesn't try to stop me. He just swallows hard and closes his eyes. I allow the tips of my fingers to start at the top of his scar just above his left eye, and slowly trail down its rough ridges to below his cheekbone. My heart physically hurts inside my chest at the thought of how much pain he must have suffered when the scar was first made.

"How did you get it?" I ask, letting my fingers try to sooth the ravages of wrath.

"It was part of my punishment," he tells me, his eyes still closed. "God made the mark to remind me of my failure."

"How can you love a God who can be so cruel?" I ask, not trying to hide my disgust.

"Because He was right; I did fail my brother Watchers. They were under my command, and I wasn't strong enough to keep them on the path we were sent to follow. It was my fault they went against His law."

"I thought you said He forgave you all for what happened in the past when you helped stop Lucifer from destroying the universe."

Mason opens his eyes, turns his head with my hand still caressing the left side of his face, and looks down at me.

"He did. But I haven't found a way to forgive myself yet. I don't think I can until the Tear is sealed. Then, maybe, I'll finally feel like I've done enough to deserve forgiveness. Until then, I wear this scar as a reminder that I'm not perfect."

I shake my head in bewilderment.

"I wish you could see yourself through my eyes," I tell him.

"Why?" he asks, his voice husky. "What do you see?"

I take a deep, shuddering breath as I attempt to drag up a braver me to tell him exactly how I feel, and what I see when I look at him.

"Excuse me; are we interrupting something?"

Mason and I pull away from each other guiltily, like we've been caught doing something we shouldn't.

I know who the voice belongs to before I even turn my head to look in his direction.

Malcolm is standing in the living room, a knowing grin on his face. Standing beside him is a man I have never seen before. He has skin the color of milk chocolate, short-cropped hair, and soft brown eyes. He smiles at me, and I'm instantly put at ease, even if Malcolm is still smirking at Mason and me.

"Yes," Mason answers, not trying to hide his agitation with Malcolm, "you are."

"Sorry, Mason," the man with Malcolm says, truly apologetic. "I asked Malcolm to bring me over so I could check on Jess again."

"Again?" I ask, not being aware there had been a first time.

"Jess, this is Tara's husband, Malik. He's the one I told you about; the one who made the medicine I gave you when you were sick."

"Thank you so much for that," I tell Malik. "You really should sell that stuff to a larger market. It's like a miracle drug."

"Well, we're thinking about expanding our operations," Malik says, pleased with my rousing endorsement. "As soon as Tara gives birth to baby number two, we might look into it more closely."

"You really need to give that child a name," Malcolm complains. "You can't keep calling her baby number two."

Malik sighs. "I know, man, but Tara is dead-set against

giving her a fairy name, and I'm set on it. We just can't seem to agree."

"Let me name it," Malcolm suggests. "That'll put an end to your squabbling."

"Yeah, right," Malik scoffs, like Malcolm has completely lost his mind. "Like Tara would actually let *you* name our child."

"Tara loves me," Malcolm proclaims. "We'll see if she lets me or not."

"Want to put a wager on that?" Malik challenges.

Malcolm holds out his hand and Malik shakes it.

"We can decide what you'll give me for winning later." Malcolm turns his eyes to me. "Now, why were you unconscious for so long?"

Mason and I fill them in on what Michael told me. I see Malcolm's surprise when he learns I am the vessel for Michael's soul.

"Will you tell Lilly?" I asked him, wondering if she should know this information or not.

"I don't see how I can keep something so important from her," Malcolm admits, even though I can see doubt clearly in his eyes. "Though, I think I should tell Brand first; then maybe we can both decide how to explain this new development to Lilly."

"He loves her, you know," I say. "Michael truly does love her, and he's so proud of what she was able to accomplish. She might want to know that."

"I will take it under advisement," Malcolm says, standing.

"We should probably get back," he tells Malik. "We told Tara we would go get her chocolate croissants before we phased back home."

"Why do you let my wife make you go to Paris every day, just to get her croissants?" Malik asks, slightly amused.

Malcolm shrugs. "It keeps her happy, which keeps Lilly happy. As long as they're both happy, we're all happy. It's not like it takes me more than five minutes a day to go get them. I've gone so often, now the shopkeeper has them ready for me before I even arrive."

I smile at the thought of Malcolm letting two rather petite females boss him around, but he doesn't seem to mind. In fact, I have a sneaking suspicion he enjoys feeling like he's needed by them.

"Let us know if we can be of any help," Malcolm tells us, before phasing himself and Malik on their run to Paris.

"Those croissants must really be good," I say.

"They *are* pretty delicious," Mason agrees.

I'm not sure what to do next. Since Malcolm interrupted the rather intimate moment between Mason and me, it just seems like the mood has been broken for the time being.

"I should go check on the soup," Mason tells me. "Why don't you stay up here and see if you can focus your thoughts, kind of like meditation, if you've ever done that before?"

"I took a yoga class once," I admit, shrugging. "I'll give that a try."

Mason grins at me and leaves the room to go check on his soup. I sit back down on the sofa and assume the lotus position. It's the only thing I remember from the one and only yoga class Faison made me go to with her. With my legs crossed beneath me and hands resting on my knees, palms up, I take a deep breath and try to clear my mind of everything except finding the other humans who are archangel vessels like me.

I focus my mind on the crackling of the fire, letting the sounds guide me along the surface of my thoughts without thinking too long on any particular one. I've always had trouble keeping my thoughts on a linear path. They've always acted like living creatures, having minds of their own, jumping from one aspect of my life to another without me consciously being aware of where they were going. Now, I'm forcing myself to clear my mind so I don't have any of the regular white noise to distract me from my purpose.

As I listen for every pop from the fire, I begin to hear a distinct hiss. At first I think it's just part of the noise of the fire, but soon realize it isn't. I focus on the sound to see where it leads me. Like a dream, a scene opens up in my mind, with white smoke swirling around a solitary figure with a blue spotlight shining down on him, giving his body a ghostly glow. It's a man, but he's facing away from me, making it impossible to see his face. His arms are lifted at his sides, and I hear the guttural beat of music fill the air.

I hear the ringtone of my cell phone and involuntarily jump, breaking the trance I was in. When I open my eyes, I see Mason standing at the entrance to the room with his arms crossed over his chest, leaned against the frame watching me.

He quickly searches his pants pocket and pulls out my cell phone.

"Hi, Lynn," he answers, walking towards me. "Yes, she's fine. Would you like to speak with her?"

Mason hands me the phone, and I immediately feel guilty. I didn't even think about calling Mama Lynn or Faison to let them know I was okay.

"Hey, Mama Lynn," I say, waiting to see how upset she is with me for not calling her as soon as I woke up.

"Oh, Jess," she says, relief in her voice, "I was worried sick about you," she tells me. "Mason called us a few days ago to let us know you had been injured on the job. We wanted to come see you, but he said you wouldn't have known we were there anyway. What happened?"

The question catches me off-guard. How much should I tell her about my dual identity? I decide to skirt the issue for now.

"I just came into contact with something, and it had an adverse effect on me."

"Something alien?" she questions, knowing since the Tear opened that we had been inundated with advanced technology and strange flora and fauna.

"Something like that," I tell her. "You know I'm not allowed to talk about some of the things I see." Which is true, but I'm using it as an excuse in this case.

"Oh, I know. But you're better? I don't need to worry anymore?"

"I'm perfectly fine," I reassure her. "I'm sure I'll be home soon."

I look up at Mason for confirmation, and he nods his head.

"Will you be back by New Year's Eve? Faison's arranged for you girls to have a spa day. She thinks it might loosen you up for your date with Mason."

My eyes dart in Mason's direction as he still stands beside me, and I hope he hasn't overheard Mama Lynn's last statement.

"One second," I tell Mama Lynn, holding the phone down to my still-folded legs. "Will I be home by New Year's Eve? Faison wants us to go to the spa that day before I go to Angela's party."

"I would like you to stay here until tomorrow," Mason says, concern on his face, "just to make sure there aren't any more episodes with Michael; but I'm sure you can make your date with Faison. I'll have you back in time."

I lift the phone back to my ear. "Tell Faison I'll be home by then."

"Ok, Jess, I'll give her the message." Mama Lynn pauses for a long time, and I know she wants to ask me something.

"Was there something else?" I ask, giving her an in to voice her question.

"How are things going with Mason?" she tries to ask casually, but I can tell she wants to know if I've decided to take her advice concerning him. It seems like everyone is trying to make me face my feelings for Mason, even when I'm not even sure what those feelings are exactly.

"Things are going good here," I say, averting my eyes away from Mason's direction, in case I inadvertently make another Freudian slip.

"He made sure to call us twice a day, you know," Mama Lynn tells me. I can hear how impressed she is with his thoughtfulness towards her and Faison.

"I'm glad to hear that," I say, letting my eyes drift back over to Mason.

"Well, anyway, I'm just glad to hear your voice. Give me a call when you make it back home."

"I will; I'll probably be back tomorrow."

"Ok, see you then."

"Bye, Mama Lynn. I love you."

"Love you too, baby."

As I end the call, I unfold my legs and stand up to slide the phone into my back pocket.

"Thanks for letting them know I was okay while I was unconscious," I say to Mason.

"I didn't see any reason for them to worry unnecessarily. If I thought you had been in any real danger of not waking up, I would have brought them here. I know how important they are to you."

"They're my world," I tell him, wondering if it's time I let one more person be included in the small microcosm I've made for myself.

"I was watching you while you were meditating," he says, not apologizing for his voyeurism. "It looked like you were concentrating on something, or I would have made my presence known."

"I saw someone," I tell him. "A man; he was standing in this white smoke."

"Fog?"

I shake my head. "No, it was like that smoke that comes out of a smoke machine. There was a blue spotlight on him and music playing, but he had his back to me. I wasn't able to see his face."

"Did you recognize the music?"

I shake my head. "I have no idea what song it was, but it did sound like something you might hear on the radio. Unfortunately, I don't listen to a lot of music on the radio."

"It's a step forward, though," he says, full of encouragement. "Whatever you did seems to have worked."

Mason holds his hand out to me, and I slip mine into his. Besides my father, Mason's the only other man I've ever held hands with. The close contact feels so natural between us I don't even try to second-guess myself for accepting it without question.

"First, I think you should come down and have some soup."

Surprisingly enough, my stomach agrees with him.

"Then I think you should go back to your room and get some more rest," he continues to instruct.

"I'm not tired," I say, even though I end up yawning right after I say it, as if my body wholeheartedly disagrees with my words.

Mason smiles.

"Soup, then bed," he orders, leading the way to the kitchen.

The moment I taste Mason's chicken soup, I agree that his is the best I've ever eaten in my life. I eat two bowls of it, one right after the other. When I'm finished eating, Mason leads me through the maze of corridors inside his villa back to my bedroom. The closer we get to my room, the heavier my eyelids feel, making me wonder what magical properties Mason's soup actually has.

Once in the room, I lay down heavily on the bed. I'm vaguely aware of Mason tucking the quilt around my body before I fall to sleep.

CHAPTER 14

In my dream world, I find myself back in my mother's garden, with Michael waiting for me in the gazebo.

"I see you've had a bit of success," he says to me as I sit across from him in the gazebo, just like the first time we met.

"Yes, I think I've had a glimpse of the person I'm supposed to find," I tell him. "I'm not going to sleep through another two days by talking with you again, am I?"

Michael shakes his head, with an amused grin. "No. You only slept that long the first time, to allow your mind to make room for me."

"Make room for you?"

"My conscious has been inside your mind since you were born, but not fully awakened until now. There are neural connections that need to be made in order for me to come to you when you want to speak with me. Each time you sleep, new connections will be made to make it easier for you to contact me, even when you aren't sleeping."

"Are you going to eventually take me over?" I ask, worried.

"No," Michael reassures me, "I would never do that to you."

I breathe a sigh of relief at the news.

Michael smiles at me. "I'm glad to see you've taken my advice about Mason."

"He didn't really help me," I say. "He ended up being more of a distraction than anything else."

"Yes, but the fact that you let him in to see some of what you feel for him *did* help you connect with that part of yourself you try to hide away. I seriously doubt you would have been able to connect with the other vessel otherwise." Michael's smile fades. "You know, I've worried over Mason for a while now. He holds on to his guilt like a blanket sometimes, using it as an excuse to not get close to anyone. You are not the only one in this relationship who has been hiding behind a protective wall. Mason's added bricks to his wall for hundreds of years, to a point where it's more like an unassailable fortress. If anything, his reaction to you surprises me more than yours to him. I've kept watch over him since he was exiled here, and I've seen him hide from the world, to a point that I never thought he would find a reason to rejoin it. It was only his willingness to help Lilly when she asked that brought him back to the land of the living. I sincerely hope his growing feelings for you are a sign that he is on his way towards letting go of his guilt."

"Me too," I say, remembering what Mason said about his scar. The scar doesn't bother me in the slightest, but it seems to bother him tremendously because of what it represents.

"So this God of yours," I say, "how could He have been so cruel to Mason, and marked him with that scar? I thought He was supposed to be all loving and crap."

Michael's eyebrows lower as he glowers at me.

"Do not speak of Him with such disrespect," Michael warns. "Our Father is like any parent; He loves us beyond all reason, but when we do something wrong, it's that love which pushes Him to punish so we can learn from our mistakes. If you have a parent who doesn't push you to be the best you can be, that parent is not doing you any favors. You have to have discipline in your life, or you will flounder and never find the true path that leads to your destiny."

"I've never had much reason to have faith in Him," I say, finding my statement ironic, considering I'm the vessel for an archangel. "I think you know my reasons."

Michael lowers his gaze to the floor of the gazebo, unable or unwilling to meet my gaze any more.

"I'm sorry for what you went through," Michael says. "I'm sorry you lost your parents at such a young age, and I wish I could have helped prevent your uncle from using you in such a vile way."

"Losing my parents wasn't your fault, but why weren't you allowed to help me with Uncle Dan?" I ask, feeling my temper begin to flare because being mad is easier than crying. "You were inside me. Why didn't you do something? Why not turn him into a pile of ash, like you did that demon? He was just as bad, if not worse."

"Because, Dan is human; a demon I can smite, but not a human. I suffered with you during those times you were abused by him," Michael tells me, a glistening of tears clouds his electric-blue eyes. "You were never alone, Jess. I was always with you."

"A hell of a lot of good that did me," I say, feeling my eyes burn, but I refuse to cry. I cried far too many times because of what Uncle Dan did, and I refuse to let him take any more of my tears. "Why would your God let me go through that?"

"Bad things are allowed to happen because it's those events in your life that help shape you into the person you are meant to become. True strength only comes from surviving adversity."

I laugh harshly. "So your God wanted me to become a person who could never see having a normal life, who never wanted to date and risk falling in love? Is that what you're telling me? Is that the flimsy excuse you're going to hide behind, that going through what I did was the only way to make me stronger?"

"I'm not trying to justify what happened. Trust me, if I had been allowed to kill him for you, I would have. I'm a fighter, Jess, and so are you. It's only because you are that you were able to go through what you did and still remain sane. Plus, you and I both know if you hadn't taken the brunt of his abuse, his attention would have fallen on another innocent."

It's only with Michael's gentle reminder that I close my eyes and finally let my tears fall.

"I couldn't let him do that to Faison," I say. "She wouldn't have survived it; she isn't strong enough."

"I know. You fight for and protect those you love. That's who we are, Jess. And that's one of the reasons you chose me to come with you here. You have an inner strength that I don't even think you realize you have. It's that strength that got you through those dark years, and it's that same strength that will lead us to victory."

I stand from my seat.

"I think I'm going to wake up now," I tell Michael.

Michael stands, and I feel as though he wants to give me a hug. I don't feel like I'm ready for such an intimate thing to happen between us, so I turn away and walk down the steps of the gazebo to force myself to awaken back in the real world.

When I open my eyes, I find myself in my bedroom at Mason's villa. I sit up and see him standing by the paned glass doors in the room, looking out at a darkening sky.

"Hi," I say.

Mason turns to look at me.

"How did you sleep?" he asks, coming to my bedside.

"Fine, I guess; if you can call having a conversation with an angel inside your head sleeping."

"Then you talked with Michael again? Did he have anything important to say?"

Mason sits down beside me, and I instantly find a piece of lint to pick at on the quilt.

"Nothing about how to find the others," I say, not seeing any reason to tell Mason that Michael and I argued more than talked.

"Do you think you could take me home now?" I ask, lifting my gaze to look at him. "I would really like to take a shower and change clothes."

Mason stands up to give me room to do the same.

"Take the crown and sword," Mason tells me. "I'm not sure exactly when or if you'll need them again, so it might be best if you kept them close to you."

"Isn't that going to look a little conspicuous?"

A lopsided grin appears on his face.

"Probably," he agrees, "but until we know what purpose they serve, it would probably be better to keep them close."

"I'll make a note to ask Michael the next time I see him."

I grab the crown and the sword from the top of the dresser. With my hands full, Mason places a hand on my shoulder, and I instantly find myself standing in my bedroom.

"Are you hungry?" he asks me.

"Yes," I admit, even though I feel like all I've been doing is eating in front of Mason. "What's the date, anyway?" I ask, having completely lost track of my days.

"December 30th."

"Umm, you wouldn't happen to have some more of that chicken soup you made yesterday, would you?" I ask, my stomach growling at just the mention of Mason's specialty.

Mason grins, and I can tell he's pleased I asked.

"I'll go get it and bring it over. Would you like some toasted garlic bread with that?"

"You know the way to my heart," I tease, only realizing after I say the words that they could be construed in two different ways.

Mason's grin widens.

"I certainly hope so," he replies before phasing back to his villa.

I hang my head and shake it. What a boneheaded thing to say. I decide I really need to start thinking before I say things to Mason.

While I'm untucking my blouse from my pants and walking to my bathroom, I hear the familiar creak of a rocking chair come from my front porch. I walk to the bay window in my room and look out.

Lucifer is sitting in one of my rocking chairs, staring out at my neighborhood as if he's waiting for something, most likely me.

I take a deep breath and try to remember the way Lilly and everyone else told me to act around Lucifer in order to glean the most information out of him. We need to know what his end game is, and the only way to figure that out is to speak with him.

When I walk out on to the porch, Lucifer looks up at me. A genuine smile graces his handsome face. I can't deny that he picked an attractive body to inhabit. I feel sure it's a prerequisite for any body he takes.

He's dressed simply in a pair of blue jeans, light blue T-shirt, and blue jean jacket.

"Jessica," he says standing up, "I've been wondering where you were. Your sister wouldn't speak with me about you. I assume you told her not to."

"You assumed right," I say, walking to the railing opposite the rocking chair he's still standing near.

Lucifer sits back down and continues to rock as he studies me.

"There's something different about you today," he says, looking at me with a cursory glance. "What is it?"

I shrug. "No idea."

"You're lying," he says confidently. "Don't you know that just makes you more interesting to me?"

Great; the last thing I need to happen. Becoming more interesting to Lucifer was not on my list of things to do today.

"So, where have you been?" he asks.

"Away."

Lucifer grins. "You know I'll find out eventually."

"Perhaps; at least it'll give you something to do beside tromp around the globe with your brand-new bestie."

Lucifer grins. "I thought you and Mason would be keeping tabs on us. Have you figured out what we are doing, or who he is yet?"

"I have no idea what you guys are doing," I say, not tipping my hat that I know the man is one of the princes of Hell he has been searching for.

Lucifer's grin grows wider. "Well, don't expect me to just

tell you. What's the fun in that? You'll have to earn the answer for yourselves. I'm not going to serve you the information on a silver platter."

"I didn't expect you to; I've always worked for what I wanted, and I've always gotten it in the end."

Lucifer narrows his eyes on me in an appraising way. "You know, for a human, you're rather impressive. Most would have broken, considering what you've had to deal with in your short life. First you were abandoned by your parents, and then abused by your adopted mother's brother."

"My parents didn't abandon me," I say. "They were taken against their will. There's a big difference."

Lucifer cocks his head at me. "Hasn't Mason told you how people are chosen to go through the Tear?"

"It's random," I say, everyone on the planet knows that. Why is he making such a big deal out of it?

Lucifer chuckles, like he's in on an inside joke. "I suppose it would be nice to think so, but no, it's not random."

I'm silent because I don't like the look on Lucifer's face. I feel as though he's about to lower the boom on me, and I'm not so sure I'll be able to survive it.

"How are they chosen?" I ask, bracing myself for the answer.

"Only people who, for whatever reason in their lives, want a fresh start somewhere else go through the Tear. I suppose it was my father's way of tempering what I did, to make it easier on those who went through. The ones who return are the ones who eventually decide they want to come back home."

"You're lying," I say, but I know he isn't. Deep down, in the inner recesses of my soul, I know what he's saying is true.

"For some reason," Lucifer says to me, "your parents didn't want to be a part of your life anymore." He pauses, letting what he just said sink in. "I'll never lie to you, Jessica. You know I'm telling you the truth. I thought you should know it too. Don't waste your time grieving over people who don't deserve it."

I push away from the railing. "I think you should leave now."

"If that is what you want, but I will be back," he says with certainty.

I nod, not trusting my voice not to betray my true emotions in that moment. Lucifer phases and I walk back into my house. I close the front door and lean my back against it. Before I know it, I'm sitting on the floor, my legs drawn up, hugging them to me. I begin to rock back and forth, trying to soothe the lost girl inside me.

What Lucifer has just said confirms what the seven-year-old me feared the most; that my parents didn't love me enough to want to stay with me. It's like having my worst nightmare brought to life. I try to reason with myself that there has to be another explanation, but no amount of cajoling or rationalizing seems to be enough to stop the lost girl's heart from shattering into a million pieces.

CHAPTER 15

I feel my world crash in around my heart, cracking its armor into so many shards. I know it will never be entirely whole again. I suddenly feel paralyzed with grief, and the first sting of tears tells me I am no longer in control of the next few minutes of my life. Sorrow and despair completely consume my body, taunting the lost girl within me with the information Lucifer has just shared. Locked away in her self-imposed prison, the child-me peeks out, and is forced to face the unadulterated truth about her parents. They never wanted her. They never loved her. If they had, they would have never left her alone in a world where people like Uncle Dan could easily use her for his own sick fantasies; acts that forced her to build walls so high and thick she never truly let those who loved her breach it completely.

An endless stream of sobs wrack my body so hard, I end

up having trouble taking a single breath, like an invisible hand is choking me. I try to force the child within to not forget the good times we shared with my parents, but she asks the same question over and over: why did they abandon us?

I don't want to believe what Lucifer said is true, but deep in my heart I know he didn't lie to me. He is often called the great deceiver, but, on this one subject, I know he has told me the unvarnished truth. I feel as though I might be the only person Lucifer will never lie to, and I know the reason without having to be told.

The reason Lucifer is drawn to me is simple... he senses Michael inside me. He may not know it consciously, but some part of him recognizes his onetime best friend standing in front of him. A part of him will never be able to lie to his best friend, even when Michael is hidden inside a human.

I cry even harder, knowing the truth of this. I have to make the lost girl inside me face the fact that our parents did abandon us. What about me was so horrible that it would make them both want to leave me? Did they regret having me? Was I a mistake? How am I supposed to recover from this?

I feel a presence beside me. Through the fog of my tears, I look to my right and see Mason's concerned face inches away from mine. He is sitting on the floor with his back against the door, just like I am. He doesn't say a word, just sits there with me, waiting.

I take a shuddering breath, intent on telling him what Lucifer has revealed to me, but the words lodge themselves in my throat to a point where only another sob comes out. I lean into Mason, needing to feel like at least one person in the world cares enough about me to stay, to not abandon me. I feel Mason pull me closer to him, offering his strength as my support if I will accept it.

"Oh, Jess," he says, holding me close with one arm, tenderly cradling my head with the other as I let my pain practically double me over it's so intense.

I feel him try to pull away, but I grab his shirt so tightly I feel him wince under me. That, more than anything else, causes me to pull away from him and look into his face.

"Did I hurt you?" I ask, taking a shuddering breath.

"Seeing you like this is the only thing hurting me," he replies, smoothing wet, wayward strands of hair away from my face and tucking them behind my ear. He stands up and pulls me to my feet in one swift motion.

Before I know it, I find myself cradled in his arms. I lay my head against his shoulder and wrap my arms around his neck. Mason carries me effortlessly to the couch in my living room and sits down, positioning me comfortably in his lap. I breathe a sigh of relief, because my heart knows he won't leave me until I'm past my grief.

I'm not sure how much time passes. Eventually, the well which stores my tears dries up, and I end up just trying to concentrate on returning my breathing to normal. I'm reluctant to lift my head from Mason's shoulder because I know he'll want an explanation for my tearful outburst, but I do because he deserves to know what Lucifer told me.

When I look at his face, I'm not prepared for what I see in his eyes.

I have often wondered how people believe in love at first sight. I've always chalked up such nonsense to some sort of involuntary hormonal reaction to the other person's physical appearance. However, I know if I were just meeting Mason for the first time, and he looked at me in the same way he is looking at me now, I would have no doubt he loved me. It's not a look I can explain or even attempt to describe. A million people have used flowery words in an attempt to describe love, but none of those phrases seems adequate to articulate the emotion I see behind Mason's eyes as he looks at me.

"Do you want to tell me what happened?" he asks gently, not pushing for an answer; just letting me know he's there for me when I'm ready.

"I do," I say, taking a shuddering breath.

I feel Mason rub my back in a circular motion, silently waiting for me to continue.

"Lucifer was here," I say.

As soon as the words leave my mouth, I feel Mason's body stiffen.

"Did he hurt you?" Mason asks; his voice low with controlled anger.

"Not physically," I tell him with a shake of my head.

"What did he say to you?"

"He told me..." I say, fighting back the last reserves of tears from somewhere deep inside me threatening to spill over. "He said that the people who go through the Tear are those who want to leave their lives behind and start new ones somewhere else." I look up at Mason and see the answer to my next question before I even ask it. "Is that true?"

"Yes," he says, not trying to temper his answer.

"Why would my parents want to abandon me?" I ask, hearing a child's heartbreak in my voice.

Mason doesn't say anything, and I feel as though he's debating whether or not to tell me something crucial.

"I don't want to say this and get your hopes up, but I can't let you sit here and think they abandoned you either," he tells me before continuing. "I'm not so sure your parents were taken through the Tear when it opened, Jess."

I stare at Mason, sure I've misunderstood him. He continues.

"When your parents disappeared, did new Tearers take their place?"

I feel my forehead crinkle at the question, suddenly realizing that that small fact has completely escaped me all these years.

"No," I say, "no one took their place."

"In every recorded incident of people going through the Tear, there have *always* been new Tearers who replaced them. Yours is the only time I've ever heard of people disappearing without being replaced. It's simply not the way the universe works. If one person disappears from here, there has to be someone else to occupy their space to keep the balance in check."

I sit up straighter. "Are you saying they're still here? They're still here on this planet?"

"Nick's actually the one who brought it to my attention when he investigated your family history. We came up with the theory that, more than likely, your parents are still here somewhere."

"But where are they?"

"I don't know, but if you want, we can look for them."

I sit there trying to absorb what Mason has just said. If what he thought *was* true, then...

"Why haven't they tried to find me? It's been 15 years."

"I don't have an answer for that question, but you shouldn't jump to conclusions," he's quick to say. "They could have been taken against their will. There's no way of knowing until we find them."

Filled with a new determination, I ask, "Where do we start?"

"I've already started," he tells me, looking a little uncomfortable with revealing this news to me.

"Don't say it like an apology," I tell him, grabbing his arm. "Thank you."

"I've had Joshua searching through the databases comparing your genetic profile with pretty much everyone in the world. You have to have some family somewhere, Jess. You didn't just appear out of thin air."

"Have you found anything yet?"

"We've found some people who seem to be distant, distant relatives, but no one who could be immediate family. Joshua's only 25% through, though. It's just going to take some time and patience."

"I've waited for them for 15 years," I say, filled with new-found hope. "A few more weeks or months aren't going to bother me."

I stare at Mason, not sure what else to say.

"Are you still hungry?" he asks me.

I nod. "Did you bring the soup?"

Mason smiles. "Not only did I bring the soup, but I brought you a special surprise too. It's why I was gone for so long. If I had known Lucifer was here, I wouldn't have made the detour. I had just bought them when I felt you in distress."

I stand up, releasing Mason from the burden of my body. Mason instantly takes my hand in his and leads me to the kitchen. The large silver stockpot with his soup is already warming up on the stove, and there is a pink box decorated with a white lace pattern sitting on the dining table.

"I intended for them to be your dessert, but why don't you go ahead and have one now? I think it might perk you up a little bit."

"What's in it?" I ask walking to the table, my curiosity piqued.

Mason walks to the stove and retrieves a bowl from the cabinet beside it.

"Open the box and see for yourself," he says; a playful grin on his face.

I flip open the lid of the box and see four perfect croissants sitting inside, drizzled with chocolate.

I gasp. "Are these the chocolate croissants Malcolm keeps getting for Tara?"

"Yes. I thought since you've been hearing about them so much lately, you might like to try one for yourself."

"This could be a mistake, you know," I warn, taking one of the croissants out of the box.

Mason looks at me curiously. "A mistake how?"

"If I really like them, I might end up bugging you all the time to go get them for me."

"I have no problem doing that for you," he tells me, his voice soft. "No problem at all, Jess."

I smile, feeling uncertain about how to react and decide to turn my attention to the Parisian perfection in my hand waiting to be devoured. As I bite into the croissant, a mixture of flaky, buttery goodness, soft chocolate, and creamy hazelnut performs a symphony of tastes inside my mouth. I moan in ecstasy and stomp my left foot twice.

"Oh… my… God," I say to Mason. "I can see why Tara loves these so much. They're better than Beau's cinnamon rolls, but don't tell him I said that," I laugh.

"You're secret is safe with me," Mason promises. "I'm glad you like them."

Mason brings me a bowl of soup, and I sit down and eat it after finishing my croissant. When I'm ready for my second bowl of soup, he also brings over the garlic bread he just toasted in my oven. Finally, he sits down with me and watches me eat. Unlike before, I have no problem with him watching me. I pretty much figure he's seen me at my worst on two occasions now: when I was sick, and just now in my living room as I cried my heart out. If he isn't scared away by now, seeing me with a little soup on my chin won't make a difference.

"I wish you had told me about my parents," I tell him, taking a bite of the bread.

"I wish I had too, Jess; then you wouldn't have taken what Lucifer said so hard. I had planned to tell you if and when we actually found something out about them; I didn't want to get your hopes up unnecessarily."

"I understand; it makes sense."

There's a knock on my door, and I start to get up to answer it.

"You stay," Mason orders. I almost feel like a dog being commanded by its master, but I let it slide because I can see Mason is just trying to make sure I stay and finish my meal. "I'll go answer the door."

As soon as Mason opens the door, I hear the voices of Mama Lynn and Faison. Before I know it, I'm surrounded by them both in a hug. Mason stands against the entryway of the kitchen, grinning at us.

"Don't worry us like that again," Faison orders, the strength of her hug rivaling that of Mama Lynn's.

"I'll try not to," I say, but it comes out muffled because Mama Lynn's poof of hair is blocking my mouth.

Finally, they both pull away from me, allowing me to breathe -some much- needed fresh air. Mama Lynn walks over to Mason, and I see his surprise as she gives him a motherly hug.

"Thank you for taking care of my baby," she tells him.

"It was my honor," Mason says.

I feel Faison slap me lightly on the arm. When I look up at her, she lifts her eyebrows in a suggestive manner. I just roll my eyes and try to finish my soup.

"Jess," Mason says to me, "I need to go back to headquarters and check on the status of some things, like what we were just discussing. I see you're in good hands now, so I'll be leaving."

"Do you have to go?" I ask, not wanting him to leave.

"It's not a matter of wanting to go," he tells me, "but I need to go. I've been away for too long."

"When will I see you again?"

"I'll be here around four your time tomorrow afternoon to pick you up for Angela and Jonathan's party. That will make it ten o'clock in London because of the time difference."

"If anything comes up and you need me," I tell him, "I'll have my phone on me. I always do."

Mason smiles. "I'll keep you up to date this time; I promise." Mason inclines his head to Mama Lynn and Faison. "Ladies, it was a pleasure to see you again. If I don't see you tomorrow, I wish you both a Happy New Year."

Mama Lynn and Faison reciprocate the sentiment right before Mason phases.

Like a pack of hyenas about to pounce on their prey,

Mama Lynn and Faison turn as one, and look at me with raised eyebrows.

"What?" I ask, scooting the pink box with the other chocolate croissants in front of me, hoping to distract them with the sugary goodness. "Want a chocolate croissant? Mason brought them straight from Paris. They're even still warm on the inside."

"Don't try to bribe us with chocolate," Faison says, even though she comes over to look inside the box and quickly snatches one with the quickness of a viper.

"So what exactly happened between you and Mason the last few days?" Mama Lynn asks while standing her ground and not allowing the call of sweet pastries dissuade her from meddling.

"It was just work stuff," I say, trying to play it off as nothing.

"What I just saw wasn't 'just work stuff'," she says back to me. She's quiet as a contemplative look enters her eyes. "Jess," she says, watching me carefully, "have you fallen in love with Mason?"

"Oh," Faison says as I see her eyes enter the fantasy realm she likes to visit every once in a while, "can you imagine the gorgeous babies they would have together? I bet each one would come out prettier than the next."

"For Pete's sake, we haven't even been on a real date yet, and you already have me married off and knocked up," I say, trying to laugh, but it ends up coming out too strained not to sound like it's exactly what I want to happen.

Mama Lynn comes over to me and gives me a big hug.

"Oh, Jess, I'm so happy for you." She pulls away from me, resting her hands on my shoulders. "I didn't know if you'd ever find a man."

"Geez, thanks for having so much confidence in me to attract someone of the opposite sex."

"She thought you might be gay."

I look at Faison, and see her nodding her head. I look at Mama Lynn and notice the red hue on her cheeks.

"Not that there's anything wrong with that, even if you had been," Mama Lynn says in her own defense, "but it would be a lot harder for you to have some grandbabies for me if you were. Now, I don't have to worry about it. Faison's right. The two of you will have the most gorgeous babies ever."

"Ok, can we stop talking about babies, please?" I beg, reaching into the box for some sugar courage. "I admit, I'm interested in Mason, but that's all you two are going to get me to admit."

"That's all we need to know," Mama Lynn says, patting my hand and sitting down beside me at the table.

"Well, he couldn't be any more in love with you if he tried," Faison says. "Did you see how he looked at her, Mama Lynn?"

"I did," Mama Lynn reaches into the box for the last croissant. "It couldn't have been more obvious."

"You guys just saw what you wanted to see," I say, trying to downplay the same conclusion they both seem to have come to on their own.

Even though I had noticed the difference in how Mason looked at me, I wasn't quite sure I was ready to believe it was real. If I did, and I was wrong, I feared the heartache would be too much for me to handle in my current state.

"We only saw what was there," Mama Lynn says, taking a bite of the croissant and having about the same reaction I did to the taste of the pastry.

Eventually, I get them off the subject of Mason and on to the subject of Faison's upcoming nuptials in April. If there is anything they love talking about more than my 'maybe' love life, it's Faison and John Austin's wedding.

By the time they leave my house, it's almost eight in the evening. After they are gone, I am finally able to take a shower. After that, I fall into bed, feeling completely exhausted. I call to Michael in my dream world. This time I choose to meet him inside my father's study.

Michael walks around the room, studying various items belonging to my father, trying his best to avoid meeting my gaze.

"You knew, didn't you?" I accuse.

"It's not that simple, Jessica," he says.

"Why didn't you tell me my parents hadn't been taken through the Tear? Do you know how long I've imagined them stranded on some strange planet? They've been here the whole time, haven't they? I could have been looking for them!"

"If you had known," Michael says, "you would have never joined the Watcher Agency, met Mason, or discovered what your true path really is."

"That's beside the point!"

"No," he says calmly in the face of my ire, "that *is* the point. It was the point of everything, Jessica. Everything you've been through has led you to this moment. You are exactly where you are supposed to be."

"Where are they?" I ask, directly. "You have to know where they are."

"I don't know, and that's the truth."

I can tell he's holding something back from me.

"What aren't you saying?" I demand.

"I made a promise to your father."

"What promise?" I ask, finding myself holding my breath, waiting to hear the answer.

"I promised I would let him explain everything to you. I'm sorry, Jess, but I can't tell you anything more without breaking that promise. I owe him the decency of telling you what happened himself."

"When is he coming back to talk to me?"

"That I don't know. But, when the time is right, he will; I can promise you that much."

"I don't think I can stand to look at you right now," I say, feeling an uncontrollable anger towards Michael. "Leave."

I wake up in my bed and turn to lie on my back. All this time, Michael let me believe my parents were Tearers, scattered somewhere in the universe, and he knew they were still on this planet. It isn't something I'm sure I can forgive.

CHAPTER 16

The next morning I am woken up by the sound of my phone buzzing, notifying me that I have a text message. Suddenly wide awake, I grab it and open the text.

Good morning. I hope you slept well. Nothing much is going on here. Just wanted to keep you informed, as promised. Don't forget I will be at your house at 4 this afternoon.

I lie in my bed and read the message from Mason at least five times before answering.

. . .

Good morning to you too. I slept very well except during a talk with a certain archangel. I will have my phone with me all day at the spa if you need me. I will be promptly ready at 4.

I pause, not sure I want to send the rest of what I'm thinking but decide to take a chance.

I look forward to seeing you in your tuxedo this evening.

I hit send and wait to see if I get a reply.

Two minutes later I do.

Have fun at the spa with Faison. I hope they pamper you well. You deserve it after what you have been through the last few days. I eagerly await seeing you in the dress Santa left for you Christmas morning....don't forget the mask, even though I would rather have people see the beauty on my arm. But, it is a masquerade ball after all...

I can't help but smile, and instantly feel my heart ache in a good way at his sweet sentiment. I ponder if I should reply or just leave it at that, but can't seem to prevent myself from writing:

. . .

*I hope you like what you see and only for you will I take the
mask off at midnight.*

I hit send and bury my head in my pillow, somewhat ashamed
and surprised by my own audacity. Nervously, I wait to see if
he replies. As soon as the phone buzzes in my hand, I peek
over my pillow to see what he has written back.

**I have no doubt I will love what I see, and I sincerely hope
I am the only man you allow to remove your mask...**

I feel my heart swell with excitement about what might tran-
spire that evening, and force myself to put the phone down.
It's already nine, and Faison warned me the night before she
would be over to pick me up at nine-thirty.

I quickly hop into the shower and don't even bother to put
on any makeup or blow-dry my hair afterwards; that's what
the spa is for.

When I grab my phone, I notice the little green light is
flashing and discover I have another text message
from Mason.

. . .

Did you receive my last text message?

I smile and respond.

Yes, I did receive it. Sorry, I just got out of the shower. Faison will be here soon to pick me up for our spa day.

I wait impatiently, tapping my finger against the side of the phone to see if he writes back.

Just wanted to make sure you got it. I meant every word… until tonight…anxiously awaiting our first date…

I feel my heart flutter with excitement, and wish I didn't have to endure more than six hours before I'm able to see Mason again.

You don't happen to have a time machine that can make the day go by faster, do you?

No. Unfortunately, time travel is not within the Watcher

arsenal of capabilities. Or I would be on your front porch to pick you up instead of sitting here with Nick going over some boring paperwork your government makes me sign every year.

So sorry to hear you have to spend time with Nick! He is my least favorite person on your team.

Nick is an acquired taste. He's a good man though. Please don't think too harshly of him.

If you vouch for him, then he must not be too bad, and I will give him the benefit of the doubt from now on.

I am glad to see you think so highly of my opinion of people...

I greatly value what you think...

The doorbell rings, and I know I have to end our conversation quickly.

. . .

Faison is here. I am sorry. I will have to go now. See you at 4.

I will be counting the minutes...

The spa Faison takes me to is owned by a girl we used to go to high school with. She is actually the person who threw the Christmas party Mason and I were supposed to attend the night I was sick.

"Hey, Shelby," Faison says, giving the woman a peck on the cheek as we enter the spa.

Shelby is waif-thin with long, flaming-red hair and pale white skin. Her large green eyes immediately captivate you with their brightness, and her kind heart is easily seen through them.

"I hope you girls are ready to be treated like queens today," Shelby says, giving me a quick hug. "I've got manicures, pedicures, facials, steam baths, and massages planned; not to mention a full makeup and hair-styling session at the end." Shelby turns to me. "Faison told me you're going to a ball in London tonight with a Watcher," I hear the swoon in Shelby's voice. "That's so romantic. I sure do envy you."

I have to admit, I would be envious of me too; it does make my life sound rather interesting.

"Ok, enough of all this; let's get the two of you started."

For the next four hours, I am scrubbed, rubbed, patted down, and basted in all of the modern conveniences to make me look presentable for my first official date with Mason. I suddenly realize it's actually my first official date with anybody. In high school, the boys were simply too juvenile to go out with. In college, I was too busy trying to earn a four-year degree in three. At the Watcher academy, fraternizing with your classmates was looked down upon, and I didn't want to give anyone an excuse to stop me from becoming a Watcher agent. For the first time in my life, I don't have an excuse to avoid dating, and, strangely enough, I don't want one, considering my first date will be with Mason.

"What are you smiling about?" Faison asks me as we sit in the salon chairs, getting our nails polished.

"This is my first date," I whisper to her, not wanting the manicurists to overhear us; otherwise, I'm sure they would think me strange.

"Why do you think I brought us here?" Faison answers. "I figured I would use some of the small fortune you gave me and treat you to a day of pampering, so you don't have time to get nervous."

It is only then that I begin to feel a swarm of butterflies invade my stomach like the Luftwaffe. A look of instant trepidation must be on my face, too, because Faison's eyes widen.

"Oh, no you don't," she says to me sternly. "You are not going to get nervous and find a reason to back out of this date."

"No," I assure her, "I'm not going to back out. I wouldn't do that to him… or me, for that matter. I have to see where things lead. I have to try, even if it turns out to be a mistake."

"It's not a mistake," Faison states as a matter of fact. "You two were meant for each other."

"What makes you say that?"

"Because you're both broken souls," she says seriously, not trying to romanticize it like she does most things. "Even I can see the two of you fit together like pieces of a puzzle. He brings out a side of you I've been waiting to see for so long, Jess. Please don't get nervous. He was meant for you, and I think he realizes you were meant for him too; so don't jinx anything," she orders. "I might not live long enough for you to find someone who fits you so perfectly."

A beautician named Maribel is placed in charge of my beautification for the ball. She ends up being somewhat perfect for me. She keeps the makeup light and airy- looking, just the way I like it. For my hair, she rolls it to curl softly at the ends, and sweeps it completely to one side, allowing it to hang over my shoulder elegantly.

By the time Faison gets me back home, it's almost three in the afternoon. She stays to help me get into my dress, since the bodice is corseted in the back and requires an extra pair of hands to tighten and tie it properly. At around three forty-five, my doorbell rings.

"Is that him?" Faison asks, handing me my matching shoes.

"No, he's never early or late," I say, dropping the shoes on the floor and slipping them onto my feet.

"I'll go see who it is," Faison tells me, walking out of my bedroom.

I take a moment for myself and examine my reflection in the antique cherry wood full-length mirror by the bay window. I've never been one to over-analyze my looks, but even I have to admit I look beautiful in the dress Mason bought me.

I hear a commotion of more than two voices out in the foyer, and go to see who exactly is at the door.

When I get there, I feel like making an about-face and finding a place to hide in my bedroom until Mason arrives.

"There she is!" Mama Lynn practically screams at me excitedly.

I try to put on a smile, but feel the strain of such an act actually start to hurt my face.

It would have been bad enough just to have Mama Lynn present with her camera at the ready, but it isn't just her. George, John Austin, Vern, Sadie, Beau, and his entire family are all standing inside my house, staring at me. George, Vern, and Sadie smile at me proudly, but John Austin and Beau are staring at me with their mouths agape.

"What?" I ask the two of them, hands on hips. "Didn't think I could clean up this good?"

Beau's wife, Fanny, slaps her husband on the back of the head, which promptly makes his three little girls giggle. I imagine such a thing is quite commonplace in their home.

"Don't take this the wrong way," I say to them, "but why are you all here… now… in my house?"

"I dropped by Beau's store to pick up some batteries for my camera," Mama Lynn says. "When I told everyone what I needed the camera for, they wanted to come see you in your new dress."

"I hope you don't mind, Jess," Sadie says. "It's just that we don't get a lot of excitement around here, and, well, when Lynn described the dress to us, I just had to see you in it. You look so gorgeous. Your date is a lucky man."

I see George cross his arms over his chest. "Am I going to need to have a talk with Mason before the two of you go on this date? I might not be your father, but I can make sure he understands what's expected of him."

"No, George, that won't be necessary." I say. "If there is anyone in this world you don't have to worry about treating me like a lady, it's Mason. He's really old-fashioned. He even pulls out the chair for me when I sit at a table."

"Awww," Beau's three girls say in unison, obviously thinking Mason must be some type of romantic hero.

"Well, I want to take some pictures of you before you go," Mama Lynn says, turning on her camera.

For the next few minutes, I let Mama Lynn take all the pictures she wants. I know what she's doing. Since I didn't go to any of my proms or winter formals, she's making up for lost picture opportunities.

"Try to relax and smile naturally," Mama Lynn instructs. "You look like you're getting your teeth pulled, not like you're about to go on your first date."

I glower at Mama Lynn for sharing this personal information with everyone, but, apparently, they already know it, and don't look the least bit surprised. I suppose that's one bad thing about living in a small community; everyone knows everything about everyone else.

Finally, the doorbell rings, and I know it has to be Mason. I watch George open the door since I am on the other side of the house, standing in front of the Christmas tree for the background Mama Lynn wants in her picture.

George is so big he fills the entire opening, making it impossible for me to see Mason at all. I hear the two men exchange greetings, and George finally moves out of the way to allow Mason entry into my home.

I feel like someone has just snatched all of the air from my lungs at my first sight of Mason, and a true smile spreads my lips.

"Yes! Stay just like that!" Mama Lynn says excitedly, snapping pictures in quick succession.

I barely hear her because my ears are filled with the sound of my own rushing blood.

Mason is dressed in a black tuxedo with a black bow tie. He's wearing a white mask similar to the one I once saw in the movie *The Phantom of the Opera*. I know why he has chosen such a mask. It perfectly covers up the left side of his face, camouflaging his scar. I instantly want to take it off him. I hate that he feels the need to hide that part of himself, and hope he didn't choose to wear it because of me.

I watch as Mason's eyes take in everyone in my house, and hope he doesn't feel like he's being ambushed by the general population of Cypress Hollow. Most of the men are standing in the foyer, and instantly extend their hands to Mason as they introduce themselves.

I hear John Austin say, "Now, Jess is like a sister to me. You treat her right."

Mason nods his head. "You have nothing to worry about. She will be treated like the lady she is."

Mason finally turns to look directly at me, and I see a slow smile of appreciation spread his lips. Our eyes lock and I feel as though the whole world fades away, allowing Mason and me to share this one moment with only each other.

"You look beautiful, Jess," he says, coming to stand in front of me.

"And you look quite dashing," I reply breathlessly.

"Now, I want to get a picture of the two of you together," Mama Lynn says.

"I'm sorry," I silently mouth to Mason, completely ashamed that Mama Lynn is treating us as if we're teenagers going on our first date.

"Don't be," Mason replies, coming to stand beside me and placing an arm around my waist as we stand together for Mama Lynn.

Mama Lynn smiles.

"Perfect," she says, and only snaps a single photo.

"We need to leave now," I tell the others. "You guys are welcome to stay if you want."

Faison walks up to us and hands Mason my mask.

"Maybe you should put it on her," she suggests. "I'm a little short to do the job right."

Mason instructs me to turn my back to him, and asks Faison to hold my hair up. I hold the mask over my eyes while he loops the silky ribbon over my ears and to the back of my head. Once the ribbon is tied, he tells Faison to let my hair go so it covers up the ribbon.

Mason holds his arm out to me.

"Shall we go?" he asks.

I nod, too excited to verbally answer his question.

CHAPTER 17

Before I know it, we are standing in the entryway of a mansion. To the right of us, I see Angela walking down a grand staircase, dressed in a red and black ball gown accompanied by a handsome man wearing a tuxedo similar to Mason's.

"There you are," she says excitedly. "Oh, my God, you look gorgeous, Jess," she tells me, giving me a kiss on the cheek.

"Jonathan," Mason says to the man at Angela's side, who I had already assumed must be Mason's son, "I would like to introduce you to Jess Riley. Jess, this is my son, Jonathan."

Jonathan smiles at me. I expect him to hold out his hand for me to shake, but instead he wraps his arms around me, giving me a hug instead.

"Thank you," he whispers in my ear, leaving me clueless as to what he could be thanking me for.

When he pulls away, he's still smiling.

"I can't tell you how much we've been looking forward to having you in our home," he tells me. "I've waited a long time to meet you."

I find his words curious since I've only known Mason for little over a week now.

Angela loops her arm through Mason's free one and says, "I want to introduce you to some people."

Reluctantly, Mason lets go of my arm and looks down at me apologetically.

"Jonathan," Angela says to her husband, "why don't you show Jess the Christmas tree? I'll bring Mason there to find you after I introduce him to Matthew."

Jonathan holds out his arm to me, and I take it. I watch as Mason is whisked away by Angela, and I know something is up.

As Jonathan walks me into the large living room area, where a 12-foot blue spruce is, I ask, "So what's really going on? I feel like I was just pulled into a game of divide and conquer."

Jonathan laughs. "No, it's nothing like that; I just asked Angela to distract my dad so I could have a moment alone with you."

Jonathan lets go of my arm, and we turn to face each other.

"Is something wrong?" I ask.

"No," Jonathan says smiling, "everything has suddenly become right since my dad met you. I just wanted to thank you in person for bringing him back to me."

"I don't understand," I say, sounding as confused as I am.

"Ever since he met you, he's been pleasant to be around. He's smiling, making jokes, letting himself be a part of our family. I've never seen him so happy. On Christmas Day, Angela and I couldn't believe how much he was acting like a young man in love. He must have checked his phone a thousand times just to make sure he didn't miss a text message from you. He's never done that, Jess; never."

I feel flush all of a sudden. I know if anyone knows Mason, it's his son.

"I've worried about him for a very long time," Jonathan says, his smile fading with the reminder of distant memories. "Now, I don't feel like I need to. Having you in his life makes him want to live again, and not hide himself in his work. He's held on so strongly to his guilt over failing the other Watchers. I wasn't sure he would ever find a good enough reason to start forgiving himself for it. You are his reason now. He wants to become a better man because of you."

I swallow hard, trying to take in everything Jonathan is telling me.

"I don't know if I deserve him," I confess.

"Even though I don't know you personally," Jonathan says, "I know that you and my dad belong together. You're helping him more than you could possibly know. He needs you, and, from what you just said, I think you need him too. It's not a question of whether or not you deserve him, or if he deserves you, because it's a moot point. You belong together.

You were made to bring out the best in one another. That's all love is, really."

"How do you know he loves me?" I ask.

"How do you *not* know that?" Jonathan asks in return.

"We're back," Angela announces, with Mason still on her arm as she escorts him to my side. Angela easily transitions from Mason to Jonathan's arm with a grace I envy.

"Would you like to go dance?" Mason asks me, holding out his arm for me to take once again.

My blood runs cold. How, in all of my preparations, did I miss the most important thing about tonight? This was a masquerade ball. Of course there would be dancing. The closest I ever came to dancing was when Faison and I went to the karaoke bar and swayed to whatever music we were singing together. And this was a ball, which meant people would be dancing fancy waltzes and things I had never even heard of.

"I can't dance," I hear myself confess. Better to get things out in the open than hide them. I felt sure if I tried to pretend I knew what I was doing, Mason's feet would suffer the consequences.

"You don't want to dance?" Mason asks, his face the picture of confusion.

"No. I can't dance. I don't know how to. I've never done it before."

Mason's face relaxes, and he smiles at me.

"Then you're in luck, because I'm an excellent teacher."

Out of the corner of my eye, I see Angela tug on

Jonathan's arm, and they walk quietly out of the room, leaving Mason and me alone.

In the background, I hear the strings of an orchestra begin to play, and the dulcet notes of a classical piano quickly join in. Mason puts his arm around my waist and pulls me close to his body. He holds my other arm out with his, and I place my free hand on his shoulder.

"Now, you don't actually need to know how to dance in order to dance, if that makes sense." He smiles. "As long as you follow where my body leads you, you'll be all right." Mason looks me in the eyes. "Do you trust me?"

Without even having to think about it, I nod. Mason's smile grows wider, and we begin to dance. At first, my body seems to have a will of its own, and fights against following Mason's lead. I apologize profusely every time I step on his toes. Mercifully, Mason finally stops to end my torture of him.

"Close your eyes," he instructs me. "I think you're over-thinking things. Maybe if you can't see what is happening, your body will adjust to mine."

"Okay," I say, not uncertain Mason knows what he's doing, but uncertain my body will relax enough to let me be led around the room, without knowing where I'm going.

I close my eyes and feel myself involuntarily grip Mason's hand and shoulder tighter.

I feel him lean into me.

"Relax, Jess," he whispers in my ear, his warm breath causing me to tingle all over. "I won't let anything happen to you. Trust me."

I loosen my grip slightly, and try to concentrate on relaxing my body enough to let Mason lead me around the room.

Mason begins to hum the tune the orchestra is playing, and I instantly feel my body respond. The tension in my muscles dissipates, and I begin to feel like I'm floating on a cloud. When the music stops, Mason brings us to a standstill.

I open my eyes and smile up at him.

"Is that how you teach everyone?" I ask, wondering who else Mason has danced with in his life. I feel sure I am not the only woman, and find myself not liking that fact.

"The humming is new," he says, "but it seemed to help you relax enough to let me lead you."

"Do you sing?"

"Not often."

"Would you sing for me one day?"

The corners of Mason's lips quirk up in an almost-shy smile. "I believe I would do about anything you ever asked of me."

"Then take me dancing."

When we walk into the ballroom, I see a multitude of colorful dresses and masked people twirling about the dance floor. One large, single mirror runs the length of one side of the room, making it appear even larger than it is. A mural of angels, I have to assume rivals the one painted by Michelangelo in the Sistine Chapel, adorns the ceiling. I estimate there are well over a hundred people in attendance.

Mason leads me in dance after dance, without any

mishaps. The more we dance, the more comfortable I feel leaning into him and trusting him to show my body where to go and how to move. Finally, I ask for a break when I become desperate for something to drink.

Mason leads me to Angela's side, since she is the only other person in the room I know while he and his son go find drinks.

"You and Mason look fabulous together," she tells me after they've left.

"Only because Mason is a great dancer."

"This is the first time I've ever seen him dance," she reveals.

"I thought you have this ball every year."

"We do. But, this is the first time he's actually come."

"Why is he here this year?"

Angela smiles at me. "I suspect it's because of you. You know, he asked me to come with him to help pick out the dress you're wearing, which, by the way, is knock-out gorgeous on you."

"So you picked the dress?"

"No, he did. When he saw it at the House of Armand, it was like he just knew it had been made for you. It's a one of a kind, you know. No one will ever have that same dress."

To know Mason went to the trouble of shopping for me warms my heart, making me feel like someone special.

"Jonathan is beyond thrilled by the change in Mason. He's been so worried about his dad. You're the first healthy relationship Mason's ever been in."

"Has he had many other relationships?" I ask, hating my sense of morbid curiosity.

"He's had a few lady friends here and there, but no one he's ever spent any amount of time with. He's not a monk, you know," Angela laughs. "He's a man with certain needs from time to time. He certainly didn't bring any of those women to meet his son. We only knew of those women because of Isaiah."

"Is Isaiah here?" I ask, hoping to see my one-time mentor.

"No, he couldn't come this year. I think he went to see Lilly and Brand."

"I thought they might be here too."

"Normally they would be," Angela says, and I can tell she's purposely holding something back from me.

"Why aren't they here this year?"

Angela gives me a sideways glance, and I'm not sure she's going to answer until she says, "Lilly wasn't ready to see you just yet."

I instantly know why.

"Because of Michael."

Angela nods. "It was a shock when Malcolm told her. Brand said she just needed some time to think, but he also told me I should probably warn you that Lilly will come to see you when she's ready."

"I'm not sure I'll have much to tell her," I say. "I only have contact with Michael when I dream, at least for now. He did say something about new neural connections being made in my brain, and me being able to call on him even when I'm awake at some point. I don't know. It didn't make a whole lot of sense to me. Anyway, I'm not sure if seeing me will help her out any."

"Well, I thought I should warn you to expect her."

"Thanks," I say; not sure if the warning helps me or makes me nervous to meet with Lilly again.

I enjoyed my time with her when we first met, and don't relish the idea of having her upset with me over something that is beyond my control. However, from what Michael told me, my soul chose to meld with his while it was still in the Guf. Why had it been stupid enough to saddle me with a tag-along archangel?

By the time Mason and Jonathan make it back with our drinks, Angela is starting to herd people towards the back terrace, since it's only a few minutes until midnight. Apparently, she has planned a pyrotechnic display of fireworks to ring in the New Year.

I soon find my hand entwined with Mason's as he leads me in the opposite direction the crowd is heading.

"Aren't we going to watch the fireworks?" I ask.

Mason looks back at me as he leads me out of the ballroom.

"Trust me," he says, with mischief in his eyes.

We end up going up the grand staircase to the second floor. We walk down a long hallway and finally into one of the bedrooms. It's only then I begin to wonder if our earlier flirtatious texts about removing masks had been code for something else entirely. Angela's words about Mason being a man and having needs are still fresh in my mind.

Without pause, we walk into the room. Mason heads directly out a set of glass doors to the bedroom's balcony. The balcony faces the back of the house, overlooking the garden area and forest beyond. I hear the chatter of the other guests below us.

"Thought it might be nicer if we had more privacy," Mason says as we stand together near the stone railing.

The winter air is chilly, and I involuntarily shiver. Mason lets go of my hand, and I watch as he goes back into the bedroom and grabs his trusty grey wool coat from off the bed. When he comes back out, he holds it open for me so I can easily slip my arms inside its warmth. Gently, he spins me around to face him and begins to button the front up for me.

"You don't have to do that," I whisper, even though I like the feeling of being taken care of in this small way.

"I know I don't, Jess," he says, glancing up at my face, "but I want to."

When he's finished, I hear the crowd below us begin the countdown to midnight, starting with 20.

"Time to take off the masks," Mason says, reaching his hands under my hair and easily undoing the bow he placed there earlier. The mask falls from my face, and he deftly catches it with his free hand.

"That's better," he says, grinning down at me.

I reach up and place my hand on his mask. He almost flinches away from me, but I don't let him.

"My turn," I tell him, reaching with my other hand behind his head to slip the silk ribbon tie free.

I pull off the mask and set it down on top of the railing. When I look back at Mason, I say, "That's better."

I hear the crowd below us reach the 10-second mark.

Mason cups the side of my face with his right hand, and I tilt my cheek into it, enjoying the rough texture of his skin against the silky smoothness of mine. I feel his other hand come to rest on the small of my back, gently bringing me in closer to his body. His eyes burn with an unasked question, and I wrap my arms around his neck in answer.

He leans his head down closer to mine, and I feel his warm breath against my lips. I close my eyes, waiting breathlessly to experience my first kiss. The crowd below us bursts into a joyous chorus of 'Happy New Year!' and then it happens.

A multitude of terrified screams shatters the happy revelry. Mason's sharp intake of breath causes me to open my eyes and see him staring at something in the sky. I turn around in his arms to follow his gaze, and witness a living nightmare.

The Tear is open.

CHAPTER 18

Through the open white ribbon of fate, I see a large red planet loom like an evil specter about to ravage our world. Mason grabs my hand and phases us directly back to headquarters.

Joshua is nowhere to be seen, but Nick is there watching the Tear on the holographic display.

"What's going on?" Mason asks, letting go of my hand.

"I have no idea," Nick says, his hands moving almost as fast as Joshua's across the control panel.

As we watch, the Tear closes, but I know it doesn't need much time to wreak its havoc on the universe.

"Show me the Antarctica satellite," Mason demands.

"What do you think I'm trying to do?" Nick asks irritably. "I'm not Joshua. I'm doing the best I can." He hits a button with finality. "There."

On the holographic display, I see Lucifer and his new

friend standing on a snowy plain, looking up at the sky, rather pleased with themselves.

"I'll be back." Mason says, as if he's about to phase there alone.

I grab his arm, forcing him to take me with him.

When we reach our destination, I suddenly wish Nick had shown us a larger view of the area where Lucifer and his friend are standing. The sun shines brightly over us, causing a glare off the pristine white snow, forcing me to shield my eyes with a hand. On the outer reaches, I see a line of 20 men dressed in black leather pants with billowing black feathered capes on their bare backs. The biting chill of the wind makes me wonder how they can stand to be here without wearing any shirts.

"Ahh, Mason," Lucifer says, like he's talking to an old friend, "I thought you might show up." Lucifer looks at me, turning serious. "You shouldn't be here, Jess. This isn't a safe place for you."

I feel Mason take hold of my hand and squeeze it tightly.

"I need to take you somewhere safe, Jess," he tells me, keeping a wary eye on the men in capes.

Instantly, one of them phases to stand right in front of us.

"It probably would have been wiser not to bring her here in the first place," the man says to Mason, but is looking directly at me, like he wants to devour me whole.

"I will kill you if you harm her," Mason threatens in a low growl.

The man looks at Mason. "You did that a long time ago,

Mason. Or have you forgotten already? You're the reason we're like we are. If you had been a better leader, perhaps we would all still be in Heaven instead of this hell hole."

"We all made bad decisions," Mason tries to reason, but even I hear the guilt in his voice, like he doesn't quite believe what he just said.

"You should have done a better job of protecting us," the other man spits out. "Then our children wouldn't have been born and made to suffer through their half-lives."

"Our father gave you a way to save your children," Mason reminds the man, "but you chose to ignore his chance at redemption. Don't put that blame on me, Baruch. You made that decision yourself, not me."

"I will always blame you," Baruch says. He turns his eyes on me, "and maybe I'll take that blame out on your little girl-friend, here, one evening when she's least expecting it. My son has become increasingly hungry for human flesh over the last 15 years. She looks like a delicate morsel he might enjoy."

"She," Lucifer says to Baruch, "you do not touch. Ever. Is that understood?"

Baruch's eyes narrow on me. "Why protect this human?"

"I don't remember giving you permission to question me," Lucifer snaps.

Baruch falls to his knees in front of us, screaming in pain as he holds his head in his hands. The intensity with which Lucifer is staring at Baruch tells me he's causing the other man's agony in some way. When Lucifer lifts his eyes to meet mine, Baruch instantly phases away to points unknown.

"How were you able to reopen the Tear so soon?" Mason asks, staring at Lucifer.

"Don't you recognize the person standing next to me?" Lucifer asks.

Mason looks more carefully at the man standing by Lucifer's side. The man smiles, but it's a sinister expression, not one meant as an indication of friendliness.

"Samyaza," the other man says, "it's been far too long."

"Asmodeus," Mason says, "I never thought I would see you again."

"Yet, here I am, brother," Asmodeus says, a smile plastered on his face. Asmodeus's gaze lands on me, and I instantly feel his lust.

"She's off limits, Asmodeus," Lucifer says as a warning to the other.

"Why is she so special to you?" Asmodeus asks, just as confused as Baruch as to why Lucifer is offering me his personal protection.

Lucifer sighs. "Honestly, I'm not completely sure why," he admits, "but until I figure that out, hands off." Lucifer turns to the remaining men in black feathered capes behind him. "And that includes all of you too. You drink one drop of her blood, and I will personally transform you and your progeny into piles of dust. Is that understood?"

The men nod their heads in unison.

"Now leave," Lucifer commands. "You've served your purpose for now."

The men phase away.

"Who were they?" I ask no one in particular. I just want an answer.

"The men Mason let wallow in debauchery," Lucifer chuckles. "Isn't that right, Mason?"

Mason remains stoically silent.

I look up at him, just to make sure he's all right.

The cold, hard look in his eyes tells me that he's not.

"What are you planning, Lucifer?" Mason asks.

"Eventually, you'll figure it out," Lucifer says, coming to stand closer to us. "Until that time, you'll just have to wonder."

Lucifer comes to stand in front of me and smiles.

"You look rather ravishing this evening," he says. "I do wish I could see the rest of the dress."

Before I know it, Mason has phased us back to headquarters.

Joshua is back in his usual seat with Malcolm standing behind him, watching the scene we just left. I stare at it as Lucifer looks up into the sky, as if he knows exactly where the satellite is, and winks. He walks back to Asmodeus, and they phase away together.

Malcolm turns to us.

"So, how was your evening?" Malcolm asks sarcastically.

Mason lets go of my hand, and I have an odd feeling the gesture has a deeper meaning, from the stiff way Mason is just standing next to me.

I look up at him, but can't seem to read his expression. He

looks completely closed off, and he doesn't even act like he knows I'm still there.

"Not as pleasant as I had hoped it to be," Mason answers, walking away from my side to stand by Malcolm.

Becoming warm in Mason's coat, I unbutton it and slip it off, setting it down on a nearby chair.

I feel someone staring at me, and look up to see Malcolm's leer.

"Well, you clean up rather nicely," he says, looking me up and down, not even trying to hide the fact that he finds me desirable.

"I didn't do it for you," I tell him, wanting to wipe the smirk off his face.

"Lucky man, Mason," Malcolm says appreciatively, grinning at me.

"Would you mind taking Jess home for me, Malcolm?" Mason says, not even bothering to look back at me as he says the words. "I have a lot to do here."

"Maybe I can help." I take a step forward.

Mason shakes his head, still not looking at me. "No, it would be better if you left so I can concentrate. I'll call you later."

"But…"

"Please, Jess," Mason almost shouts, half turning his face so all I can see of him is his left side. The scar seems to be pulsing red for some reason, almost like it was freshly made. "I need you to go. I don't want you here."

An ice pick to the heart would have hurt less than his words.

Malcolm walks to me and places one of his hands on my shoulder. Before I know it, we are standing on my front porch.

I stand there, trying to figure out what just happened. How did one of the best nights of my life instantly turn into one of the worst?

"Don't take what he said to heart."

I look up at Malcolm, and see compassion for me in his eyes.

"I don't understand what just happened," I say, feeling completely lost.

"Lucifer reminded Mason that there are still Watchers who butcher humans for their own pleasure. He wanted to make sure Mason didn't forget his part in our fall so it keeps him unbalanced and easier to manipulate; but you should know one thing," Malcolm says so earnestly I find myself holding my breath to hear his next words. "Mason would have never taken you to meet his son if he didn't care for you a great deal. As far as I know, he has never allowed Jonathan to meet any of the women he….how do I put this to a virgin so you're not offended…."

"How do you know I'm a virgin?" I question.

"I've intimately known a lot of women in my life," Malcolm says, with no shame in the fact. "And you remind me of the one virgin I once tried to seduce; simple deduction really. Anyway, as I was saying, as far as I know, Jonathan has never met any of the women Mason has been with. Give him some time to regain himself. He's never let go of the guilt he feels. Lucifer just reopened an old wound, one we all hoped Mason had found a reason to stop using as an excuse to hide from the world. Don't give up on him if you really care for him. He needs you, but he'll probably act like an ass for a while, just to push you away."

"How do I help him?"

"Just be there for him when he finally realizes how much he needs you. Listen when he's ready to speak to you about things that have happened in his life. They won't be pleasant memories for him to relive, so prepare to hear the worst."

"How long do you think it will take before he wants to be around me again?"

"I don't know. Only he knows that."

"Why are you being so nice?"

Malcolm looks surprised by my question then busts out laughing.

"I guess I deserve that after the way I treated you concerning Lilly's safety."

I smile. "Yeah, you kind of did."

"I will leave you now so you can get some rest. Let Mason make the first move. Don't try to call him, or you'll just push him further away. He has to realize how much he needs you; it's the only way you'll have a chance of making it."

Malcolm squeezes my arm reassuringly before phasing away.

I stand on my porch for a while, letting Malcolm's words act like a healing balm on the hole Mason made in the middle of my heart. Malcolm didn't seem like someone who would say what he did to me if he didn't truly mean it. I make a promise to myself then and there that I won't contact Mason. I will flush my phone down the toilet if my fingers even twitch to write a text message. I vow to remain resolute in allowing him to make the first move, no matter what.

CHAPTER 19

"Oh for Heaven's sake, would you just call the man already?"

I look at Faison sitting across from me at the table in my kitchen, and scrunch my nose up at her.

"I can't. He has to make the first move. I've already explained this to you."

"Why does he have to be the one who makes the first move?"

"Because."

"Because why?"

"Just because!" I say in complete frustration.

"Now, don't get mad at Faison," Mama Lynn says, bringing over a plate filled with scrambled eggs and Polk sausage. "She just doesn't like seeing you so sad."

I sigh. "I know. And I'm sorry, Fai, but you badgering me doesn't make me feel any better. Don't you think I want to call him? My fingers are itching to text him just to make sure he's still alive, but I can't. He's got issues he needs to work through, and I just have to be patient."

"Patience is overrated, if you ask me," Faison says before stuffing her mouth with a forkful of Mama Lynn's scrambled eggs.

Mama Lynn pats me on the back. "He'll call, baby. Don't you worry your pretty little head about that. Now, how much longer are you supposed to be working at the Tunica station anyway?"

"Until Mason calls," I say.

The day after the Tear opened, Isaiah came to me in person and asked if I could come in to work to help them out. I didn't ask how he knew I would be free because I felt sure Mason had arranged the request. If I wasn't going to be working with the Colorado team for a while, he probably thought it would be a good idea to keep me busy here at home. I assumed Mason thought if he kept me occupied, I wouldn't have time to dwell on what went wrong on New Year's Eve.

How did we go from almost sharing our first kiss to completely ignoring one another? I say ignoring. I still ended up thinking about him almost every minute of the last six days, going on seven. Unfortunately, it was Friday, which meant I would have two days off to do nothing but think about Mason. I let out a heavy sigh.

"Oh, Jess," Mama Lynn says as she stands by the sink, cleaning the pan she used to make breakfast. "I just hate seeing you like this."

"I'll be fine," I say, standing to covertly throw away my half-eaten breakfast before Mama Lynn has a chance to chastise me for wasting food.

"You want a ride to the hospital?" I ask Faison as she stands up to put her dish in the sink.

"Yeah, if you don't mind; that'll save me from having to bring my car back home. John Austin can just meet me at the hospital for our date."

I kiss Mama Lynn goodbye.

As Faison and I are driving in my car, she insists on changing the station to one playing the latest pop rock. As usual, Faison seems to know the words to all the songs and serenades me on the drive. Even her god-awful singing doesn't make me want to smile.

As I pull into the hospital's parking lot, a song comes on that I vaguely recognize. A vision of a man standing in a blue spotlight, with swirls of smoke surrounding him, flashes in my mind.

"Who sings this song?" I ask Faison, my personal encyclopedia of useless information.

"Geez, Jess, get with it. That's just the one and only Chandler Cain. The song's been number one on the charts for weeks."

"Thanks, Faison," I say, my heart thumping so hard I fear it might bruise the inside of my chest.

Faison says goodbye and gets out of the car.

I immediately call Isaiah and tell him I may know who one of the other six archangel vessels is.

"Ok, Jess. I'll get in touch with Mason and see what he wants you to do next."

After I hang up, I realize how depressed I feel. I had hoped Isaiah would just tell me to call Mason myself, considering the importance of the news. It would have been the perfect excuse to call him first. Why hadn't I just called Mason instead of Isaiah in the first place?

I bang my forehead on the top of the steering wheel three times. Stupid, stupid, stupid….

The phone buzzes in my hand, and I look down at it, expecting it to be Isaiah calling me back. It isn't. It's Mason.

I take a deep breath and answer.

"Hello?"

"Isaiah says you know who the vessel is that you saw during your meditation. Who is it?"

No 'hello'? No, 'hey how have you been this last week, nice to know you're still alive'? Nothing? Just straight to business. Well, two could play at that game.

"Chandler Cain. His song is number one on the charts right now."

"I know who he is."

There's a long pause. I can hear Mason breathing on the other end of the phone, but he remains silent.

"What do you want me to do?" I ask, holding my breath, waiting to see what the answer is.

"I'll call you back."

And he hangs up.

I sit there, feeling my heart tighten into a knot in my chest at his rudeness. I haven't done anything to deserve it, and begin to wonder if I just imagined Mason's interest in me. He wasn't even treating me like a co-worker. He was treating me like dirt on the bottom of his shoes that just wouldn't go away, no matter how hard he stomped.

I felt the threat of tears and force them to go back from whence they came. I will not cry. I won't give him the satisfaction. Slowly, I feel my tried and trusted wall of protection reassemble itself, because I refuse to be a victim of his whims. I have survived a lot in my life, and I feel determined to survive this.

The phone buzzes in my hand.

"Where are you?" he asks brusquely.

"Sitting in my car."

"Which is where exactly?" he demands, sounding irritated by my obtuseness, which only makes me feel like I've had a small victory.

"Tunica Central Hospital."

"Meet me at the emergency room entrance."

And he hangs up again!

I sit in my car for a good 15 minutes fuming. I refuse to jump when he says jump. If he wants me to keep helping him, he is going to have to learn how to treat me with a little bit more respect than he's shown me thus far this morning.

Eventually, I get out of my car and casually walk over to the emergency entrance.

When I see Mason, my heart involuntarily lurches inside my chest, happy to see him and mad, all at the same time. I focus on the mad because it's easier to deal with.

Mason sees me and stops his agitated pacing. For just a split second, I think he's going to revert to the easy-to-make-smile-Mason I had become used to, but then I see the curtain behind his eyes close, and know he's intentionally blocking me out. Rationally, I understand this is his way of keeping me at a distance, but emotionally it threatens to make me a complete wreck.

"I thought you said you were already here," he says irritably. "What took you so long?"

I stop in front of him and cross my arms, taking a defensive stance.

"Let's get something straight," I tell him. "I don't jump when you say jump. You should know by now I don't respond well to rudeness. You either treat me with respect or I walk away. Am I making myself clear, or are you just so mad at me for whatever reason, we won't be able to work together anymore?"

Mason's eyes remain impassive, and I can't tell what he's really thinking.

"I don't expect you to jump when I say jump," he finally says. "I've never expected that from you, Jess. And us working together," he pauses, like the next words are hard for him to say, "well, we don't have much choice. You're stuck with me, for the moment, to try to help you figure things out."

"I don't feel stuck with you," I say in a low voice, treading the waters carefully to see how he responds.

Mason laughs harshly. "We're stuck with each other whether we want to be or not. It's not like either of us has a choice."

I look down at the sidewalk at my feet, not wanting him to see the tears that are suddenly clouding my vision. I force them back, promising myself a good cry when I get home, but not now; not when he's standing right in front of me, watching me. I won't give him the satisfaction.

I blink a few times to clear the tears away and look back up at him. He's watching me quietly with hooded eyes, and I wonder if he knows how much his words have hurt me. I force my mind to turn back to the work at hand.

"So do you know where this Chandler Cain guy is?"

"Yes, Nick found him. He's staying at a hotel in New York. Apparently, he has a concert tonight at Madison Square Garden."

"Does he know we're coming?"

"He should by now. I had Isaiah go over and lay the groundwork for us. Ready?"

I nod.

Mason places his hand on my shoulder, and I close my hands into fist as I realize he didn't even try to hold my hand.

We are instantly standing in the hallway of a nice-looking hotel. Mason walks down the corridor without waiting to see if

I'm following him. I do follow him, but just because he seems to know where he's going.

The sounds of an electric guitar come from down the hallway, and I have to assume it's where Chandler Cain can be found.

Mason knocks on the door, and Isaiah answers it.

"What did you tell him?" Mason asks Isaiah.

"Just the basics; that we need his help, and that he doesn't have much choice in giving it to us." Isaiah smiles, rather pleased with himself.

"Are those the people we've been waiting on?" I hear a man ask from inside the room.

Isaiah opens the door a little wider, and I see Chandler Cain sitting on a white L-shaped sofa in a mostly white and black decorated living room, holding a glossy black electric guitar in his lap. Our eyes lock, and I feel an instant connection with him. Without taking his eyes off me, he sets the guitar on the floor, leaning it against the couch he's sitting on, and walks directly to me like we're tethered to one another by an invisible string.

If I had to put a picture of a rock star in the dictionary, it would most certainly look like Chandler Cain. He has a strong square face with a dimpled chin, full lips, and brown eyes so dark they almost look black. His tawny brown hair is gelled into a messy style only the rich and handsome seem to be able to get away with wearing and actually make look good. He's dressed simply in a white T-shirt and faded blue jeans ripped around the thighs.

When he reaches the door, he smiles at me and holds out his hand.

"I know you, don't I?" he asks.

"The answer to that is yes and no," I say, placing my hand in his, and instantly feeling like I've found a long-lost friend.

He tightens his fingers around mine and gently pulls me into the room. He's still holding my hand when he urges me to sit with him on the couch he was sitting on when I arrived. The ardent way he's looking at me doesn't make me feel uncomfortable. In fact, I feel more comfortable in his presence than most of the people in my life.

"You feel it too, don't you?" he questions, a smile lifting the corners of his mouth, not trying to hide the joy he feels being in my presence.

"Yes," I say, finding it impossible to keep a smile of my own from appearing.

Chandler reaches up with his free hand, because his other one is still holding mine, and gently traces the side of my face with the tips of his fingers. I close my eyes, reveling in the contact. Our closeness isn't sexual in nature; it's the complete opposite for me. I feel like I'm finally with someone who would never leave me or hurt me intentionally. I know without any doubt that I can trust Chandler to fight by my side and stay with me, no matter what dangers the future might hold for us.

"What's your name?" he finally asks me, letting his hand drop back into this lap.

"Jess Riley."

"Chandler Cain," he says, which makes me smile.

"Yes, I know who you are," I tell him.

He holds my hand tighter. "I can't seem to make myself stop staring at you," he apologizes with a small laugh. "I'm not freaking you out, am I? I'm not normally this stalker-like. It's usually me who gets stalked."

I shake my head. "No, it's all right. I understand what you're feeling."

Finally, I make myself drag my eyes away from Chandler's face to look at Isaiah and Mason.

Isaiah is grinning at us, but Mason's expression almost breaks the peace I've found just being in Chandler's presence. It's almost as if a dark shroud is covering Mason's face as he glowers at how Chandler and I are reacting to one another. If I didn't know better, I would have said he was angry about something.

I decide to not let Mason's dark mood intrude on the happiness I've found being with Chandler, and turn my full attention back to my new friend.

"So, do you know what's going on?" Chandler asks me, still completely confused as to why we're sharing such a deep, instant connection.

"Yes," I tell him. "It's going to be hard for you to believe, but you have to trust me."

"I trust you," Chandler says. I can see how surprised he is to say the words. "I don't know how or why, but I know I can trust you completely. Please, tell me what's going on, Jess."

I tell Chandler everything that's happened to me since

killing the Owen changeling. When I come to the part about finding the crown, the fiery sword, and meeting Michael for the first time, Chandler's eyes fill with pent-up excitement.

"So I'm a vessel for an archangel?" he asks me.

I nod.

"That is so wickedly cool! Which one do I have?"

"I don't know. We'll have to find your crown and whatever talisman you were assigned before you can make first contact with your archangel."

"So, where do we start? How do we find my crown?"

I sigh heavily. "Yeah, that part might not be as easy as I made it sound. My crown didn't reveal its presence until after I killed the demon. I'm not sure what your trigger will be, but I suspect it will be different for all of us."

"But, I'm meant to find it, right?" he asks like an excited child. "If it's fate, then I have nothing to worry about. I've led a pretty charmed life so far."

It's not something I have trouble believing about Chandler. He's so open to everything. I can't imagine he's had a life filled with anything less than perfection.

"And now I've found you," he says, smiling at me brightly. "Or, I guess you found me. Either way," he shrugs, "charmed life."

Mason clears his throat to gain our attention. "Now that the two of you have…found each other," he says, making it sound almost dirty, "maybe you should spend the rest of the day together."

Although Mason is suggesting I spend the day with Chandler, his stiff demeanor seems to indicate he doesn't really want me to.

"Great!" Chandler says, reluctantly letting go of my hand to stand and walk over to a built-in bar in the room. "Want something to drink, Jess? I don't have alcohol, never liked the stuff myself, but I do have soda, water, and juice."

"Water is fine," I tell him.

I stand up and walk over to Isaiah and Mason.

"So, any clue as to what might help trigger his crown to send out a homing beacon like mine did?"

"No," Mason says in a clipped voice, "we'll just have to wait and see what happens. I'll have Joshua comb through Chandler's records and pinpoint locations where it might show up. It's probably just a matter of time."

"Then you just want me to stay here and keep an eye on him? For how long?"

"Does it matter?" Mason asks brusquely. "The two of you seem to be getting along rather well. I didn't think you would mind spending the day with him."

I feel myself bristle.

"Why would I?" I ask, refusing to let him leave thinking otherwise. "He's handsome, sweet, and actually seems to want to be around me. What girl on this planet wouldn't give her soul to spend a day alone with Chandler Cain in his penthouse suite?"

I see Mason ball his hands into fists.

"Call me when you're ready to go back home," he says tersely. "I'll come get you."

With that, Mason turns his back to me and phases.

"Let us know if you two need anything," Isaiah says to me in a kinder voice than Mason's.

I feel as though he wants to say more, but thinks better of it before he phases away too.

"Wow," Chandler says from the bar, pouring water over ice in a glass. "You could cut the tension between the two of you with a knife...literally. What's the story there, Jess?"

"There is no story," I say, going back to the couch and sitting down heavily on it. I lean my head back on the soft cushion and close my eyes, feeling tired all of a sudden.

I feel Chandler's weight dip the couch as he sits down beside me, and I open my eyes. He holds out the glass of ice water to me and I take it. After drinking almost half of its contents, I set the glass down on the black lacquered coffee table in front of us.

"Ok, spill," Chandler says to me. "What's going on between the two of you?"

"Nothing," I say. "At least, nothing now; I thought there might be something, but now I think I must have just been deluding myself."

"I don't think you were, not from the way he was looking at you before he left. Trust me; a man doesn't act that way unless he really cares about you. To me, it looks like he cares about you more than he wants to admit to himself, though."

My heart lifts a little with hope from Chandler's words, but I don't let it last long. I let Mason in once, thinking he would be different, but I wasn't going to do it again until I knew for sure what his feelings for me were. I won't torture myself with what might be.

Chandler and I spend most of the morning talking about our lives. I tell him everything, not leaving anything out. I have to assume it's our archangels making us so comfortable with each other, and, strangely enough, I'm okay with that. I have so few people in my life who I can confide in, and I feel as though Chandler isn't a new friend, but an old one.

Compared to Chandler's life, I realize just how screwed up mine has been. Apparently, he grew up in a small town in Georgia with the whole two-story home, white picket fence, two dogs, a cat, and loving parents who never argued scenario. I almost envy him but realize there's no reason to. His life was meant to make him into the man he is and mine was meant to... what? Make sure I was as screwed up as possible? I push the thought aside because I don't want to taint my time with Chandler dwelling on things in the past that I have no way of changing.

That afternoon, Chandler asks me to attend his concert at Madison Square Garden.

"I have to get over there soon to do the sound check and make sure things are set up right. But, I want you to come see me perform."

"Okay," I say, truly excited. "This will be my first concert."

Chandler stares at me like I've suddenly grown horns on my head.

"You're kidding, right?"

"No," I say shaking my head a little. "This will be my first concert."

"Hmm, well then, you have to let me indoctrinate you into the life style of a rock star."

He fishes his cell phone out of his pocket and makes a call.

"Hey, Deon, it's your favorite rock star," Chandler says into the phone. "I need to hire you for something." He pauses. "Tonight. I have a friend I want you to pamper for me." He pauses again and grins at something Deon says. "No, not that type of friend. This one is a real friend, not one of the girls. Well, she is a girl, but not one of the usual girls. I want you to come over and get her ready for my concert tonight. No, I don't care what you need to get. You have my card. Okay, see you in a few."

Chandler looks over at me with mischief in his eyes.

"Ok, who is Deon, and what's wrong with the way I look now? Watcher uniforms not allowed at concerts these days?"

"Well, you are definitely going to have to leave the plasma pistol behind," Chandler laughs. "I know you could probably get away with carrying one to the concert, but I would rather you didn't. Sends the wrong vibe, and I like for people to listen to me sing without having to worry about being shot."

I laugh. "Okay, I can do that for you I guess. But, seriously, what is this Deon person going to do to me?"

"Now that would just ruin the surprise," Chandler says, leaning over and giving me a peck on the cheek. "Trust me."

I purse my lips at him and shake my head, wondering what I've just gotten myself into.

CHAPTER 20

When Deon and her crew arrive at Chandler's hotel suite, she doesn't exactly match up with the picture I had in my mind. I suppose I was being judgmental. Since we are in a rock and roll environment, I assumed Deon would dress edgy and over the top. She actually comes in looking like she just stepped off a runway in Milan, with her crisp white suit and perfectly coiffed straight hair.

She holds out her hand to me when Chandler introduces us, and her skin is like black velvet it's so soft.

"Pleased to meet you," Deon says. "And may I say I'm happy to see you are nothing like the regular girls Chandler has me tend to. I'm glad he's found a nice girl this time," She takes in my Watcher uniform, "but that uniform is going to have to go; otherwise, you'll scare off half of Chandler's fans."

"Okay, I'll leave you in Deon's capable hands," Chandler says, giving me a peck on the cheek. "I've got to meet my agent downstairs and head on over. Deon will bring you to the concert for me." He turns to Deon. "Treat her good. I don't care how much you need to spend."

Deon lifts an eyebrow. "Dangerous words to speak to a stylist."

Chandler laughs. "I trust you, Deon."

After Chandler leaves, Deon asks me to go shower and wash my hair so she and her crew of two women and one man can get me ready for the concert.

When I emerge from the shower, I'm not sure what to put on. I rummage through the clothes Chandler has, and find a button-down shirt and a pair of shorts, which are too large, but I refuse to go out without something on down there.

Deon and her helpers set to work on me immediately. While the girls curl my hair into a multitude of spiral curls, I see Deon and the man looking at a rack of clothing they must have brought in while I was in the shower. Out of the corner of my eye, I notice Deon pull out something bright red.

"This will show up nicely on stage," she says to the man.

I see that the dress is made out of a red nylon/spandex-mix material with a square neckline, thin shoulder straps, and horizontal sections of material that gives it a bandage effect. There is a long zipper in the back, which tells me I will never be able to put it on by myself.

"On stage?" I question. Chandler didn't say anything about me having to be on stage.

"Oh, just in case," Deon says with a wave of her hand, as if I have nothing to worry about.

For Chandler's sake, I hope she's right.

At around six that evening, I call Faison to let her know where I will be, since Mama Lynn didn't answer her phone.

"You're going *where*?" she practically screams at me. I hold the phone away from my ear.

"Chandler Cain's concert at Madison Square Garden," I tell her a second time.

"I definitely picked the wrong job," Faison whines. "Bring me back a T-shirt!"

"Do you want it signed?"

"Oh, my God," she says, enunciating each of her words dramatically. "Are you telling me you're actually going to meet him?"

"I pretty much spent the day with him," I tell her, and she squeals, forcing me to pull the phone away from my ear again.

"Well, if I had to pick someone for you to rebound with, it would be Chandler Cain. He is *beyond* gorgeous."

"He's just a friend, Faison," I tell her. "Now, do you want him to sign the T-shirt or not?"

"Yes, yes, yes!"

After I get off the phone with Faison, Deon dismisses her crew and escorts me to the ground-floor of the hotel to an awaiting black stretch limousine. It doesn't take us long to get to Madison Square Garden. Apparently, Deon is like one of Chandler's crew, because we breeze by his security team when they see I'm with her. She escorts me to a private room, where Chandler is getting ready.

I guess I understood he was a rock star, but find it amusing when I see him all gussied up as one. He has makeup on, with his eyes outlined with black eyeliner. His hair looks similar to his natural style but seems to be standing up on end a bit more dramatically. His outfit is somewhere between punk rock and neo-Victorian, with its stiff collar and cravat around his neck. The white shirt he is wearing has puffy sleeves. A pair of black, skintight leather pants and matching vest complete his look.

When Chandler sees me, he hops out of his makeup chair and twirls around in front of me.

"What do you think?"

I smile, because he's like a big kid.

"Very rock-starish," I say. "You'll have the girls swooning in no time."

He smiles, and it literally lights up the room.

Chandler runs his gaze up and down my body, and whistles, "Deon does know how to dress a lady. You're looking wicked cool tonight, Jess."

Chandler introduces me to people in his entourage, but I don't pay too much attention to their names. I seriously doubt any of them will become very important to me. When it's time for the concert to begin, I'm told I can watch everything from the side of the stage.

I didn't want to admit it to Chandler, but this is the first time, besides the song I heard on the radio in my car, that I have actually listened to his music. I instantly know why he is so popular, especially with the female population. His love songs are sweet and sentimental, just like he seems to be. The faster, more upbeat songs are catchy, and I find myself tapping my foot to the beats.

Near the end of the concert, Chandler turns and motions for me to come to him on stage.

I shake my head and take a step back, only to find a pair of strong hands pushing me gently forward.

"Go on out," I hear Deon say to me.

A man on Chandler's road crew brings two stools out onto the stage. When I step out, I feel like I need sunglasses, because the spotlights are so bright.

"I'd like for you to all welcome my friend, Jess, to the stage," Chandler says into the microphone.

I can't see the crowd because of the glare of the lights, but am silently thankful I can't see them. Otherwise, I feel sure I would probably faint from the sheer number of people.

Chandler points to the stool beside him, indicating I should take a seat. Someone brings an acoustic guitar to him and, before I know it, I am being serenaded by Chandler Cain, in front of thousands of people. I silently pray I don't end up as a viral video clip on You Tube, but know such an occurrence is inevitable in the age we live in.

When the song ends, Chandler gives me his million-dollar megawatt smile, and I can't help but smile back at him, though I do vow to kill him later for making me come out on stage, but that's just a small detail.

Chandler gets up and thanks the crowd for coming to the show before wishing them all a good night. The curtains close and he grabs one of my hands to escort me off stage.

"I can't believe you made me do that," I tell him, shaking my head in disbelief.

"Oh, come on, I couldn't just let the most beautiful woman here stand on the side of the stage. They deserved to see you in that knock-out dress."

I just continue to shake my head, but am silently flattered by the compliment.

I do, however, wish I had prepared myself for what was waiting for me off-stage: a scowling Mason.

"I came to check on you, since you didn't call," he says. I hear the anger in his voice and don't understand why it's there. His gaze travels the length of me, and he looks disgusted by what he sees.

"That's my fault, man," Chandler protectively positions his body between Mason and me. I have to assume he's concerned for my safety from the murderous way Mason is glaring at me. "I wanted Jess to see my concert. I should have remembered what you said about calling. If you want to blame somebody, blame me."

"No, *she* should have remembered me," Mason says in a low voice, almost as if he thinks I completely forgot he existed.

I touch Chandler on the shoulder, which makes him turn to face me.

"Thank you for the concert and Deon and everything. I had

a great time, but I should probably be getting home now."

Chandler takes my hands in his and holds them to his chest. "When will I be able to see you again?"

"It'll be soon. I promise. We have a lot of work to do."

Chandler leans into me and kisses me on the cheek.

"Call if you need me," he whispers into my ear. "I put my private number in your phone."

I nod. "Okay, I will."

Before Chandler can even let go of my hands, I feel Mason grab my arm roughly, and instantly find myself standing inside his house in Colorado. We are in the same room I first phased to the night we met, when he asked me to be a part of his team.

I yank my arm out of his grasp.

"That was rude," I say. "You know I don't like rudeness."

"Is it that, or is it that you just didn't want to leave your new boyfriend so soon?" Mason asks scathingly.

"He's not my boyfriend," I say, as if the idea is ridiculous, which it is. "I can't expect you to understand our connection, because I don't fully understand it myself."

"Just how 'connected' are you?" Mason questions hotly.

"What concern is it of yours?" I ask, my own temper flaring. "I think you've made it pretty clear from your silence the last few days where you and I stand with each other now. You have no right to question who I spend time with, or how we spend that time together."

I didn't think it possible, but Mason's expression actually darkens.

"Just how *close* did you two get today?" he growls, demanding an answer.

"Why do you care?" I shout.

Mason looks away from me. "It's just a question, Jess. Why can't you answer it, or would explaining the details be too embarrassing for you?"

"We're friends," I tell him, completely exasperated. "There's nothing for me to be embarrassed about. We didn't do anything but talk and get to know one another."

"Is that all?" Mason asks; I can hear his relief even through the hard edge of his voice.

"Yes, that's all," I tell him, feeling my anger slowly ebb as I suddenly realize why Mason has been acting so strange since my first meeting with Chandler... He's jealous. "I don't want anything more than friendship with him, and I can safely say he feels the same way. We can't help the way our archangels make us feel towards one another."

Mason looks back at me. His gaze travels all over my face, as if looking for any telltale signs that I'm holding something back from him about my feelings for Chandler. Satisfied that I'm telling the truth, he says, "So, do you have any idea how we're supposed to activate his crown so we can find it for him?"

I sigh heavily. "No. Not a clue. From what Michael told me, Chandler will have to display some of his power before it will reveal its location. How we get him to do that? I'm not sure. I don't exactly want to throw him in a room with a demon just to see if he sinks or swims."

This gains a reluctant chuckle from Mason, the first one I've seen in a long time. It makes me smile, because I know the Mason I've come to know and care deeply about is still lurking behind the surly façade he's been hiding behind all day.

"I agree," he says with a lopsided grin. "We probably shouldn't throw a demon at him to see how he reacts, but we will have to figure out something."

Joshua walks into the room, dancing to some music only he can hear. When he sees us, he takes his ear buds out.

"Hey, Jess. Long time no see," he says with a smile, truly happy to see me.

"Hey, Joshua. What are you listening to?"

"Mason told me you were at a Chandler Cain concert and it made me want to listen to some of his music. Hey," Joshua says, quickly coming to stand closer to me. "Do you think you could score me a couple of tickets to his next concert in Denver? It's on Valentine's Day. I'd really like to take Caylin to it. I thought it might be a nice first date. What do you think? Do you think she would like that?"

"I'm sure she will. I can probably get backstage passes for you guys if you want."

Joshua's eyes grow large with excitement, and he grabs me by the shoulders and kisses me on the cheek.

"You're the best!" he says excitedly. "And Jess, could you please come back to work here? Mason's been unbearable since you've been gone."

"Joshua…" Mason says, warning Joshua to be careful with

what he says.

"Come back to work," Joshua mouths to me silently. "Please," he begs, holding his hands in front of him, as if in prayer.

Joshua turns around, avoiding direct eye contact with Mason, and quickly heads out of the room.

"So," I say, "are you going to let me come back to work here, or are you going to keep me in Tunica doing busy work?"

"Right now the most important thing you can do is help Chandler figure out what power he has, and try to work together to find the next vessel. If what Michael said to you is correct, then you should be able to find the third person more easily with his help," Mason says. "I'll have Isaiah take you to Chandler each day, until the two of you can work something out."

"Why Isaiah?" I ask. "Why not you?"

Mason stares at me, and I can't read his expression; the intensity of his gaze is almost stifling.

"Mason," I say, taking a step towards him, but he takes a step back, like it's vital for him to keep a certain amount of distance between us. "Talk to me," I implore because I know, unless he opens up, there's no hope for us.

"I can't," he finally says, breaking off our eye-contact and averting his gaze to the floor.

I suddenly feel like this might be my last chance to make Mason face his feelings for me. The longer I let him hide behind his ancient guilt, the harder it will become for him to let me in. Desperation claws at the box my heart is in, tearing it asunder until all I have left is a raw need to let him know how I feel.

"I'm falling in love with you," I tell him, proud of myself and amazed at my finally saying it out loud and daring to take a chance with my heart.

Mason's head jerks up at my words, and he looks at me like he's in shock, mouth slightly open and eyes wide.

"You don't have to look *that* surprised," I say, feeling awkward all of a sudden. "And before you even try to deny it, I know you feel something for me too. That's the only reason you've been avoiding me."

"I haven't been avoiding you...directly."

"Then what would you call having Malcolm take me home the night of the ball and not contacting me for almost seven days? Do you know how worried I was about you? Do you even care?"

"I care about you more than I have a right to," he says, so quietly I have to strain to hear him.

"Talk to me," I tell him again, knowing this is the only way we're going to have a chance. If he can't talk to me about what he's feeling and thinking, we'll always have his silence keeping us apart.

"I don't know if I can," he finally admits.

I take heart in the fact that he didn't completely shut me out and tell me he would never be able to share his thoughts with me. I'm given hope.

The look of indecision on his face prompts me to walk to

him before he has a chance to hide again. As I stand in front of him, I notice he's staring at the tips of my Louis Vuitton black high heels.

"Nice shoes," he comments, purposely trying to avoid lifting his eyes to look at me.

"Mason," I say, "look at *me*, not my shoes."

I watch as his eyes slowly travel up my body and seem to stop at my chest, but he doesn't seem to be focusing on my breasts intentionally, just avoiding direct eye-contact with me.

"Uh, my eyes are a little bit higher than that," I gently remind him.

Mason suddenly looks up.

"That wasn't on purpose," he says, completely chagrined.

"Stop before you say anymore, or you might unintentionally insult me," I tease.

"No, I don't mean it that way either. Your breasts are beautiful," he grimaces, and he tilts his head back to look at the ceiling. "Anything I say will come out wrong in this situation, won't it?"

I laugh. "Yes, it will." I put my hands on either side of his head and gently make him look down at me. When our eyes meet, I say, "Talk to me. Please."

"I haven't led a charmed life like Chandler. My story is much darker, too dark for most people. Are you sure you want to hear it?"

"Yes."

"Then I need to take you somewhere so you can fully understand."

CHAPTER 21

Mason reaches up and pulls my hands from his face to hold them both in his. Before I know it, we're standing in a cavernous space within a mountain. There is a solitary opening high overhead at the apex of the mountain. There isn't much in the cave except for a few broken and rotted wood items, which seem to have been chairs, cots, and a table at one time.

Faint light streams down from the mountain opening, letting me know it's daytime wherever we are. The hole appears to be the only way light and air can enter the cave.

"Jonathan and I used to live here," Mason tells me, his voice far away as he remembers his days in this dank, cold space with his son. "I couldn't let him harm anyone, and this was the only place he couldn't escape from at night when he was a child. It was good for me, too, because no human could reach us. When we needed food, I would phase out and get it. We stayed hidden here for a hundred years." Mason pauses, and I can see the weight of so much time on his shoulders as he remembers his self-imposed prison sentence. "By that time, I had my hunger for human blood under control, and Jonathan was just entering puberty. I saw the toll this type of life was having on him, and made a vow to myself to provide him with a better existence, because he deserved it. I'm not sure you can understand the toll it takes on a parent to be the cause of so much pain to their child. Every night I watched him transform into the cursed creature he had to endure because of me. I felt I owed him that much for being the cause of his suffering."

I grasp Mason's hands even tighter, urging him to continue.

"When we left this place, we lived in a small village. I didn't think either one of us was ready to deal with having a lot of people around. I'm not sure if it was fate or just another part of my punishment, but the first village we picked to settle down in was already occupied by a Watcher and his child. The child was female, and Jonathan instantly fell in love with her when they met. Our children bond for life, just like real wolves do, so, there wasn't any way for me to prevent them from being together. He had made his decision, and wouldn't back out of it no matter how much I begged him to."

"Why?" I ask. "Why didn't you want him to be with her?"

"She and her father preyed on humans. He drank their blood while she ate what was left over. They were both damned, and I didn't want that fate for Jonathan. I had kept him in this place," Mason says, looking around at the cave, "for a reason, to protect his soul. Charlotte urged Jonathan to go on hunts with her and her father. I think the only reason he refused was because he knew it would rip my heart apart. One night, the Watcher came back home from a hunt, but Charlotte wasn't with him. When we asked what happened, he said she was dead, killed by a group of hunters that had set a trap for them. I thought I lost Jonathan that night. He told me he hated me. I could take the scorn of the other Watcher, but not Jonathan's hatred; it was too much for me to bear. I have a lot more to repent for, Jess; more than just this one story. Why would you want to settle for someone like me? You deserve better than what I have to offer you."

"I deserve to finally be happy, and so do you." I tell him. "Are you happy when you're with me?"

Mason draws me in closer to him. "The happiest I've been in a very long time."

"Then stop pushing me away," I beg.

"You scare me," he admits.

"Why do I scare you?"

"If I let you inside my heart, I'll never want to let you go."

"Is that so bad?" I ask, mirroring the question he asked me once.

"No, it's not bad," Mason says, closing his eyes and resting his forehead against mine. He's so close his nose tickles mine, and I smile contentedly.

He pulls away slightly to look down at me. Even in the

dim light, I can see his desire for me in his eyes, and I instantly know his intention.

I step back from him, letting his hands go.

He looks at me in confusion.

"Not here," I say, shaking my head slightly. "I don't want my first kiss to be here in a place you hate," I tell him, looking around at the cave - Mason's own personal prison.

Mason looks at me even more confused. "Your first kiss? Is that what it would be for you? Are you telling me you've never kissed a man?"

"Not willingly," I say, not having to go into any further detail.

Mason holds a hand out to me.

"No, your first kiss shouldn't be here," he agrees. "Plus it's late. I should get you back home."

I walk back up to Mason and take his hand. Before I know it, we're standing in my bedroom.

"I'll leave you now to get some rest for tomorrow," he says, bending to kiss the back of the hand he still holds.

"Will *you* take me to see Chandler tomorrow?" I ask.

Mason smiles. "Yes, I'll take you. I won't try to hide from you anymore. I don't think you would let me now, even if I tried."

"Damn straight," I say.

Mason laughs. "Good night, Jess."

"Good night, Mason."

Mason phases, and I sit down on my bed. After I kick off my shoes, I lay down, promising myself I will get back up and take a shower. I just need to close my eyes for a few seconds to gather the strength to do it.

The next thing I know, I'm being woken by my phone buzzing. Bleary-eyed, I look over on the other side of my bed and see it laying there. I raise myself up on an elbow and find everything I left at Chandler's penthouse lying on the other side of the bed from me. I reach for my phone and look at the text message. It's from Mason.

Thought you might need your stuff back. I don't think a Watcher Agent is supposed to leave their plasma pistol in a rock star's apartment.

Why didn't you wake me up when you dropped my stuff off?

You looked too beautiful to disturb...

Flattery will get you anything...

Anything?

I stare at the text, not sure I'm ready to commit to the word. I wasn't sure how far 'anything' would mean in Mason's world, so I chicken out and ignore it.

What time will you be picking me up to take me to Chandler?

Is an hour long enough?

Ok I will be ready

I wait to see if he replies and pushes me on the 'anything' but he doesn't. I feel a bit disappointed and figure his old-fashioned gentleman gene has kicked in, preventing him from continuing the sub-sexual banter. So, as a woman of the modern age, I text back:

And yes...anything...

I toss the phone on the bed and go take a shower. I dress casually and comfortably because I want to try meditating with Chandler during the time we're together that day to start searching for our third member. I put on the same clothes I wore when I met Lilly.

The doorbell rings and my heart races. I take a deep breath and walk to the door with my coat in my arms. When I open the door, Mason is standing there with one perfect red rose in one of his hands.

"Good morning," he says, handing me the rose.

"Good morning," I reply, taking the rose and bringing its soft petals to my nose to breathe in its heady aroma.

"Would you be interested," he says, "in coming to my villa tonight for supper?"

I smile. "Yes, I would. I like it there."

"Perhaps while we're there we can discuss what this 'anything' entails."

"Perhaps..."

Mason holds out his hand for me to take. I instantly find myself standing outside the door to Chandler's penthouse.

"He's waiting for you," Mason tells me, still holding my hand. "I'll let you two get to work."

Mason bends and kisses the back of my hand. I attempt to withdraw it from his hold, but he gently prevents me by tightening his fingers around it. I watch as he turns my hand over, palm up. He kisses the middle of my palm gently before performing the same action on the inside of my wrist. The gentle pressure of his lips on my sensitive flesh causes me to shiver pleasantly. I see Mason smile, pleased by my reaction to him.

When he stands up straight again, he leans into me, drowning me in the scent of him.

"Call me when you're ready for me to come back," he whispers in my ear, kissing my neck lightly before phasing away.

I end up standing in the hallway for a good five minutes, just trying to get my hormones under control. Was this what they call a slow seduction? I had no way of knowing for sure, but if it was, it was working like a charm. I couldn't help but wonder what it would feel like to share a real kiss with Mason...and possibly more.

After I feel sure my cheeks are cool once again, I knock on Chandler's door. He instantly opens it, as if he was waiting on the other side the entire time.

He smiles at me, as if he knows something he shouldn't.

"Were you watching us?" I asked him, and his guilty smile widens.

He holds up his hands palm forward. "I swear, Jess, I was just looking through the peephole to see if you had made it here yet or not. I didn't do it on purpose."

I swat Chandler on the arm, like he's my little brother snooping into my private business.

"Make your presence known next time," I scold him, trying to be firm, but finding it almost impossible to be mad at him.

"But if I'd done that you wouldn't have had...you know... *the moment*," he says popping his eyebrows up and down. "Why were you just standing out there for so long by yourself after he left?"

"None of your business," I say, feeling my cheeks redden. I walk further into the penthouse and drop my coat in a chair, placing the rose Mason gave me gently on top of it.

Chandler closes the door. "He got you that hot and bothered with four little kisses?"

"Chandler," I say, "drop it."

Chandler tucks his fingers inside the front pockets of his jeans and leans against the door with one foot propped up against it, giving him a rebel-without-a- cause look.

"Oh, my God," he says, realization dawning on his face, "Jess, are you a virgin?"

"Why does everyone make that sound like it's a bad thing?" I ask in exasperation. "And how can you people tell? Do I have a sign on my forehead saying *Beware: Virgin Territory?*"

Chandler laughs. "No, it's just a little unbelievable," he says. "But I guess I know why you still are, because of what you told me yesterday."

I sit down on the arm of the chair my coat is on.

"Mason flusters me," I confess. "I'm scared and excited all at the same time when I'm around him, if that makes sense. I've just never felt like this around someone else."

"It's called love, Jess," Chandler says, pushing off the door with his foot to walk over to me. "Is this the first time you've felt it?"

I nod.

Chandler's smile widens. "Then enjoy it. Real love is hard to find, almost impossible for a lot of people, including me."

"You've never been in love?" I ask. "What about all those great love songs you sing? I thought for sure you had been in love at least once."

"Oh, I've loved a few women in my life, but not to the point where just an innocent kiss from one of them made me have to stand completely still for five whole minutes just to get over it," he teases.

"Am I that pathetic?"

He shakes his head. "No. I envy what you're feeling. Don't let it go. Keep it for as long as you can. This type of love only comes around once in a lifetime. Fight for it."

"I am," I say, and tell Chandler what happened the night before after Mason so rudely phased me away after the concert.

"Yeah, I knew he was jealous," Chandler says. "No man acts that stupid unless he is."

"Well, I hope we're through the worst of it. I feel like he's finally opening up to me, even if I had to push him to do it."

"It sounds like he's held onto his guilt for a long time. I think you've just worked a small miracle, getting him to tell you what he has so far."

"All right, enough about my love life. I want to try something with you."

"Should I be scared?" Chandler laughs lightly.

"No. I want to meditate with you like I did when I had to find you on my own." I look around Chandler's penthouse but don't see a fireplace. "We need something to concentrate on, though. The first time I did it I used the sounds from a fire."

"Hold on; I might have something," Chandler says, running up the metal staircase to the second floor. He comes back down with a little white machine in his hands.

"I use this when I can't sleep sometimes," he tells me, pressing a button on the machine and instantly filling the room with the sounds of ocean waves.

We pick a spot on the floor and sit down in the lotus position with one another, but, instead of holding our hands palm-up on our knees, we hold each other's hands.

"Okay, when I did this," I tell him, "I cleared my mind of everything except the crackle of the fire. So, let's concentrate on the wave noises and see what happens."

I watch Chandler close his eyes before I close mine too.

I'm not sure how long we sit there trying to concentrate on finding the third member of our archangel group, but eventually Chandler says, "This isn't working for me."

I open my eyes and have to agree.

"Me neither," I reluctantly admit. "I'm not sure why it isn't working. Michael said it would be easier once there were two of us."

I pull my hands away from Chandler's, and we both stand up.

"We'll figure it out," Chandler says, not worried in the

slightest. "Now what?"

"We need to find a way to activate your power."

"Any idea how to do that?"

I sigh. "Not really. I had to almost be killed by a demon before mine kicked in."

"Hmm, well, you know any demons that can attack me?"

I laugh. "No. I don't think that's the best idea.

"Maybe we're just thinking too much," he suggests. "Let's go do something."

"Like what?"

"Let's go do something touristy. I've never been to the Empire State Building, have you?"

"No, my visits to see you are the only times I've been in New York."

"What?" Chandler says, like it's completely scandalous. "Well, then, let me be your guide to the little-known parts of this city. First stop, though, is the Empire State Building."

"And just how are we supposed to go to these places without hordes of your adoring fans chasing after us?"

Chandler takes my hand. "Come on; you can help me put on my disguise."

"Disguise?"

I soon learn what Chandler's disguise is. He makes me help him put on a blond wig while he adheres a matching beard and mustache to his face. With a pair of sunglasses and a cowboy hat, he barely looks like himself. He proceeds to dress in a cowboy shirt, faded jeans, and cowboy boots.

"Hmm," I say after his costume is complete, "you look

like you belong in a rodeo. Is that at all comfortable?"

"Not really," he says, scratching at the beard on his face. "But it's either this, or get accosted wherever I go. I'd rather just be a little scratchy. Plus, if you keep that pistol of yours on your leg, I don't think I will get as much attention as you. You look kinda hot with it slapped to your thigh like that."

I hit Chandler on the arm. "No talk like that from you. It sounds pervy. You're like my little brother."

"Uhh, you wound my male ego," Chandler says, dramatically clutching at his heart while laughing. "Yeah, I know what you mean. You're like the abusive big sister I never had."

I laugh and hold out my hand to him. "Okay, little bro, take me to see the city."

I soon learn that Chandler has a bodyguard who stays in the background wherever he goes. I'm introduced to him before we leave the hotel. His name is Ben, and I'm surprised by how slim and normal looking he is. In my mind, I always imagined a bodyguard to be bigger than life, just to scare off anyone who might be thinking to cause trouble with his sheer size. But Ben is someone who can slip in and out of a crowd unnoticed, which seems to be important to Chandler. It's obvious he didn't want a bodyguard who would attract much attention.

As Chandler and I travel through the city that day, Ben takes separate cabs from us and discreetly keeps his distance. I barely know he's there during my day with Chandler. I suppose that's why I didn't notice him missing until it was too late.

CHAPTER 22

All through the day, I kept in constant contact with Mason, just to let him know where we were and what we were doing. I reason with myself that it's work-related and not just me wanting to stay close to him, even if we were separated by a few thousand miles. We keep the texts simple and short, not delving into any innuendos, which, I'll admit, was a bit disappointing. I was happy to see him reply almost instantly to my texts. It made me think of what Jonathan said on New Year's Eve, about his dad acting like a young man in love by constantly checking his phone to see if I had sent him a message. My heart felt all warm and fuzzy inside just from the thought of him waiting for my texts.

"You know you're making me feel like a third wheel," Chandler says to me as we're riding in a horse-drawn carriage through Central Park. "Hell, I'm the one you're with, and I feel left out!"

I giggle, which is something I never do, and it almost sounds alien to my own ears. Faison is the giggler in the family, not me. But Faison had been in love with John Austin since she was seven. Was this what love did to you, make you giggle like an idiot?

"I'm happy," I say to Chandler. "Leave me alone." And I stick my tongue out at him.

Yep.

Love makes you act like an idiot, and, strangely enough, I was all right with that.

It's almost five in the afternoon when I decide I should ask Mason when he wants to have supper at his villa.

What time do you want to pick me up for supper?

As soon as possible…

Give me 30 minutes so I can take Chandler home. I would feel better knowing he is safely returned there.

I will be at his door in exactly 30 minutes

If we get there sooner, I will let you know

I can't wait to see you…

I was just about to put my phone back in my coat pocket when it buzzes one more time.

I mean it Jess…I want to see you…

I want to see you too…I'll hurry…

Please do…

"How much longer is this ride?" I ask Chandler.

He sits back in his seat and crosses his arms over his chest. Narrowing his eyes at me, he says, "What's the rush? Don't you like spending time with me?"

I roll my eyes. "You know I do, but I have a date."

"Oh, with Mr. Moody?"

"He is not moody," I defend. "He just has issues."

"Why do you girls always fall so hard for guys with problems? You would think someone, like me, for example, would be more perfect."

"Perfection is overrated. And it's not that we like guys with problems. It's just that those guys tend to be more serious, unlike you for example. You've had it so good all your life, you see the world through rose-colored glasses."

"Do you think that's bad?" Chandler asks, becoming serious.

I shake my head. "No. It's not bad. It's good actually. But someone with a life as screwed up as mine tends to look for someone just as screwed up. And I found him."

Chandler smiles. "Yeah, that's kinda messed up, but it makes sense in a way."

"So, how long is this ride supposed to be?" I ask again, but Chandler doesn't have to answer because the driver brings the horse to a stop in the exact spot we started out on the south side of Central Park. When we get out of the carriage, I instantly look for Chandler's bodyguard, thinking he should be in the carriage behind us, but it doesn't have a passenger.

"Where is our shadow?" I ask Chandler as he steps down from the carriage to stand beside me.

Chandler looks at the next carriage to roll in and says, "I thought he was behind us."

Before I know it, a man in a black feathered cape appears

at Chandler's side, and grabs his arm before disappearing with him in tow. It happens so quickly I seem to be the only one who sees it.

I frantically dig for my phone in my coat pocket to call Mason, but someone grabs my wrist, and I find myself not in Central Park anymore.

A cool wind blows through my hair as I'm faced with a vast expanse of rolling hills made of sand. The full moon hanging in the night sky illuminates not only the desert, but also the nightmarish creatures standing in front of me.

Three men wearing black feathered capes stand ten feet from my position. Chandler is struggling against the firm grip of the Watcher who abducted him, in a futile attempt to escape. I can tell he's mad, not scared by the situation. I feel a sense of pride that he is able to command such strength, considering the dire straits we find ourselves in.

A few yards to the left of the Watchers is a pack of three nightmarish creatures, feasting on what appears to be the remnants of a human corpse. The crack of bones, rending of flesh, and suckling sounds as they swallow the meat makes me sick to my stomach. I pity the person who is being devoured whole by the children of the Watchers.

One of the Watchers walks toward me, and I instantly recognize him.

"Didn't Lucifer order you not to harm me?" I ask.

Even in the dim light of the moon, I see the Watcher named Baruch smile.

"I know I'm not allowed to harm *you*," Baruch says, "but

he didn't say anything about the humans you associate with, like this one." Baruch tilts his head in Chandler's direction.

"Don't worry about me, Jess," Chandler calls out to me. "Get out of here!"

"I'm not leaving without you," I promise him. I look to Baruch. "Why are you doing this? I haven't done anything to you. I barely even know you."

"Mason loves you," Baruch spits out. "That's reason enough. You can thank him for what I'm about to do to your life. Everyone you love, everyone you consider a friend or even an acquaintance, anyone you might remotely have feelings for will suffer the same fate as this boy. I will make your life a living hell because, if you're miserable, Mason's miserable. Lucifer is the only reason I don't rip your throat out myself and feed you to my boy over there."

As if knowing his father is talking about him, I see one of the werewolves lift its head from what remains of the corpse, and sniff the air in my direction.

"Who is that?" I ask looking pointedly at the body the werewolves are eating, suddenly frightened to learn the answer.

"That boy's bodyguard. We didn't want him drawing undue attention to us while we brought you here. Plus, our children were hungry. It was as good a meal as any. And after we feed the boy to them, they should be sated for tonight."

I feel my blood boil, not with anger but fierce determination. I vow to myself that Chandler will not suffer such a death. Deep within my soul, I know we will survive this transient moment in time, because our destinies aren't supposed to end like this.

I stand a little straighter as I tell Baruch, "I *will* kill you. If you let him go, I might let you live."

Baruch laughs, almost doubling over because he seems to find what I've said funny. When he finally regains control of himself, he turns to the Watcher holding Chandler and says, "Kill him."

The next few seconds become a blur of motion. I watch as the Watcher holding Chandler sinks his teeth into the base of my friend's neck, causing Chandler to cry out in excruciating pain. His cry awakens something buried in the well of my soul, and I feel the flames of righteousness burn bright. Instantly, I find myself holding the flaming sword given to me as my talisman on Earth.

The arching flames of the sword blaze across the dark desert sand, drawing the attention of the others.

"Let him go," I demand of the Watcher holding Chandler. Out of sheer fear, the Watcher instantly lets Chandler go. Chandler falls to the sand on his hands and knees, gasping for air.

"How did you get that?" Baruch hisses. I see the terror in his eyes, not scared of the sword itself it seems, but scared of me now, since I possess the ability to call such a weapon to my side.

"Do you think you're strong enough to keep it?" Baruch asks me. "If I take that sword from you, I can kill Lucifer with it and finally be free of him."

I tighten my grip on the hilt of the blade. I've never swung a sword in my life, and I have no idea if I can fight off the dark angel standing in front of me, but I know I would rather die than let him take the sword from my grasp.

"I guess you'll have to see for yourself if I'm strong enough." I take a deep breath and wait for the attack.

I've always wondered why action movies show fights in slow motion, and now I understand why. The next few seconds seem to move slower in my mind than I know they are in reality. Baruch rushes me, his cloak billowing behind him, making him look like a bird of prey. I duck away from his initial attempt to tackle me to the ground and swing the sword at his back, setting the black feathers of his cloak on fire. Baruch rips the flaming cloak off his back in a swirl of motion, and throws it to the desert sands. He whips around to face me again. He's so close the flames of my sword are reflected in his dark eyes.

"Give me that sword," he growls menacingly.

"Come and get it," I taunt.

Baruch phases almost on top of me, grabbing the arm which holds the sword by the wrist, and twisting so hard I hear my delicate bones break. The pain is almost unbearable with the added weight of the sword, and the hilt begins to slip out of my hand.

I feel cool fingers pluck the sword out of my grasp and see Chandler holding it, standing behind Baruch. With one mighty swing, Chandler buries the blade in Baruch's back.

Baruch looks at me in dismay, not understanding what's just happened.

As I watch Chandler slide the sword out of Baruch, the Watcher's body explodes into a pile of glistening black ash, covering the pale desert sand between Chandler and me. Cradling my broken wrist to my chest, I look where the other two Watchers are, because I don't understand why they aren't attacking us. I see them kneeling on the desert floor, their faces buried in their hands, sobbing uncontrollably. Their children are whining beside them, not understanding what is happening to their fathers.

"What's wrong with them?" I ask Chandler.

"I think I found my power," he tells me, breathing heavily from the exertion of the fight. "I don't know how, but I knew if I touched them I could make them feel their deepest sorrow."

Before I have time to ask my next question, Mason and Lucifer suddenly appear on either side of Chandler.

"Better late than never, I guess," Chandler says to Mason, before completely collapsing from exhaustion and blood loss.

I run to him and turn him over onto his side. The wound on his neck is deep and still bleeding.

"We need to get him to a doctor," I tell Mason.

Mason picks Chandler up, cradling him in his arms, while I grab my sword.

I see Lucifer look from the sword to me.

"I suppose I'll have to wait for an explanation as to how you obtained such an item," he says to me before his eyes glide over to the other Watchers and their children. "It's probably a good idea if you take them both away now, Mason. I seriously doubt you want Jessica to see what I'm about to do to them."

I grab Mason's arm without having to be told to do so. I suddenly find myself in a bedroom similar to the one I occupied the last time I was at Mason's villa.

"Shouldn't we be taking him to a hospital?" I ask as Mason eases Chandler's body down onto the bed.

"Hospitals ask too many questions," he tells me. "I'll go get Malik. He'll be able to heal the wound. He's done it before."

Mason turns to me and pulls me into his arms. I let out a whimper of pain, which makes him instantly let me go.

"Where are you hurt?" he asks in sudden alarm.

"My wrist," I say, still cradling the injured arm to my chest.

Mason kisses me on the forehead. "I'll be right back."

He phases away, and I go to sit beside Chandler on the bed.

He opens his eyes and tries to smile at me.

"We make a pretty good team," he says weakly.

I nod. "Yes, we do."

Only a few minutes pass before Mason returns with Malik. Malik sets to work on Chandler immediately, and I feel confident he's in good hands. Mason phases me to the hospital in Tunica to have my wrist looked at. Since everyone there knows I'm a Watcher agent, my injury doesn't send up any red flags; they simply consider it part of the dangers of my job.

Faison is on duty, and makes the nurse attending me go away so she can do it herself. Ten minutes later, Mama Lynn and George are at my side, treating me like I'm a 10-year-old kid. Mason stands in the background, watching as I'm cared for by my family.

Once my wrist is set, I'm ordered by the doctor to take it easy for a few days and get some rest. I tell my family I need to go see a friend who was also injured in the same fight. They're reluctant to let me go, but simply don't have a choice.

Mason takes my hand and phases me back to his villa, but we don't immediately go to Chandler's room.

Instead, Mason phases us to the living room and gently holds me in a tender embrace.

"What happened Jess?" he asks, since he has no way of knowing everything that transpired in the desert.

I tell Mason everything that happened between my last text message to him and his and Lucifer's sudden appearance in the desert. I leave out the reason Baruch said he wanted to make me suffer, because I know it will only cause Mason to feel more guilt unnecessarily.

Mason pulls away from me at the end of my tale, not asking any questions, and phases me to Chandler's side.

Malik is still there, holding Chandler's wrist as if he's checking his pulse. Chandler tries to smile up at me, but it comes out more of a grimace because of the pain he's experiencing.

"How is he?" I ask Malik.

"He'll be fine. Just make sure he takes that medicine," Malik says, nodding his head at a glass vial filled with blue liquid, sitting on the table by the bed. "He refused to take it until you got back."

"It's going to make me sleep," Chandler says in a weak voice. "I wanted to speak with you first, Jess."

Malik stands up. "I've pretty much done everything I can for the moment. It's just going to take time to heal, but you shouldn't have much of a scar from where the Watcher bit you. I did the same thing for Tara when she got bit way back when, and you can hardly see the place on her neck anymore."

"Thank you for helping him," I say to Malik.

"Any time; but now I need to get back to my wife before she worries too much about me." Malik gathers up his bag of medicine and turns to Mason. "Give me a lift home?"

Mason puts his hand on Malik's arm, and they phase out of the room.

I sit on the side of the bed by Chandler.

"What did you want to speak with me about?" I ask.

"You need to tell Mason why Baruch took us," Chandler tells me.

"I'm not telling him."

"Jess, I seriously doubt those people are the only ones with a vendetta against Mason. You might be protected because of Lucifer's order, but the rest of your friends aren't."

"Even if I told him, what difference would that make?"

"At least he would know it's because they think that, by

hurting the people you love, they can hurt him too. Tell him so he can help you protect the people around you."

I shake my head. "He doesn't need to know. Mason's dealt with enough guilt in his life. I'm not about to add to it."

"Jess?"

I close my eyes at the sound of Mason's voice behind me, and wish he had made the popping noise to let us know he had phased back.

I reach for the vial of medicine on the table by the bed and open the top.

"Get some rest," I tell Chandler as he opens his mouth, and I pour in the liquid.

Almost instantly, Chandler falls asleep.

I stand to face Mason and his questioning eyes.

"What guilt would you be adding to?" he asks.

"It's nothing," I say, hoping against hope he won't push the matter. "Could you take me home so I can take a shower and change clothes? I feel dirty."

Mason takes hold of the hand that isn't half-covered with a cast, and I suddenly find myself standing in my bedroom.

I look up at Mason and still see his question in his eyes. I quickly look away because I don't want him to ask it again. I want to act like everything is all right and that Chandler hadn't almost been killed because of my feelings for Mason. Was I being selfish? Was I putting the other people in my life in danger because I wanted what might be my only chance to love someone?

"Jess," Mason says, and I hear the desperation in his voice, "look at me."

I stare at his brown leather shoes instead. I don't want to tell him what he wants to know because I know how much pain it will inflict upon him, but what if Chandler is right? Maybe I need to tell Mason so he can help me keep my friends and family safe from any other attacks.

Mason places his fingertips underneath my chin, forcing me to look up at him.

"What are you trying to hide from me?" The question is softly spoken and full of concern for my welfare. It makes me hope he won't take what I have to say as badly as I fear.

"If I tell you," I say, "do you promise not to overreact?"

Mason narrows his eyes, obviously not understanding why I would ask for such a promise from him. "Tell me."

I take in a deep breath. "Baruch took me because he wanted to hurt you."

Mason's body stiffens, like I just stabbed him with my words. I immediately want to take them back, but know I can't. There is no way to win in this situation. I can try to hold on to the rest of the information, and hope he doesn't delve any further, or I can tell him everything, and be completely honest.

"And why did he take Chandler?"

"He said since Lucifer told him he couldn't harm me that he planned to harm everyone I cared about to make my life miserable."

"Because you being miserable would hurt me too," Mason says, understanding the workings of Baruch's sadistic mind.

I nod, watching and waiting to see how Mason reacts to this news.

Mason lowers his eyes and turns his back to me, walking a couple of feet away to put some distance between us.

"Mason, this wasn't your fault," I tell him, but know my words will be useless.

I've come to realize Mason is built to harbor guilt, and I know what I just told him has only added weight to his already-overburdened heart.

"I'm sorry, Jess," he says, his back still to me. "I'm sorry he tried to make you pay for my sins." Mason turns to me, and I see the curtain has returned behind his eyes, shielding his true feelings behind a mask. "I made a mistake, thinking I could find happiness and keep it. You deserve a man who doesn't have so many enemies in his life."

I take a step forward.

"Don't do what I think you're about to do," I say. "Baruch is gone. He can't hurt anyone anymore."

"Can you honestly stand there and say that one of the other Watchers who still hate me won't try to use you to get back at me? Do you want me to be the cause of you losing Lynn or Faison or George? You would come to hate me," Mason says, and the man behind the curtain peeks out and shows me the pain he feels at the mere thought of something like that happening to me. "You've lost too many people in your life as it is, Jess. It's better to lose me now and keep those you love safe."

"But I love you," I declare, not surprised by my words, but surprised I had the courage to say them to Mason. "I love you, and I think you love me."

"It doesn't matter what either of us feels," he says, running his hand through his hair. "We can't be together."

"Don't say that," I beg, my eyes burning with tears. "Do you think I go around telling people I love them every day? You're the only man I have ever or will ever say that to."

I walk up to him and place my hand on his arm. "Please, Mason. Fight for me."

Mason looks at me, and I see the pain in his eyes like it's a permanent tattoo.

Without saying a word, he pulls away from me and walks over to the bay window in my room, staring out at the night.

"I'm going to put Isaiah in charge of you from now on," he tells me, keeping his voice neutral. "I'll help when needed, but I'll stay in the background and only contact you when it's necessary."

"Mason," I sob, letting my pent-up tears flow freely now because I know what his next words will be to me, and I can't bear to hear them. Not from him.

He looks over his shoulder at me, like he's taking a mental picture, and I know, without a shadow of a doubt, that he never intends to see me again.

"Goodbye, Jess."

He phases away before I can say or do anything to change his mind.

Feeling cold to the bone, like I'm in shock, I lay down on my bed, letting the reality of what has just happened sink into my heart. A series of pained sobs wrack my body as I feel my heart implode inside my chest, never to be whole again. How could he just give up on us so easily? Maybe his love for me wasn't strong enough to make him want to fight by my side. Perhaps the simple fact was that he just didn't love me as much as I did him.

I hear a knock on my door.

Wiping the tears from my face, I rush to the front of my house, thinking it has to be Mason. The dead weight inside my chest opens slightly, hoping he's come back to tell me he made a terrible mistake, and that nothing on this Earth can make him stay away from me.

I yank the door open. My tears instantly stop.

It's not Mason.

I look at the man before me. The golden glow of his aura surrounds him as he stands on my front porch, looking just the same as he did 15 years ago.

"Daddy?"

THE END

AUTHOR'S NOTE

Thank you so much for reading **Broken**, the first book in **The Watcher Chronicles.** If you have enjoyed this book please take a moment and leave a review. To leave a review please visit: Broken mybook.to/Broken-1

Thank you in advance for leaving a review for the book.

Sincerely,

S.J. West.

THE NEXT IN THE WATCHER CHRONICLES

Kindred

The Watcher Chronicles, book 2

Get the second book in the series today, and continue Jess &
Mason's story

It's available at Amazon & Free on KU.

mybook.to/Kindred-2

ABOUT THE AUTHOR

Once upon a time, a little girl was born on a cold winter morning in the heart of Seoul, Korea. She was brought to America by her parents and raised in the Deep South where the words ma'am and y'all became an integrated part of her lexicon. She wrote her first novel at the age of eight and continued writing on and off during her teenage years. In college she studied biology and chemistry and finally combined the two by earning a master's degree in biochemistry.

After that she moved to Yankee land where she lived for four years working in a laboratory at Cornell University. Home-sickness and snow aversion forced her back South where she lives in the land, which spawned Jim Henson, Elvis Presley, Oprah Winfrey, John Grisham and B.B. King.

After finding her Prince Charming, she gave birth to a wondrous baby girl and they all lived happily ever after.

As always, you can learn about the progress on my books, get news about new releases, new projects and participate on amazing giveaways by signing up for my newsletter:

FB Book Page: www.facebook.com/SJWestBooks/
FB Author
Page: https://www.facebook.com/sandra.west.585112
Website: www.sjwest.com
Amazon: author.to/SJWest-Amazon
Goodreads:
https://www.goodreads.com/author/show/6561395.S_J_West
Bookbub: https://www.bookbub.com/authors/s-j-west
Newsletter Sign-up: http://eepurl.com/bQs0sX
Instagram: @authorsjwest
Twitter: @SJWest2013

If you'd like to contact the author, you can email her to:
sandrawest481@gmail.com

Made in the USA
Monee, IL
28 December 2023

50697257R00193